NISEMONOGATARI

FAKE TALE

PART 01

NISIOISIN

VERTICAL.

NISEMONOGATARI
Fake Tale

Part 01

NISIOISIN

Art by VOFAN

Translated by James Balzer

VERTICAL.

NISEMONOGATARI, PART 01

First published in Japan in 2008 by Kodansha Ltd., Tokyo. Publication rights for this English edition arranged through Kodansha Ltd., Tokyo.

Published by Vertical, Inc., New York, 2017

ISBN 978-1-942993-98-8

Manufactured in the United States of America

First Edition

Vertical, Inc.
451 Park Avenue South, 7th Floor
New York, NY 10016

www.vertical-inc.com

CHAPTER SIX KAREN BEE

CHAPTER SIX
KAREN BEE

001

Karen Araragi and Tsukihi Araragi—my sisters. I doubt there are many in this world who would be interested in hearing their tale in the first place. And even, supposing, there were a class of people so peculiarly predisposed, given the choice, for my own part I'm quite certain I would not be interested in telling their tale. If I were to explain why I'm sure most anyone would understand, but by and by, and by and large, few these days care to bare every last detail of their home lives, and I certainly have no interest in bucking that trend. But even putting such general objections aside—Karen and Tsukihi are an unusual case. If it weren't for the fact that they are my sisters, I'm sure I would have never had anything to do with them. And even supposing we did come in contact, they're the type of people I would have almost certainly ignored. Due to the odd experiences I've had these past few months, I've made more than my share of strange acquaintances—for instance, Hitagi Senjogahara, Mayoi Hachikuji, Suruga Kanbaru, and Nadeko Sengoku—but if there's something in me that has allowed me to go more or less tit for tat with them, the attribute can be traced back to having been raised under the same roof as my sisters.

Of course, I suppose it wouldn't be fair if I wasn't up front about the fact that feelings of inferiority and jealousy might be coloring my view.

While I spent my high school life slacking off and wound up a loser, Karen and Tsukihi always had their act together—they're still in middle school, though, and up through middle school I had it together too, so there's probably no need for me to be so hard on myself. But looking back from my current vantage point, I have to admit that they have promise. Whenever the relatives get together, almost like clockwork one of them is sure to say to me, "Koyomi, you must be so proud of your sisters." Yes, they're those kind of sisters. By the way, I've never heard anyone tell my sisters, "You must be so proud of your brother." Then again, with a brother as shabby as me, I suppose that would be asking for too much.

However, let me make one thing clear, loud and clear.

My sisters may not be losers, but they're still problem children. They may be girls of character, but that character is bankrupt.

As their brother, I have the habit of always speaking about them as if they were a set, but obviously they each have their own distinct personality and idiosyncrasies, so let me take a moment now to explain them individually, in turn.

First, the older little sister.

Karen Araragi.

Currently in the third year of middle school, Karen turned fifteen at the end of June—and back to being just three years younger than me. Ever since elementary school she's generally kept her hair tied back in a ponytail. But apparently, once, around the time she entered middle school, she had actually dyed her hair—a garish shocking pink, too, like some character out of an anime. Or so I heard. I still don't know why she did it, but the predictable consequence was that our mother smacked her upside the face (for the sake of my mother's honor, let me just state that it was the first and last time the mild-mannered woman ever raised a hand against one of her daughters) and Karen re-dyed her hair black that same night (with calligraphy ink, of all things). Since Karen's hair was actually only shocking pink for a few hours, from when she dyed it in her own room to when our mother came home, and I was at school at the time (still in my first year, I was teetering on the brink of loserdom but still scrambling to hold on), I unfortunately never got to witness that look. As much as I wish I had, if it had been me who discovered her hair instead of our mother, honestly I might have been the one to smack Karen upside the face. So who's to say? In this remote country town, hardly anyone even lightens their hair, and just unbuttoning the top button on your school uniform is enough to brand you as a delinquent, so in light of the kind of off-the-wall middle-school debut Karen was looking to make, there's probably no need to say any more about her personality, all things considered.

The figure she cuts is, to be blunt, not cute.

If anything, I'd say she's more handsome or cool.

She's a bit taller than me, which might sound vague, but just how much qualifies as "a bit" I will leave up to your imagination. I don't want to give away too much about my own height, which I'm using as a standard of measurement. Whereas I stopped growing in my second year of middle school, in her second year, Karen shot up like a leaf. This has developed into an unfortunate complex for us both. Honestly, it's mortifying. I have to look up to my little sister. Can you imagine a bigger humiliation? To make matters worse, Karen does martial arts so her posture is magnificent, making her look about two inches taller than she really is. As a result, Karen refuses to wear skirts. She says they "make her legs look too long." Instead, she always wears a baggy, loose-fitting sports jersey to school. The jersey actually suits her, boosting her tomboy image.

By the way, the martial art Karen studies is karate. Ever since she was a kid she's been the sporty type, but apparently the best outlet for her talent was violence. She took her black belt in no time. There's a picture of her hanging in our living room, dressed in her *gi*. The black belt is tied around her waist and she's making the V sign at the camera. Both the outfit and the pose suit her way too well. There isn't much femininity to Karen. I wouldn't go so far as to call her mannish, but there's definitely something boyish about her—her hawkish, slanted eyes are

11

probably a factor. If I were to compare her to anyone else I know, I'd probably say that Suruga Kanbaru is the closest match. If you took away Kanbaru's respect for me, maybe you'd be left with Karen—although, the thought is kind of chilling.

And then there's the younger little sister.

Tsukihi Araragi.

Currently in the second year of middle school, Tsukihi's birthday is in early April. In other words, she is currently fourteen—unlike her older sister, Tsukihi's hairstyle changes from mood to mood and season to season. Honestly, since she never seems to keep the same hairstyle for more than three months at a time, I'd be hard pressed to tell you whether her hair is "her thing" or she actually just doesn't care. Not long ago she was keeping it long and straight, but at the moment she has it in a shaggy Dutch bob. I've never been interested enough to ask, but apparently she has a favorite salon she goes to. Maybe that sounds a little precocious for a middle-school student, but then again, these days that might just be what kids do. Besides, in Tsukihi's case it's not the exterior that's her problem so much as the interior. Karen's insides more or less match her outsides, but Tsukihi's outsides belie her insides— her insides, however, do not belie her outsides, which is an important distinction. Tsukihi has gentle, downward-tilted eyes (a contrast to her sister) and a small frame (an even bigger contrast to her sister), as well as a slow, distinctive way of speaking that is nothing if not girlish. But deep down she's even more aggressive than Karen, with a temper to boot. When Karen gets into some fight, listening to the story afterward, more often than not it was Tsukihi who was behind it. She has a temper that borders on hysteria. The sharp contrast with her gentle appearance tends to leave people scratching their heads in bewilderment—her one saving grace, I suppose, is that when she does get angry it is only ever on someone else's behalf.

For example, there was an episode that occurred when Tsukihi was in her second year of elementary school. During recess, a ball kicked by one of the older students landed in the sunflower bed tended by

Tsukihi's class. When the older student came to get his ball, Tsukihi's classmate, who had been watering the flowers, tried reprimanding him, but the older student got nasty and made her cry. Not that unusual of an occurrence for an elementary school. But as soon as Tsukihi heard about it she sprang into action, ascertaining which class the boy belonged to and then launching a full-out attack on the classroom (Karen, by the way, went with her). By the time the commotion, which later came to be known as the Ikedaya Incident (the assassins of the late shogunate and restoration era were popular at the time and I doubt the name was chosen for any special meaning) died down, the older student had been sent to the hospital and nearly all of the fixtures in the classroom had been destroyed. And then in a finishing touch, they sent a get-well bouquet to the hospital. Sunflowers.

Any way you looked at it, they had gone overboard. Maybe the girl stopped crying, but she probably did so out of pure fear. The whole incident was atrocious.

Tsukihi joined the tea ceremony club at her school, but only as an excuse to wear a kimono—she has such a thing for traditional Japanese clothing that she even wears a *yukata* to bed instead of pajamas. Supposedly they're teaching her about the peaceful spirit of tea, but sadly that doesn't seem to have translated to a change in her personality. Then again, any art form that was dominated by a difficult, short-tempered priest who'd go nuts just because someone sprinkled sugar on a watermelon probably just fans her hysteria instead.

Either sister, as you can see, would be a handful on her own, but matters are complicated by the fact that there are two. Forget about just handfuls, it takes feet and shoulders to juggle them both. As their extraordinarily bland older brother, I'm constantly at a loss over how to respond in the wake of each new scandal they cause. The real problem may be how well each sister complements the other.

The older sister: always ready for a fight. The younger sister: always ready to find a reason to start a fight. It's why they are known as the Fire Sisters of Tsuganoki Second Middle School.

According to Sengoku, my sisters are quite the famous duo among other junior-high kids in the area. Tsuganoki Second Middle School is private, while Sengoku attends a public school (my own alma mater), a little further away by bus. If the rumors had circulated that far, it was certainly no laughing matter.

I never heard this story from Karen herself so I can't speak to its veracity, but apparently on her first day of school she earned a name for herself among junior-high kids by challenging and defeating, in a one-on-one throw-down, the juvie boss leader who'd lorded over the middle schools in our area—no, there's no way that could be true. I mean, just look at how many weird phrases there are in those three little lines. Those kind of words don't belong in the twenty-first century. Someone had to have made that up. Still, I suppose the fact that a rumor like that could float around, unchallenged, is proof enough of Karen and Tsukihi's fame.

The Fire Sisters of Tsuganoki Second Middle School.

Karen Araragi, the enforcer, and Tsukihi Araragi, the strategist. As a pair, they spent their days…I don't know. Running around rescuing those in need? Righting wrongs and making the world a better place? In any case, playing at being make-believe defenders of justice. Of course, if I said that to the girls, I know how they'd reply.

Karen: "It's not make-believe, Koyomi."

And Tsukihi would almost certainly add: "We aren't 'defenders of justice,' we are justice itself."

But as their flesh and blood, I can confirm that their activities are not nearly so lofty. It's just an outlet for their excess energy. And if they keep it up they're going to get themselves into trouble someday—at least that's what I kept telling them, but the one who keeps getting into trouble these last few months has actually been me. And since I haven't been able to get my own act together, I guess nothing I say sounds very persuasive—then again, knowing it all probably goes in one ear and out the other, I can say it loudly and repeatedly.

Karen and Tsukihi Araragi. In the end, the Fire Sisters are nothing

more than make-believe defenders of justice.
My sisters, whom I must be proud of.
The truth is, they're just hopelessly fake.

002

The development seems so entirely out of context that I can only apologize, but apparently I was kidnapped.

The date was July twenty-ninth, approximately ten days after the start of summer vacation—well, I had a feeling that I'd been unconscious for some time, so I suppose it was possible that it was already the thirtieth. In fact, for all I knew the thirty-first had come and gone and it was August. If I could see the watch strapped to my right wrist, I'd be able to ascertain the date and hour, but with my hands bound together behind a steel beam, that was easier said than done. Nor could I extract the cell phone sitting in my pocket. Which is not to say that I had no estimate of the time—it was pitch black outside the window, allowing me to surmise, at least, that it must be night. I say window, but in reality the glass was missing, and the wind blustered into the room. Midsummer or not, the location was far too exposed. I could probably manage to stand up if I tried since my feet weren't bound, but there didn't seem to be much point in doing so. I kept my butt planted on the floor and stretched my legs out instead.

I can't believe Oshino and Shinobu lived like this, I thought absently to myself.

That's right. I was being held captive in a location I knew all too well, the ruins of the former cram school. It was a four-story affair strewn with garbage and rubble and on the verge of collapse. To someone unfamiliar with the building, every floor and classroom probably looked the same, but if you knew the place as well as I did, small differences were apparent. I could tell that the classroom where I was being held was one of three on the fourth floor, the one farthest on the left viewed from the stairwell.

A fat lot of good it did me, though.

Oshino, of course, was no longer in town, let alone in these ruins, and Shinobu had left them to take up residence in my shadow. Perhaps, at this very moment, she was feeling nostalgic. Or perhaps she wasn't feeling anything at all. How was I to know what a five-hundred-year-old vampire might be thinking.

So, what to do?

Despite a throbbing pain in the back of my head (I must have been struck there when I was abducted), I went over the situation with a calmness that seemed at odds with my predicament. People can be surprisingly levelheaded at such moments. After all, it's not like losing your head got you anywhere. The most urgent task, really, was to take stock of the status quo.

I had assumed my hands were tied behind my back with a length of rope or something, but it seemed it was actually a pair of metal handcuffs keeping them in place. If they'd been the toy variety, I probably could have resorted to brute strength to rip them apart—but I tried and they didn't budge. I'd end up ripping my own wrists to shreds before I even put a dent in the cuffs. If there's any distinction between real and fake in the handcuff world, these were clearly the real deal.

"Still—vampiric strength would have let me escape without even breaking a sweat."

Forget about the cuffs, I'd demolish the steel beam, too. Hell, even if I mangled my wrists, the trademark healing skill would restore them soon enough. Six of one or half a dozen of another.

"Vampire…" I muttered, sweeping my gaze over the ruined classroom once more. Even if I couldn't use my hands, there might be something I could reach with my feet.

My eyes fell on my own shadow. However dark the darkness, it always appeared a shade darker in relief.

"......"

Over spring break, I was attacked by a vampire.

A beautiful vampire with blond hair who drained my blood.

All of it. Every last drop. And as if that weren't enough—

Drained of blood, I became a vampire.

Over that spring break I'd spent not as a human being but as a vampire, these cram school ruins had served as my lair where I hid from prying eyes.

Usually, people who've turned into vampires are saved by vampire hunters, or Christian special ops, or even kinslayer vampires who hunt other vampires, but in my case, it was some older dude who was just passing by—Mèmè Oshino.

Saved by another. Oshino never stopped disliking that presumptuous way of putting it.

But that was how I became human again, while the beautiful blond vampire was reduced to a pale memory of her former self, robbed of her strength and even of her name (Shinobu Oshino was the one she received in exchange), to be sealed inside my shadow in the end.

I suppose you could say we had it coming.

Both Shinobu and me.

That was all there was to it.

Only, I couldn't leave it at that—and so she and I existed as we did. There was no way for me to know how Shinobu felt about it all, but even if it had been a mistake, I don't see what other choice we had.

Anyway.

The ruins were all full of memories for me. Maybe I should say awful memories, but that's beside the point.

The issue, at the moment, was that while I once possessed the strength of a vampire it was a long time ago, and only a faint vestige of that attribute now remained. Tearing through a set of metal handcuffs was only wishful thinking. If I were Lupin the Third, I'd dislocate the bones in my wrist and slip out of the cuffs as if they were a pair of gloves, but since I was just a high school third-year and not, in fact, Lupin the Third, such sleights of hand were beyond me.

Come to think of it…

Come to think of it, Tsukihi had also been kidnapped, recently—well, maybe "kidnapped" is overstating it, but it was still no laughing matter. Some enemy organization (?), doubting it was a match for Karen in combat prowess, instead hatched a plan to take Tsukihi hostage. Before I could even worry, I had to shake my head at all of them for staging, in real life, hijinks worthy of a weekly boys' comics magazine, but fortunately, when push comes to shove, Tsukihi can shove back. Getting herself kidnapped had been a ruse, and she ingratiated herself into the "enemy organization" (lol) and managed to bring it down from the inside.

The formidable Fire Sisters.

Incidentally, both girls kneeled before me afterwards and begged, "Please, don't tell mom and dad!"

They shouldn't have bothered. I wasn't about to bring something crazy like that to our parents' attention. Kneeling down along with her sister spoke well of Karen, but maybe also poorly.

I mean, girls of their age shouldn't fall on their knees to apologize about nothing. It's just immature, okay?

"As for me, I bet falling on my knees wouldn't even cut it… Those two are quick with the waterworks despite their own antics. So, what to do?"

Honestly, though… I already had a pretty good guess as to how I wound up in this situation. A pretty clear picture, you might say.

The truth was staring me in the face, yes indeed.

Whether I wanted to admit it or not.

The writing, as they say, was on the wall.

"Hmph…"

Just then.

Almost as if timed to coincide with my waking up, the sound of footsteps, climbing stairs, echoed through the ruins. Light seeped into the classroom from beyond the door—all of the electricity in the building was dead, so the source was probably a flashlight. It was moving in a beeline straight for the classroom where I was being held.

The door opened. The light was intense, momentarily blinding me—but my eyes soon adjusted.

Standing in the doorway....was a woman whose face I knew well.

"Ah. Araragi, you're awake."

Hitagi Senjogahara.

Her tone of voice was aloof, as always, as she pointed the flashlight in my direction.

"Phew, I was worried you might die without ever waking up," she added.

"..."

I was at a loss for words.

There were plenty of things I wanted to say, but not a single one coalesced into words. Senjogahara closed the door and strutted in my direction, barely acknowledging the approximation of a grimace that crossed my face.

There wasn't a hint of hesitation to her stride. It was the attitude of a person who harbored no doubts over what she was doing.

"Are you okay? Does the back of your head hurt?" she asked, setting the flashlight to the side—her concern was very touching, in and of itself.

Yet...

"Senjogahara," I said. "Take off these handcuffs."

"I will not," she replied.

She had given it exactly zero seconds of consideration.

Man...

I took a deep breath, wanting to make sure I had plenty of air in my lungs before shouting. And then shout I did.

"So you're the culprit after all!"

"Ah, you make a compelling case. But you'll never prove it was me," Senjogahara uttered a line that sounded like something out of the last chapter of a mystery novel. The speaker was always the culprit.

"The moment I saw I was being held in these ruins, I had a feeling it was you! Besides, no one else I know would have such heavy-duty handcuffs!"

"You have quite the imagination, Mr. Araragi. You don't mind if I take notes, do you? I could probably use them when I write my next book."

"In this case, I don't give a damn about twists where the culprit is a mystery novelist! Just take these handcuffs off already!"

"I will not," Senjogahara repeated. Lit from below by the flashlight, her stony expression was even more intimidating than usual.

Talk about scary.

"I will not," Senjogahara said again, her face still a mask. "Also, I cannot. I already threw away the key."

"You what?!"

"Also, I filled the keyhole with putty to make sure it can't be picked."

"Why would you?!"

"I also threw away the antidote."

"I've been poisoned on top of it?!"

Senjogahara's face finally cracked into a smirk. "I lied about the antidote," she said.

As relieved as I was to hear that, apparently that meant she was telling the truth about throwing away the key and filling the keyhole with putty. I slumped my shoulders in defeat. How was I going to get out of these cuffs now?

"Oh well," I conceded, "I should be glad that the part about the antidote was a lie…"

"Right. Don't worry, the antidote is safe and sound…"

"So you did poison me?!"

I tried to thrust myself forward as I quipped, but the handcuffs caught on the steel beam and I didn't make it very far. Maybe it wasn't a big deal, but for someone like me, that's extremely stressful.

"I lied about the poison, too," Senjogahara told me. "But if you won't be a good boy, who knows?"

"…"

Scary!

So, so scary!

"I float like a butterfly, sting like a butterfly."

"Butterflies don't sting!"

"My mistake. You must be so proud of yourself, pointing it out. Are you gonna brag about this for the rest of your life?"

"What a novel way of admitting your mistake!"

"Correctly, it's bee."

"Bee poison—is potent…"

I gulped hard, taking another look at the woman standing in front of me—at Hitagi Senjogahara.

One of my classmates.

She had a pretty face and looked smart, which in fact she was. With grades regularly in the top ten of our year, she had a reputation for being a cool beauty. What was known to only a select few, however, was that those who got too close to her were guaranteed, without exception, to pay the price.

The beautiful rose has its thorn. But in Senjogahara's case it was nothing so poetic—Senjogahara, herself, was one beautiful thorn.

In terms of a disconnect between interior and exterior, my sister Tsukihi rivaled her, but in Senjogahara's case there was no question of hysteria, just composed antagonism. Tsukihi was touchy, while Senjogahara was always on a combat footing at her normal temperature. She was like a security device programmed to lavish indiscriminate attacks on anyone who approached within a certain perimeter.

For instance, in my case, I got a staple punched into the inside of my mouth. One wrong step could have spelled disaster—and step I did, so it's a wonder everything worked out in the end.

Well, Senjogahara did have good cause for acting the way she did. Back in May we managed to resolve that issue, even if it was a compromise of sorts—but unfortunately that programming was a part of her, and disabling it was proving to be quite a challenge. Which brings us to today.

"Still, you've actually been pretty quiet lately. Why up and kidnap your boyfriend out of the blue? Is this some new trend in domestic violence I haven't heard of?"

By the way, Senjogahara and I were going out.

We were boyfriend and girlfriend. Sweethearts.

Not to be hokey, but you might say she stapled together our hearts—okay, I suppose that's a little hokey. Besides, you don't staple ties, you weave them.

"Relax," Senjogahara stated. I felt like I was talking to a brick wall. "Relax, Araragi, I'm going to protect you."

"…"

So scary!

The horror!

"You won't die. Because I'm going to protect you."

"As much as I appreciate the random *Evangelion* allusion, Miss 'Gahara…"

Miss 'Gahara. I'd come up with the nickname recently.

It wasn't catching on very well. Sometimes, it seemed like I was the only one trying to make Miss 'Gahara happen.

"I'm starting to get hungry," I continued, "and…maybe a little thirsty, too? Do you think we could get something to eat around here?"

I didn't have much choice but to ask nicely—for the moment, my life was in Senjogahara's unrelenting hands. If I didn't tread lightly I might get stung for real, no joke about it. Regardless of how she was these days, Senjogahara would never come into a situation like this unarmed, though I had no idea what kind of stationery it might be…

"Hah," Senjogahara snorted. It sounded nasty, like she was jeering at me. "Hungry, thirsty… You're like an animal, all you do is eat and sleep. It's disgusting. Why don't you try living in a productive manner for a change? Oh, I'm sorry. I guess 'living' is too lofty a demand for Koyomi Araragi."

"..."

What had I said to deserve that? Nothing, right?

"But when it comes to dying in a productive manner," she elaborated, "I'm sure you're second to none. A tiger leaves behind its fur upon dying, or so the proverb goes, and in that sense I suppose you're a tiger."

"That doesn't sound like a compliment, either."

After all, she was still calling me an animal.

Did she think I wouldn't notice?

At any rate...

Judging from the level of venom, Senjogahara wasn't actually angry or in a bad mood. She had an acid tongue and was always lashing out, so there were only a few people in the world capable of gauging her mood. Myself, and I guess Kanbaru and Senjogahara's father, and that was it. Normally you'd take her to be someone who was irritated all the time.

"Fine, Araragi. I'll be kind this once and show you mercy. I knew a pathetic bug like you would ask for food, so I bought all sorts in advance."

Senjogahara proudly thrust out her other arm—the one not holding the flashlight—at pathetic bug-like me to present what appeared to be a plastic convenience-store bag.

It was semi-transparent so I could make out its contents.

Beverage bottles, rice balls, and such.

Rations, for my confinement.

How unexpectedly considerate of her...how unpleasantly considerate.

"Ah, I see—then water, first. I need water."

Originally I had asked to eat hoping she would untie me, but it was true that I was feeling hungry and thirsty. Thanks to the aftereffects of my past vampirism I could hold off on eating, but even I had my limits. Who knows how long I was unconscious for, and in particular, water was a necessity for humans.

Senjogahara reached into the bag and pulled out a plastic bottle— mineral water—and unscrewed the cap. Since I was tied up, I expected her to help me drink, but she held the mouth of the bottle just a hair's breadth from my lips before yanking it back.

I should have known… Senjogahara had a mean streak that went deeper than words.

"Aww, you want some wa-wa?" she teased.

"W-Well…yes…"

"Huh. But I'd rather drink it myself."

Senjogahara began gulping it down.

Some people just have a way of doing things, I guess. Drinking straight from the bottle didn't make her seem crude. In fact, she looked downright classy.

"Ahh, that hit the spot."

"…"

"My my, such a greedy expression. Who said I was going to let you have any?"

Um, was she sure about that? That almost made it sound like she'd gone out of her way to buy water just to make me watch her drink some once I got thirsty.

Not that she wouldn't ever do such a thing.

"Heheh. Araragi, did you think I'd pass it to you mouth to mouth? You nasty boy. You little perv."

"Only Kanbaru would expect that in this situation."

"Is that so? What about the other day when we traded a big sloppy kiss…"

"Don't be talking about that now!"

I'd yelled. Not that there was anyone else to overhear, but I didn't like her talking about that stuff so openly.

We boys are delicate that way.

"Fine," she said. "If you want a drink of water that bad, I could let you have some."

"I want a drink of water that bad…"

"Ha! Does this man have no pride? Bleating a shameless line for a mere sip of water… How about just dying, at this point? If I were you, I'd bite off my tongue instead."

Senjogahara seemed to be enjoying herself…

I hadn't seen her so animated in a while. She must have really been bottling it up lately…

"Fine. I can hardly turn a blind eye to such deplorable begging. I'll show sympathy and allow you to quench your thirst. I hope you're grateful, you dippy bird."

"'Dippy bird' isn't exactly an insult…"

"Heheh."

With a more sinister laugh than ever, Senjogahara tipped the plastic bottle over and began dripping water onto her other hand. What in the world was she up to? Actually, considering how spiteful she could be, I already had a perfectly clear picture.

She held out her fingers, wet with mineral water, toward my lips.

"Lick it," she ordered. "You said you were thirsty, didn't you? Then stretch out your filthy tongue and slurp like a giraffe."

"……"

That wasn't exactly an insult, either… But with Senjogahara, somehow nearly anything could come out sounding venomous.

"Uh, Senjogahara…"

"What? I thought you were thirsty. Or were you lying? Liars need to be punished—"

"I'll lick! I'll lick it! Please let me lick it!"

I was already in a horrible fix without extra punishment.

I did as she said. I stretched my neck out toward Senjogahara's fingers like a giraffe (whatever that meant) and extended my tongue.

"Absolutely disgraceful," Senjogahara continued to belittle me. "I've never seen anything so pathetic. Who'd go so far for just a sip of water? I bet this is what you wanted all along, isn't it? You're probably just a pervert who likes to suck on girls' fingers."

Miss Senjogahara was definitely getting into this.

Regardless, licking her fingers helped quench my thirst some.

Now then.

"Araragi, that was an excellent image. I almost want to use it as the waiting screen on my cell phone."

"Oh yeah? How top of the line. Maybe we could move on to those rice balls?"

"Why not? I'm feeling unusually generous today."

No wonder, after all she'd done. You'd feel at least a little magnanimous.

"What filling would you like?" she asked me.

"Any."

"You don't seem very excited. Did you prefer bread by any chance?"

"Not really... Besides, as far as I can tell, you didn't buy bread."

"Nope. All I have are rice balls."

"There's no point in asking for what I can't have."

"If they don't have bread, why don't they serve us cake instead?"

"What an oppressive regime!"

There'd be a revolution in an instant.

It took the tart.

"I had a sheltered upbringing," Senjogahara claimed. "I don't know the ways of the world."

"I think it's your own ways that are the issue here."

"I can't help it, I was spoiled. I was the apple bee of my father's eye."

"'Apple'! Just 'apple' sounds plenty painful coming from you!"

As we continued to banter, Senjogahara took out one of the rice balls, carefully removed the plastic wrapper, and suddenly shoved the whole thing into my mouth.

"Nmph! Ngh," I sputtered. I could barely breathe. I couldn't but lodge a complaint. "What the heck?!"

"Well, asking you to open your mouth and say 'ahh' was kind of embarrassing."

"So you just shove it in my mouth? Khak! Th-There's rice stuck in my throat. W-Water! Water! Quick, the whole bottle!"

"Wha… No. It'd be like we were kissing indirectly."

"You're feeling shy about that after making me slobber all over your fingers?!"

Senjogahara did supply me with water, but it was by cramming the bottle into my mouth. While the grains of rice stuck in my throat got washed down, it also felt like I was about to drown—a unique experience on dry land.

"Uh oh. Look at the mess you made," Senjogahara deadpanned. "You're a bad little boy."

I didn't know if "acid tongue" was the right term anymore. If Japan ever lost its freedom of speech, the first one to be locked up would almost certainly be her.

"If you don't mind," she announced, "I'm going to take my meal too… Today I only had the time to bring convenience-store fare, but don't worry. Tomorrow it'll be a proper, homemade lunch."

"……"

"What? You have a problem with my cooking? I've been getting pretty good lately, if I do say so myself."

No, my problem was with the fact that my confinement seemed to involve long-term planning. I'd been playing along so far figuring it was some sort of game, but I had no idea what her goal was.

Hmm? Ah, of course…

She'd told me, hadn't she?

—*Relax.*

—*I'm going to protect you.*

To…protect me. I had a feeling she was being serious. If she was really trying to protect me, I shouldn't be dismissive.

Though maybe that was less kind than spoiling.

Probably because I'd been struck on the back of my head, my memory was fuzzy—but it was all starting to come back.

Protect—what she meant by the word.

How this situation had come to pass.

"I have to say, Senjogahara, you've got some skills up your sleeve, knocking me out with a single blow to the back of the head. According to my sister, it's a lot harder to knock someone out than you'd think."

"What single blow?"

"O-Oh?"

"You refused to pass out. It took me twenty tries."

"You could have killed me!"

Unbelievable.

Well… Speaking of unbelievable, there was something else I had to ask her.

Honestly, I'm not sure I wanted to know. But I didn't have much of a choice.

"Senjogahara… You said you'd make lunch next time, and I'm grateful, I really am. But while I'm here, how am I supposed to, you know… do my business?"

I lobbed—the mortifying question.

But as cool as a cucumber, without so much as raising an eyebrow, as if she had thought of everything, Senjogahara reached into the plastic bag and pulled out an adult diaper.

"M-Miss 'Gahara? You're kidding, right? Is that, like, a joke item? As always, what an edgy sense of humor."

"Relax, I'm prepared to do anything for your sake, even change diapers." Her face was expressionless as she spoke. "Don't you know? I love you, Araragi. So much that even if you were covered in filth from head to toe, I'd embrace you without a moment's hesitation. Starting with respiration and ending with excretion, I'll control every nook and cranny of your body, including your brain."

……

Oh, the weight of love!

0 0 3

Let me try to piece together the course of events leading up to this lamentable imprisonment. Indeed, to get it all straight—I should probably start from around the morning of July twenty-ninth.

Although it was summer vacation, I was determined to shrug off the mantle of loser and take college entrance exams, so there was no time to dally. Senjogahara, who had some of the best grades in our year, and Hanekawa, who had the very best, switched off each day to tutor me. It was hard work for me, studying every day, but if I stopped to think about it, I couldn't have asked for a better arrangement.

With those two as your tutors, anyone would improve. They turned out to be a choice combo of carrot and stick.

Or should I say honey and whip?

On even days I was taught by Senjogahara, and on odd days, by Hanekawa (with Sundays unconditionally off), but of course they also had their own plans, in which case those took precedence. That included July twenty-ninth, one of Hanekawa's days, when she told me, "Araragi, I'm so sorry! There's something I can't get out of! I promise, we'll make up next time! The day after tomorrow, to be precise!"

And so I wound up free.

Since I was the one asking for private tutoring, there was no reason for her to be so apologetic... As usual, Hanekawa was just too nice for her own good.

I assumed the thing she couldn't get out of had something to do, once again, with her parents. It wasn't my place to stick my nose in, so I didn't ask too many questions. I'd do anything for Hanekawa's sake, but "anything" sometimes had to mean "nothing at all," depending on the situation.

Well. In short, I had nothing to do that day.

Obviously I could have studied on my own, but according to Hanekawa, it was important to take time off now and then—Senjogahara never dispensed remotely similar advice, but on these matters, I tended to heed Hanekawa's.

And who could blame me?

Two days off in a row!

I say that, but I already had something planned for Sunday. Thinking I might take a long-overdue trip to the bookstore, I reviewed some stuff anyway before heading down to the living room. My parents had already left (they both work, even on Saturdays), and Tsukihi, dressed in a yukata, was sprawled out on her back on the couch and watching TV with her head upside down. Given her attire and posture, she might as well have been naked, her chest a disaster area, but she didn't seem to care. Not that I was one to talk about appearances, and as long as she dressed properly outside, it was no big deal.

"Ah. You're done studying?" Tsukihi switched off the TV (she seemed not to have been watching out of any interest) and turned toward me. The drooping curve of her eyes made her look drowsy, but considering the hour, that seemed unlikely. "Your home tutor took today off, huh?"

"Yup."

Actually, on Senjogahara's days I went to her house, and on Hanekawa's days we went to the library, so "home tutor" wasn't accurate.

Going to a cram school or taking exam-prep courses had been an option, but sadly, my parents weren't persuaded. Let's just say that my behavior until then had taken its toll. I had a lot of catching up to do.

"Am I going to have to study for college entrance exams too?" my sister wondered out loud. "Ugh."

"Right, you guys don't have to take any for high school."

The blessings of an integrated secondary school—both of my sisters had passed their junior-high entrance exams without even studying... How so clever of them.

"It won't be for a while yet, even if you decide to," I reminded Tsukihi. "Isn't it a little early for you to be thinking about that?"

"Yeah, I suppose, but seeing you get so serious all of a sudden has me worried."

"My sincere apologies... Hey, where's what's-her-face?"

"What's-her-face?"

"The bigger sister."

"Karen's out."

"That's weird."

What was weird wasn't that Karen was out, but rather Tsukihi lying around on the couch at home when Karen had left—the Fire Sisters usually operated as a team. And anytime they worked separately, chances were it was because they were up to no good.

"You two better not be stirring up trouble."

"We're not stirring up anything, thank you very much," Tsukihi said. "You're always like that—treating me and Karen like we're kids. You worry too much."

"I'm not worried. I just don't trust you, that's all."

"Isn't that the same thing?"

"No, one's worry and one's trust. There's a pretty clear difference between the two."

"That's just mincing wor—phew..."

"At least finish your sentence!"

What a stupid exchange. Then again, if it was so stupid, why bother finishing a sentence? Back to the topic at hand.

"So," I asked, "where did the bigger sister go?"

"Like I told you, she's not getting up to trouble. In fact, she's clearing up some trouble."

"That's what I mean by trouble."

"Really?"

"Just tell me what happened, before the trouble turns into trauma. Confess and wear the badge of traitor with honor. Whatever's happened, it may still be early enough to do something about it."

"Gross. Don't go around sticking your nose into middle-school fights, it's lame. Fighting, I'll have you know, is a very important form of communication. There are far too many people who don't know how to fight constructively these days, don't you think?"

"Well, when you put it that way, it almost sounds right—"

"The problem isn't in fighting. It's in not knowing the right way to fight," Tsukihi got carried away and started to sound full of herself. She looked smug.

"You say that, but when you two get in a fight, it's nearly always accompanied by violence. I don't see how you can call that the right way…"

"An eye for an eye and a tooth for a tooth."

"That's B.C. thinking. You know it's the twentieth century?"

Okay, the twenty-first, actually.

"In that case," Tsukihi countered, "how about a tooth for an eye, and blunt-force trauma for a tooth?"

"You'd triple it?!"

"Oh, shut up!" she exploded in a sudden fit of temper.

The smug look from just moments before was nowhere to be seen.

"Just leave me alone! I don't know anything! Whether it's bigger or little or middle!"

"Since when are there three of you…"

Tsk, this is what I meant when I said they weren't worth worrying about.

At any rate, motivated by other people's troubles and concerns as the Fire Sisters were, they weren't keen to spill the details of whatever they had on their plate at the moment. And I wasn't about to wade into some complete stranger's privacy.

I guess it didn't really matter. They'd probably come talk to me when things got to be too much for them to handle. Just so long as it didn't involve another kidnapping rigmarole.

I muttered, "Seriously, though…I'm not going to tell you to grow up, but maybe grow a little quieter."

"You're one to talk!"

Tsukihi grabbed the remote control by her side and threw it at me. Cripes. Was she crazy? I couldn't just dodge it, so I caught it somehow and set it back down on the table.

All things considered, I suppose growing "quieter" was the taller order. Growing up is just part of getting older.

Being as quiet as, say, Sengoku is a problem in its own right.

If Karen and Tsukihi could be about a tenth as quiet as Sengoku, and Sengoku could be about a tenth as active as Karen and Tsukihi, then everything would be just right.

Unfortunately, life isn't that easy. You can't just divide and multiply people that way.

"Ah, right…Sengoku," I came up with what I should do today. Or rather, remembered.

Come to think of it, I'd been putting off a promise to go hang out with her. The bookstore could wait.

Nadeko Sengoku.

She was actually one of Tsukihi's classmates from back in elementary school. One of the friends my sister invited over to our house to play—at the time I shared a room with Tsukihi (and Karen), so Sengoku became an acquaintance of mine as well, even though we were in different grades. I stopped seeing her after Tsukihi entered a private middle school, but the other day I ran into Sengoku again under unexpected circumstances.

Very unexpected.

Namely, aberration-related.

Anyways, after we cleared up her problem, Sengoku came over one day to hang out. That was thanks to my good offices: I figured bringing her and Tsukihi together again would be cool.

As Karen and Tsukihi's brother, I find their characters highly dubious, but kids their own age seem to dig the same traits and flock to them, of all things—I don't know if "personable" is the word I want, but they possess some mystery charisma skill that I'm failing to appreciate. In any case, it did the trick with an old elementary school friend whom Tsukihi hadn't seen in a long time, and she and Sengoku were soon playing together like they used to.

On her way out, our guest had said, "Come over to Nadeko's place next time to hang out," and I'd nodded yes.

That was a good while ago, in fact. Not that I'd forgotten, but a lot happened in the meantime, and I also started getting serious about studying for my entrance exams.

Maybe it was cold of me.

Now seemed like as good a time as any, though. I decided to give Sengoku a call.

Like most junior high schoolers out in the country, she didn't own a cell phone, so I had to ring her at home. I pulled my device, which had the number saved, from my pocket.

I'd received but not made a call to her in some time. It was still before noon, but since this was Sengoku, she'd already be up.

"H…Hewwo?! Sengoku rezdensh!"

I'd expected her parents to come to their home phone, but it was Sengoku who picked up. Except she was lisping like she was Hachikuji.

Hmm? Had I woken her up? I hadn't seen that coming.

Sengoku didn't seem like the type to sleep in all morning just because it was summer vacation.

"Big Brother Koyomi, long time no hear… What's wrong?"

She spoke clearly this time. Huh, but I hadn't said anything yet. How did she—ah, of course, you didn't need a cell phone to have caller ID these days.

"Sorry to bother you out of the blue like this," I said, "but remember when we talked about hanging out at your place? I was thinking, what about today?"

"Wh-Whaaat?!"

She sounded surprised. Way too surprised.

Odd, I could have sworn we had a promise.

Maybe she'd forgotten.

"Is this too sudden? If today's no good—"

"Y-Yes! Today, today, today! I'm busy almost every day but today!"

I couldn't remember Sengoku ever being so adamant. I didn't know she could holler like that, either. "I see. If you're that busy, then I guess it's got to be today… Can I head over right now?"

"Yes! Almost any time other than right now is no good!"

Geez. Talk about a murderous schedule.

Middle schoolers these days had it tough… I wish my sisters would take a hint instead of squandering their precious youth running around playing defenders of justice. More than just a tenth, too.

"I'll be there soon," I said, hanging up.

Then I looked over at Tsukihi.

She'd switched the TV back on and tuned in to a morning talk show (Saturday edition) to catch the latest celebrity gossip, this time with seeming interest. She liked to pretend she was above that stuff, but she was basically a fangirl. I wish she'd use her charisma skill on me, too.

"All right, you heard me," I said.

"Huh? Come again?"

"Weren't you listening?"

"Am I being scolded for not eavesdropping on people's calls?"

"Ahh…" She had a point. "I was just on the phone with Sengoku."

"And you're heading over to Sen's, yeah?"

"So you were listening."

"Have fun." Tsukihi waved half-heartedly, not even looking up as she spoke. "I'll mind the fort."

"Not so fast. You're coming along."

"Excuse me?" Tsukihi turned around like she was surprised.

37

"If I'm going to Sengoku's house, obviously you're coming with me."

"From what I did hear, I figured you'd be going by yourself. Besides, I'm pretty sure that's what Sen is expecting."

"Really? I doubt it."

On the phone, I'd assumed Tsukihi would be coming with me. Did I forget to mention that?

"Whatever, I don't care," my sister said. "But I'm pretty sure I'd just be in the way, so why don't you go alone? That's probably what Sen would prefer."

"What the heck. Why would you be in the way if we went to see Sengoku? Besides, how busy could you be?"

"How busy could you bee?"

"That doesn't even make sense unless it's written down!"

"Ah, I almost forgot. I have club activities today."

"I seem to recall your tea ceremony club getting suspended for the whole summer."

That was thanks to a Japanese-clothing fashion show they'd put on for their culture festival. The originator of the cute plan was a certain junior-high girl who happened to be right in front of me. True, the brunt of the blame belonged on her shoulders, but personally, I thought the club members (and advisor) who let themselves be talked into it needed to have their heads examined as well.

"It's independent study. Independent study."

"Hush up, you kimono cosplay maniac. There's more to fashion than looking good in something."

"I don't need lessons from someone whose idea of fashion is jeans and a hoodie."

"You've got a point there… I still don't get it, though. Why are you being so weird about coming with me?"

"A-N-Y-W-A-Y-S…" A moment away from blowing a fuse, she said tensely, "I'm not such a jerk that I'd get in the way of a friend's crush, even if it's not meant to be."

"Crush? Like cans? I don't think we'll be doing anything like that.

Sengoku is a prim girl. You know, unlike my sisters?"

"I actually noticed it back in elementary school, but I mean, you only met a handful of times, so talk about devoted… How many years has it been, anyway? I could never pull it off, myself. Not that I'd want to."

"Huh?"

"Let me ask you something. Do you believe that boys and girls can be just friends?"

"Of course I do." Not too long ago, I probably would have retorted that I didn't even believe in friendships between the same sex, but my reply was immediate. "Look at me and Sengoku, we're good friends."

"I see. Fine then. Okay, have fun."

"……"

Hmm, she wasn't budging. There didn't seem to be any point in arguing further.

"Sure," I backed down, "I guess I'll go on my own. Take care of things here. And when the bigger one comes home, tell her I need to talk to her."

It was probably futile, but I'd try my luck with Karen, too.

"All right, see ya," I said.

"One more thing…"

"Huh?"

"Lately, you don't get into serious scuffles with Karen. Why is that?"

That…

I hadn't anticipated being prodded from that angle.

Had it been on Tsukihi's mind?

I was bewildered that she'd bring it up just then, but maybe she'd been wanting to ask for some time now.

"No reason…" I sounded like I had something to hide, despite myself. "It's just that Karen is getting so strong these days, I almost expect to hear a level-up sound effect. If I fought her for real, I'd lose. Even though she's surpassed me in height, you'd think I'd be stronger, but I guess I'm no match for a real martial artist."

"Maybe that's true for Karen, but when I started to get hysteric just now, you backed down right away. It's like you're being mature or something."

"Hm… Maybe…"

"Before, you'd have wrung my neck for sure."

"I never went that far!"

Actually…I'd be lying if I said never.

Once or twice…or maybe three or four times.

"It makes getting our way easier so that works out for us," Tsukihi said in a flippant tone that reminded me more of Karen, "but I don't know. I mean, could you please not grow up all alone? It's boring."

Growing up was just part of getting older.

It didn't seem like the right time to say so.

004

It's not like I could tell Tsukihi the real reason, though. "The truth is, while you guys weren't looking, I went and got turned into a vampire. Luckily I was able to become human again, but the aftereffects haven't gone away, so I have to be careful not to get into fights with you two just in case I slip up and accidentally kill you." How was I supposed to say something like that with a straight face?

But I was probably worrying about nothing.

My current relationship with Shinobu Oshino—the vampire who lurked in my shadow—was deceptively simple. Confusing in its straight-forwardness. I was still Shinobu's thrall and servant, but she existed in a reduced state as a vampire and as an aberration, neither able to live nor die without me.

To clarify, I could still become part-vampire by providing blood to Shinobu, and she, by drawing blood from me, could regain a modest amount of her vampiric strength. Put another way, unless it was imme-diately after giving blood to Shinobu, the aftereffects consisted of just accelerated healing—so I probably didn't need to worry about getting into a fight with Karen, or rather, I might lose against such a martial arts adept, as I'd told Tsukihi. Still.

I knew, now.

What fighting, battling, meant.

Not just sparring, but warring.

Not just punching each other, but killing each other.

What warring and killing each other meant.

As a result—I just couldn't get into fights with my sisters like before. Until Tsukihi brought it up today, I was doing my best not to think about it, but deep down I had.

—*I mean.*

—*Could you please not grow up all alone?*

—*It's boring.*

Karen had said the exact opposite to me.

You know, Koyomi—that's why you never grow up.

In the end, Karen probably had it right. It's not that I'd changed on the inside.

Only, I knew now.

Of course, I doubt Tsukihi wanted me to wring her neck—but to borrow her phrase, there definitely was a right and a wrong way to fight.

Thinking such thoughts.

I got dressed appropriately to visit someone's house (though as Tsukihi nailed it, my fashion sense begins and ends with jeans and a hoodie) and left the house.

Sengoku actually lived fairly close. The first time I walked her home I was surprised at just how close. Since we'd attended the same public elementary school, that made perfect sense when I thought about it—you didn't even need a bike and could walk there in ten minutes.

Just because it was close, though, didn't mean I couldn't take my bike. But Sengoku might want some time to get ready, so I decided to stroll over there on foot.

Along the way, however…

I spotted someone from behind that I recognized. It wasn't her back so much as her backpack.

"Huh, it's Hachikuji."

A giant backpack strapped to a tiny frame. Pigtails and a visibly cheeky profile. It had to be Mayoi Hachikuji.

A fifth-grade girl.

We first met when I called out to her as she was wandering around lost. She seemed to live in a different town now, but still liked to haunt ours. Even so, since she was just a grade schooler, I didn't have any way to contact her, and the best I could hope for was to run into her by accident like this. Hanekawa and I saw Hachikuji as a lucky item that brought you good fortune if you encountered her on a given day. This was my first time since summer vacation began—in fact, hadn't it been even longer than that?

Hmm… Hmm… Hmm…

Sengoku was waiting for me, after all.

To begin with, I didn't even like Mayoi, the little brat—actually, I downright hated her, okay? We weren't buddies, so why say hi just because she happened to be passing by? We could be standing face to face, and I might still ignore her!

But hey, as a high schooler and her elder, taking such an attitude would be rather small of me. A grown man knows how to interact with people he doesn't like. Why not give a little kid the time of day, it's only proper, eh? Seriously, it wasn't like I was happy to see her or anything, but wasn't pretending that I was just common courtesy?

Ha, I'm too nice.

I dropped into a cold sprint, dashed toward her at record speed, and hugged her as tight as I could.

"Hachikujiii! I missed you, kid!"

"Eeeek?!" screamed li'l miss Hachikuji, grabbed suddenly from behind. Ignoring it, I rained kisses down onto her soft cheeks.

"Ahh, I haven't seen you in so long, I thought you were gone, I was so worried! Aaah, let me feel you more and hug you more and lick you all over!"

"Eeek! Eeek! Eeek!"

"Tut! Stop squirming so much! I can't get off your panties!"

"Aiiieeeeeeeeeeee!!"

She kept screaming at the top of her lungs, and then…

"Grrah!"

She bit me.

"Grrah! Grrah! Grrah!"

"That hurt! What the hell?!"

Once again—

Both halves of it should have been directed at myself.

Anyway, you got me. The truth is I'm crazy about Hachikuji.

Leaving a bite mark on my arm that I thought might never disappear, she slipped free of my demonic grasp (?) and leapt back.

"Fssssk!" she hissed.

Feral mode.

"W-Wait! Hachikuji, look! It's me!"

Given my behavior, seeing it was me meant next to nothing, but I was glad I gave it a shot because her eyes, which had turned feral, alert, and red (so inhuman), slowly returned to their normal color (not green, let me note just in case).

"…Ah…" Recognizing my face and drawing back her claws, she said, "Who is it but Mister Araragi. Yomiko Araragi…"

"That's so close, but would you mind not confusing me with a 'paper master' attached to the British Library Special Operations Division? My name is Koyomi Araragi."

I was pretty sure that having pronounced my last name correctly, she'd gone out of her way to mess up my first.

That was me and Hachikuji's thing. I sexually harassed her whenever and however I liked, and in return she mangled my name whenever and however she liked. It was a gentleman's pact.

"Hold on just a minute, Mister Araragi! I haven't heard of a treaty that one-sided since the Kanagawa Convention!"

"Really? Seems pretty fair to me…"

"Besides, your idea of sexual harassment is starting to border on the criminal! I'm starting to fear for my feminine virtue!"

Hachikuji's complaint sounded sincere.

It wasn't like I had no idea what she was getting at. More like the opposite.

Why was I unable to control myself when it came to Hachikuji?

"What are you talking about?" I lied. "That was just a hug. They do it all the time in America."

"Since when do people sneak up from behind to give a hug?!"

"That's the problem with this country, no one's ever open to new things."

"Just where do you think you're from?! And also, Mister Araragi, maybe you just meant to kiss me on the cheek, but you missed and touched the corner of my lips a couple of times!"

"I did?! I'm sorry!"

Obviously I didn't mean to go that far!

What an unfortunate accident!

"What can I say," Hachikuji sighed. "With all the squeezing and grabbing you do, I feel like my breasts have gotten bigger. Maybe that old wives' tale about them growing when a man fondles them is actually true."

"Really? You can grow?"

"Excuse me!"

Hachikuji's pigtails stood up straight. Had she commanded them to? What kind of system was she running on?

"But," I said, "I thought part of what made you special was that you don't grow up."

"What a foolish observation. And next time you do something like that, I might have to tell Miss Hanekawa on you."

"Ugh… That would suck."

I meant it. Lately, Hanekawa and Hachikuji were getting along too well for my liking.

That alliance spelled trouble for me.

Well, maybe it was more of a survivors' group.

"By the way, were you headed somewhere?" asked Hachikuji, neatly changing the subject.

She could be easygoing.

So easygoing that I worried about her, sometimes.

"No, not exactly," I answered.

"Searching for a new member of the Araragi Harem?"

"I haven't been putting together such a tasteless outfit!"

"After all, a member of the first class, Mister Oshino, has graduated. You'll have a hard time filling that hole."

"Even if there were an Araragi Harem, why count him as a former member?! He's an aloha shirt-wearing geezer!"

"Be careful, with too many, developing the narrative will become a chore."

Hachikuji made the meta remark nonchalantly.

It was also a realistic point.

The harem bit was nonsense, but it's impossible to be fair to all of the people, all of the time. Taking someone's side means not taking somebody else's. It means being on somebody's opposite side.

Defenders of justice—only ever sided with justice.

They were enemies of all but justice.

You couldn't fake it.

In short, justice is—ready to betray us all.

"Good point," I admitted, "I'll keep it in mind."

"Please do. Then again, as long as no one tries to take my spot, I guess I don't care how many new members you get."

"Since when did you get tenure?!"

Let me make one thing clear! The only official members are Shinobu and Hanekawa (damn straight)!

"You're still just 'today's special guest,' Hachikuji."

"If you say so. Maybe you'd better start moving this program along, then."

"I messed up?!"

The MC was being called out by a guest! Oh, the humiliation!

"Well, okay," I moved things along, "have I mentioned Sengoku to you before? She's an old acquaintance. I was making my way over to her place to hang out today."

"Uh huh," Hachikuji nodded, always brisk with her rejoinders. "But why should you look so unhappy about it?"

"I do?"

"Yes, you look morone."

"That almost sounds like a word!"

Morose, she meant.

True, I had been thinking gloomy thoughts. Keeping secrets from your family, who lived under the same roof as you, was unpleasant anyway you looked at it.

"Still," I said, "I didn't think I was bothered enough that you could tell just by looking. Did I seem so unhappy?"

"You did. It was an awkward expression, like if a story that constantly made self-deprecating jokes about not getting made into an anime did get adapted out of carelessness."

"That specific a facial expression?!"

"Relax. It's not as if an anime adaptation would force you to continue a story that already has a neat conclusion."

"What the hell are you saying now?!"

Hachikuji's speech broached a different dimension at times.

This girl.

"It's understandable to be nervous about unexpected good fortune," she consoled me. "Yet there's always something to gain from branching out into new territory."

"I'd appreciate your words, if I had such worries…"

Come to think of it, Oshino used to go on about anime adaptation this and anime adaptation that. I had no idea why, but maybe he and Hachikuji could have a constructive conversation.

Hmm. Now that I mention it, they've never met or talked to each other, directly or indirectly, have they?

Anyway, I decided to play along with Hachikuji, and not just because I'd been reminded of Oshino. "What do you mean…something to gain?"

"In a word? Money," replied Hachikuji.

Just one word, but a word too many!

"There's gotta be something else," I objected.

"Huh?" Hachikuji wrinkled her nose in disgust, and her brow knitted together in contempt—oi, what a face for a grade schooler to make. "What else is there in this world besides money?"

"There's plenty! Like...love!"

"Mm? Love? Ah, of course, of course. They were selling it at the convenience store the other day."

"They were selling it?! At the convenience store?!"

"Right. 298 yen."

"So cheap!"

"When it comes down to it, what are humans but a transportation system for money?"

"Geez, what happened in your life to screw you up so bad?! If you want to talk about it, I'm all ears!"

"Think about it. Between Billionaire A, who says 'money makes the world go round,' and Billionaire B, who says 'money isn't everything,' don't you actually prefer Billionaire A?"

"That's relative!"

I prefer neither!

"Money talk aside, Mister Araragi, I'm dying to know what sort of dance they'll have us do for the ending song."

"Why is dancing a premise?!"

"I hope it's something sexy, like for *Cat's Eye*."

"If you don't mind just being in silhouette!"

Honestly, though...what a dated reference for a grade schooler. A classic or not, these days not even teenagers knew the ending animation to *Cat's Eye*.

"That's not it, Hachikuji. Actually, I can talk to you about it, can't I? Remember my vampiric nature?"

"You don't say?!"

"Don't forget such a crucial bit of backstory!"

Hachikuji looked so genuinely surprised, it didn't seem like an act.

"I thought you were just some guy who likes ramen noodles," she said.

"Since when is liking ramen part of my backstory?!"

"Didn't you know every instant noodle flavor in the country?"

"I didn't and I don't!" What kind of sad expertise was that? At least have me sampling real ramen.

"Koyomi Araragi, the man who sampled every local ramen... If I recall correctly, your current favorite is Yubari King Melon instant ramen, correct?"

"There's no way that's a real flavor!"

Then again...I wouldn't bet against it. They sell some pretty weird specialties as souvenirs sometimes.

"Hmph." Hachikuji crossed her arms and frowned. "I stand corrected, Mister Asuragi."

"I almost want to change my name now, that sounds so badass. But I keep telling you, Hachikuji, my name is Araragi."

"Sorry, a slip of the tongue."

"No, it was on purpose..."

"Spill of the tongue?"

"It wasn't?!"

"Pills on my tongue?"

"I'm not a convenience store!"

Love, too? Were we going to go buy love?

298 yen!

"I see, Mister Araragi," Hachikuji pronounced my name just fine. "A vampire. Now that you mention it, you might be right. Well, what about it?"

"Hey, I can't just come out and tell them even if they're family. I'm starting to wonder how much longer I can keep it a secret, though. Sure, I'm human again, but the aftereffects remain."

"There's such a thing as being too honest, isn't there? It's only natural to keep a secret or two, even from family members."

"Hachikuji…"

Right. With everything she'd gone through, Hachikuji had her own distinct perspective when it came to family issues. Mine might just sound trivial to the point of being insensitive.

"After all," she said, "when you tell someone a secret, you get that person involved, whether they want to be or not. Maybe sharing would make you feel better, but wouldn't you just be burdening them?"

"Hm…true."

"Besides, if I had a son and he came home one day with some delusional story about being a vampire or aberration or whatever, I'd rush him off to the hospital to be committed."

"Too true!"

But there was certainly that.

Maybe they didn't commit her, but in Senjogahara's case, that's the way her family, at least, saw it. They treated her aberration as an illness. And then there was Kanbaru. Hers meant that her left arm still hadn't returned to normal… How was she coping with it? She couldn't keep her family from noticing simply by wrapping her arm up in bandages, could she?

"Mister Araragi, what you need right now is…yes! The courage to keep secrets!"

"Ah! Now that's inspiring!"

"All I did was add 'courage to' to make it sound positive. Actually, it's just a secret!"

"You let yours out of the bag!"

"Pretty much anything can come out sounding positive if you just slap 'courage to' on it."

"Come on… Language isn't as simple as that. It's a sophisticated communication tool formed over millennia. Have a little respect, Hachikuji."

"Want me to prove it?"

"Go ahead. If you can convince me, I'll do a handstand right here in the middle of the street."

"A handstand."

"Yeah, think of it as advanced genuflection. But if you can't convince me, then you're the one who has to do a handstand…skirt and all! You're gonna expose your kiddy underwear to the public gaze until I say okay!"

Case in point!

I still sounded like a creep, no matter how cheerfully I said it!

There's language for you!

Hachikuji replied, "Fine, I accept your challenge."

"Hmph. At least you've got guts."

"You're like a phoenix to the flame, Mister Araragi."

"That sounds kinda cool?!"

"Ahem," Hachikuji cleared her throat. She was showboating. "Let's start off small… The courage to lie to your lover."

"Gulp."

That wasn't half bad.

You were just lying to your boyfriend or girlfriend, but adding "courage to" made it sound like a pious lie—without even trying to make the point.

"The courage to betray one's friends."

"Gosh."

That was amazing. In the end, you merely betrayed your friends, but—without even trying to make such a point—it sounded like you were trying to protect them.

"The courage to do harm."

"Ungh…"

A groan escaped my lips. You were just being a nuisance, but why did I see a man willing to suffer pariahdom in order to do the right thing? Without even trying to make the point, too.

"The courage to grope."

"Sh-Shit."

This was turning into a bloodbath.

Even a crime as low as groping sounded like it was driven by some higher purpose for whose sake the perpetrator had no choice but to stand falsely accused. Without even trying to make the point, again!

"The courage to be indolent."

"I-Incredible…"

My back was against the wall.

You were just wasting time and doing nothing, but it sounded like you were abasing yourself and living in poverty for some great cause—without ever trying to make such a point at all!

B-But!

It was still too early to admit defeat!

"The courage to admit defeat."

"…I admit defeat!"

Ahh!

Enchanted by the sound of it, I'd gone ahead and admitted defeat!

There's language for you!

It's quite a simple thing, really.

"Now then, Mister Araragi, let me see how advanced your genuflection is."

"Of course…the courage to stand on one's head."

I dropped into a handstand.

In the middle of my own neighborhood.

I was glad Karen and Tsukihi weren't here to see this. Well, in fact… Tsukihi aside, Karen used to walk to school on her hands all the time before she started junior high. She'd been a laughingstock. She'd boast that she was training her arms, but what she was really working out was my capacity for shame.

"Yikes…" winced Hachikuji. "Watching someone your age do a handstand just feels wrong. You can stop now."

"…"

"Really, you can stop, Mister Araragi."

"…"

"Seriously, I'm begging you. It's even more embarrassing to be watching next to you. Why persist on standing on your head like it's a promise to a friend who passed away?"

"Actually," I said, staring up at Hachikuji from my upside-down position, "as disappointed as I am that I didn't get to see you do a handstand, from this angle I can see your panties just fine."

Our wager.

Either way, I was never going to lose.

"Hnnrk?!"

Li'l miss Hachikuji flushed red in embarrassment, but her first reaction wasn't to "hold down her skirt" but instead to "kick me in the face." Thanks to the angle, her low kick hit me full-force square in the face. Not many situations where a low kick does that.

"Mister Araragi! You pervert!"

"The courage to be branded a pervert!"

"Wow, cool! When you put it that way, I'm tempted to let you look all you want! Especially since you managed to maintain your handstand even after getting kicked in the face!" It was a near miraculous feat of balance, if I do say so myself. "The very technique I created, turned against me... Oh, the irony!"

"Ahaha! Your hubris was your downfall, Hachikuji! I stole your secret technique and perfected it!"

"Wh-What have I done... I've unleashed a monster!"

"I'm sorry for saying you were wearing kiddy underwear, though. I would've never imagined you'd be wearing see-through black panties."

"Excuse me?! What are you talking about, look closer! You're going to damage my brand! I know what's demanded of me and stick to kiddy underwear! Can't you see the bunny on them?!"

"I don't see any bunny. If you want me to, you're gonna have to come closer."

"L-Like this?!"

Well.

I really didn't want my neighbors to start gossiping about this. I shifted my weight over and planted my feet back on the ground.

Aw, shucks... My hands were dirty.

I clapped them together to clean them.

It was probably my soul that was stained now, but there was no clapping it.

"Anyway, Hachikuji, what were we talking about?"

"About how much you love panties."

"Honestly, I could take them or leave them. Just ask Hanekawa."

"……"

Hachikuji offered no rejoinder, which was rare.

Had Hanekawa told her something?

If so, I was in hot water. Damn, the survivors' group was a menace. I was going to have to nip it in the bud.

"Ah, right," I brought the conversation back on track, "we were saying it would be better if I kept all the aberration stuff secret."

"Yes, indeed."

"Well, I suppose I wouldn't like being committed. Since I'm still a tiny bit undead, they might turn me into some sort of science experiment."

"True, I hope they just treat you as a nutcase." With that callous preamble, Hachikuji reminded, "*To know about aberrations is to become involved with them. If that's true, forget about other people—you're the one who'll wind up getting sucked into more funny business.*"

To know about aberrations is to become involved with them.

Hadn't Oshino said something like that?

Coming into contact with an aberration, even just once, supposedly gave that world a hold on you, and you got sucked in, unable to escape.

Hanekawa, enchanted by a cat.

Senjogahara, met by a crab.

Hachikuji, misled by a snail.

Kanbaru, heard by a monkey.

Sengoku, entwined by a serpent.

And of course, it went without saying…

Me, bitten by a vampire.

We were all semi-denizens of that world now. It was like having one foot in the grave—and not just metaphorically. In which case…

If I cared about the other person. If I cared about Karen and Tsukihi… It was safer for them not to know.

Hachikuji continued, "You could lay everything bare, including the risks, so that your family is steeled for whatever may come. But that option seems pretty risky."

"Yeah. It would definitely be high-risk, plus it doesn't sound like it would be very high-return. In that case, I'd rather go the low-risk, low-return route."

"Loli-risk, loli-return? Oh my. What a stunning philosophy."

"I've never heard of such a route!"

Hachikuji liked to pretend I had a Lolita complex. Which wasn't true. I don't have a pedophiliac bone in my body.

Just look at my actual girlfriend, Senjogahara. There's not an ounce of Lolita about her. If anything, she's mature beyond her age.

"But you're just a sham couple, right?" asked Hachikuji.

"Why would you think that?! I guess there are sham marriages, but a sham couple?"

"You've got a Lolita complex and are actually in love with me, while Miss Senjogahara is a lesbian who is in love with Miss Kanbaru."

"Ack, that doesn't sound like a joke! I don't want to think about it!"

I like you well enough, Hachikuji, but the second half is too much! The Valhalla Duo is getting too cozy lately! As if they have some emptiness to fill!

"Anyway, Mister Lol-ing Araragi…"

"I don't need a funny tag line! And 'lol' doesn't have any pedo nuance, okay?"

"You say that, but when you move out to live on your own, I bet you'll be rolling out a carpet."

"These days most apartments don't have tatami mattresses, but so what?!"

"When you go fishing, try trolling."

"Damn if I knew what you meant!"

What a compendium of rhymes! And she was a grade schooler, too!

"Phew," Hachikuji sighed.

She was using a pause as punctuation.

"Anyway, Mister Claragi…"

"That's actually some fine wordplay, Hachikuji, but this isn't *Girl of the Alps*, and I'm not a well-off young lady trying to stand up from her wheelchair. Miss Claragi is going to stay put. My name is Araragi."

"Sorry, a slip of the tongue."

"No, it was on purpose…"

"I slip on the tongue."

"It wasn't?!"

"I slip on the dung."

"What a place to land on!"

Hell, the way she talked…these weren't slips of the tongue but somersaults.

"Anyway, Mister Araragi," she said—or re-said. "Aberrations are the backstage, so to speak."

"The backstage?"

"Usually, all you see is the actual stage—that's what we know as reality. But sometimes some lame-o comes along who wants to peek behind the curtain."

"…"

"It's the sort of thing where, if you don't need to know, it's better not to. You might convince yourself that by knowing what goes on backstage you're unraveling the secret mysteries of the world—but in fact, by learning about aberrations, all you're doing is creating more questions without answers."

"I see…" I was surprised. Since when did Hachikuji get so astute?

Back in the day, she didn't even seem to understand aberrations at all—or perhaps, what she didn't was her own self.

And as far as not knowing goes—we don't really know.

But that allows you to say certain things.

In which case…maybe I needed to follow her lead.

"You worry too much," she said. "Why make things so complicat-ed? However insurmountable it seems now, in a hundred years we'll look back on it and laugh."

"That's a long time to wait!"

I'd probably be dead by then! As a doornail!

"Yes," she agreed. "In other words, after all that time worrying, we'll laugh at you after you die."

"That's terrible!"

"They say that gossip only spreads to seventy-five people."

"That many?!"

"We live in the internet age, so if seventy-five people know, so does the world."

"Why tell me that?!"

"If worrying about something doesn't lead to a solution, then it's not worth worrying about in the first place. You're like a voice actor complaining that she sounds like an anime character."

"That does sound pretty pointless…"

"Putting that aside, how come when one manga author says, 'Thank you for all your fan letters, I make sure to read every one!' and another one says, 'Thank you for all your blog comments, I make sure to (search for and) read every one,' even though they're basically doing the same thing, for some reason it still leaves a different impression?"

"What a stunning insight into the millennial generation!"

Yes, that's an exaggeration.

"Anyway," said Hachikuji, "if one of your family members ever does step behind the curtain—you can be there to guide them. But until then, it would be better if you just did nothing."

"Oh…"

Doing nothing—was an option.

She had a point.

"Or to be blunt," she added, "stop thinking about it so much."

"Yeah, you're probably right." Why not get into the occasional scuffle with my sisters? After all, I wasn't nearly as grownup as Tsukihi seemed to think.

It was just that I'd taken a glimpse behind the scenes. When it came down to it, we were just kids, me included.

"Yes, Mister Araragi. To be blunter, stop thinking about your *little sisters* so much."

"Why the emphasis?! You're making it sound like something else!"

I'd said "family" precisely for that reason. But I guess I wasn't fooling anyone!

"We really got into this," I muttered.

I was on my way to Sengoku's house. It was about time I got going.

"Sorry, Hachikuji. I didn't mean to keep you. You were probably on your way somewhere, too."

"Oh no, not really. I just wander the streets lost like this, all the time."

"Come on…"

"Or to be bluntest, I was just taking a walk thinking, *Didn't Mister Araragi live around here? I haven't run into him lately, but maybe I will?*"

"Hey."

Really. What a nice thing to say.

"Good girl. Hachikuji, from now on, when you spot me, you can be the one to run up and hug me."

"I'm afraid I'd rather not. Don't get the wrong idea, please. You're totally not my type."

"I've been dumped by a grade schooler!"

The shock! The impact of being asked not to get the wrong idea by a girl who wasn't a tsundere!

"Who's your type, anyway?" I asked her.

"I go wild for hermits, especially the old mountain-dwelling variety."

"I've heard of liking older men, but that's ancient!"

I'd have to live a few more centuries before I qualified! That was too high a hurdle.

"I don't get it," I persisted. "We've been on countless adventures and even had brushes with death together."

"So what if we did?"

"Have you ever heard of the suspension-bridge effect?"

"You mean the psychological thing where you're alone with someone on a suspension bridge, and you suddenly want to shove the other person off even though you don't dislike him?"

"It's nothing so scary!"

Well. There probably was something like that in psychology.

Like an impulse to shove the person in front of you onto the tracks, for no reason, when you're waiting on the platform for a train.

The exact opposite of the suspension-bridge effect.

"Actually," Hachikuji objected, "I've never gone on any adventures or had brushes with death with you."

"What are you saying? How many times have I used my Avan-style sword-kill technique to save you?"

"You're a disciple of Avan, as in the *Dragon Quest* anime?!"

"That's right. A hero, who kills."

"I don't remember at all."

"Ah, I see. During the climax of our adventure, you tried to protect me and took a blow to your head. The injury must have brought on amnesia."

"Such an affecting conclusion!"

"Indeed. I'll never forget the first thing you said to me when you finally woke up in the hospital."

"'Who am I, and how did I get here?'"

"No, 'Who are you, and do you go to a good school?'"

"Struck with amnesia, and still a captive to our educational system!"

"But even if you've forgotten me, Hachikuji, I'll never forget you."

"So you were caring for me devotedly as the credits rolled!"

"No, it ended with me marrying your little sister."

"You forgot me!"

"No! You're always there, in my heart!"

"I thought I was in the hospital!"

True.

Besides, Hachikuji doesn't even have a sister. She's an only child.

"Listen up, though," I said. "Before long, I'll be the kind of man you can fall for. But don't try crawling back to me then because it'll be too late."

"Are you sure?"

"Uh, sorry, I was being difficult. Please declare your love to me whenever, even if I'm already on my deathbed."

How pathetic. Who'd ever fall for a guy like that?

"Until next time," I told her.

"Yes, see you again."

"Um, Hachikuji—" I blurted out lamely when we'd said goodbye. I couldn't help but ask. Maybe I shouldn't have, but I couldn't help it. "You're not going to disappear, are you?"

"Huh?" Hachikuji cocked her head at me in response. She seemed genuinely confused.

"It's just—I meant it when I said I was worried after not seeing you for so long. Oshino went somewhere, and one day, you might disappear too…"

No.

Hachikuji had her own stuff to worry about.

In fact, it might be better for her—if her family circumstances demanded it.

But still.

Even so.

"Teehee."

A tinkling laugh escaped Hachikuji.

Her expression was so childlike.

"Mister Araragi, who's usually so busy accommodating everyone else, can only act needy like this with me, I bet, and maybe Shinobu."

"Hmph."

"I was right, you are Mister Lol-ing Araragi."

"H-Hmph."

I wish she wouldn't say that.

In the first place, Shinobu was five hundred years old—not a Lolita but a Granny Dolores.

"I'm honored, really," I was assured.

"Hachikuji—"

"Let me ask you a question, too, Mister Araragi. If I were ever in real trouble and needed help, could you please come save me?"

Save.

Oshino detested that word.

For my part, though—I still felt as if that's what he'd done for me.

And.

I wanted to do what he did.

"Of course," I answered right away. "I'd be there so fast that no one else would have a chance to save you first."

"I can come to you when I need to talk?"

"Hey, if you didn't, I'd get mad at you."

"I thought you might say so," Hachikuji noted as though to parry my words. Her smile looked—almost forlorn. "There must be some reason that I'm able to stay in this town even when I'm not lost anymore. Until that reason becomes clear, I won't be going anywhere."

She was talking about herself as if she were discussing a stranger. In a sense, I suppose she was. If you didn't understand yourself, who could be more of a stranger?

"A reason, huh?"

"Yes," she said. "So even if it wasn't going to be an anime, there would have been a sequel."

"......"

She was talking nonsense again.

She was losing me, but she went on. "Besides, wasn't the previous ending a little negligent towards me? After heading out to search for Shinobu, where on earth did I go?"

"Don't ask me... Only you know where. You probably just got lost again."

Hmm. Come to think of it, she didn't make an appearance in the epilogue.

Maybe the MC really was off his game.

We needed to hold a review meeting.

"But Hachikuji," I said, "if it means you going away, I don't want any sequels. So what if we never found out what's keeping you here."

"I'm glad to hear that. Well, even if I do disappear one day," she seemed to be telling herself more than me, "I'll make sure I say goodbye to you first."

"I see…" I couldn't help thinking of Oshino, who'd made a similar promise and left without a word in the end—but nodded. "Okay. By all means, please do."

"Yes, it's scary when someone gets mad at you."

Having said that as if she were deflecting my words again—

Hachikuji extinguished her smile.

005

Nadeko Sengoku, second-year middle schooler. While some might point to her unusually quiet personality, if I were to pick her most distinctive feature, I would say that it was her bangs. Instead of parting her long bangs to the side, she let them hang down in front, half shielding her eyes like Kaede Rukawa. Sengoku seemed to be able to peek out from the slits, but for those looking at her it was almost impossible to see her eyes. Her distinctive hairstyle might have made her seem a little peculiar, but then again she actually wore her hair that way out of shyness, so I suppose it couldn't be helped.

Speaking of which, Sengoku usually wore a hat when she went outside. Apparently a hat is a metaphor for defenses you build around yourself. Oshino, too, thought of her as a bashful little birdie, but she took avoidance to a level that went beyond being bashful or reserved. It was more like she distrusted people.

As her honorary big brother, I worried about her future.

How was she going to get through life?

At least, that's what I was wondering as I rang the bell to Sengoku's home (She lives in a normal, two-story house. Not a rundown apartment, like Senjogahara, or an overgrown samurai manor, like Kanbaru. Just normal).

When the door opened I was in for a surprise.

No, surprise didn't even begin to describe it.

I was flabbergasted.

Fllabberrgasted.

Sengoku's bangs were pushed back.

They were held in place, along with the hair on the side of her head, by a cute pink headband (an understated pink, not shocking). And her eyes were in plain view. In fact, her whole face was on display.

So that's what she looked like.

I knew she was cute—but she was even cuter than I imagined. Even though she was younger and a little-sister figure to me, I felt my pulse quicken just a bit.

Sengoku had a habit of staring at the ground, but today she came to the door with her head held high. Her cheeks even seemed a little flushed.

Was she looking forward to hanging out that much?

"Sengoku... Is this how you usually dress at home?"

"Uh...um..."

She was flustered.

That was the Sengoku I remembered.

I was starting to worry if I had the wrong house. No one but Sengoku, though, could get so agitated over a simple question.

"Wh-What do you mean?"

"It's just, your bangs."

"M-My bangs? Wh-What's wrong with them?" Amazingly, Sengoku played innocent. But there was no way she didn't know what I meant. "I-I-It's not like I worked up the courage just because you were coming over for the first time."

"Hmm..."

Well.

I guess, if she said so.

She probably always used a headband at home—just as her skirt, which was short enough to expose her pale thighs, her pretty camisole, and the whisper-thin cardigan she wore on top were her usual attire. After all it was August, the middle of summer.

Phew. For a second there, I almost started to think that she'd gone out of her way to get all dolled up for me. Can you imagine? That would almost make it seem like she was thinking of me as a boy.

No way, no chance. It wasn't even possible.

"Please, Big Brother Koyomi. Come in, come in."

"Y-Yeah... Hm?" As I stepped inside, I noticed something. There were no shoes by the entrance. There was a pair of school shoes, yes, which I figured had to be Sengoku's. But where were her parents' shoes?

"Sengoku, your mom and dad..."

"They both work on Saturdays."

"Oh, mine do, too... So that's why you answered the phone when I called."

Wait...

Should I be barging into a girl's house while her parents were out and she was alone? I'd assumed they'd be here... Crap, I knew I should've forced Tsukihi to come with me. In fact, it wasn't too late, and we could still reschedule for another day.

While I was deciding what to do...

Click.

Clock.

Sengoku locked the front door.

It was a double lock. She even put on the chain.

Hmph, Sengoku took security very seriously... I suppose it was fine, then. It meant she trusted me.

It was up to me to meet that trust. My duty as someone who was older.

"My room is on the second floor, up the stairs."

"Kids' rooms usually are."

"I've already gotten it ready."

"Oh."

I climbed the stairs, as directed.

Sengoku's room, about a hundred square feet in size, was a typical middle school girl's. Every inch (right down to the wallpaper and the curtains and the doorknob covers) exuded a girly aura of strawberry hues. It was so unlike my sisters' den.

Huh.

The closet door, however, seemed to lack the same feminine, strawberry aura. In fact...

"Sengoku, that closet—"

"Don't open it," she commanded, almost sharply. She'd interrupted while I was still on the "l" and finished speaking before the "t" had left my mouth. "I won't forgive you for it."

"......"

Who knew "won't forgive you" was part of Sengoku's vocabulary? It was always worth visiting someone at home.

Clack.

As soon as Sengoku saw I was fully in the room, she locked the door behind us. I guess it only made sense that a girl her age, just hitting adolescence, would have a lock on her door... Hold on.

I understood locking the front door, but hers too?

Was I trapped?

No, I was being silly. Sengoku would never. Why would she, anyway?

It was probably just out of habit... She was bashful and reserved. There was nothing strange about her making a custom of it.

There was a tray set down on the carpet with soda and snacks on it. That must have been what she meant by getting ready.

How cute.

"Okay—please sit there," Sengoku said.

"You mean on the bed? Are you sure?"

"Yes. You're not allowed to sit anywhere else."

"......"

I guess Sengoku wasn't one for options. Everything else was out, only this.

Was she an "eliminationist" as in the process of elimination? Not that I've ever heard of such an ism.

I sat down on the bed, and Sengoku sat on the swiveling chair in front of her homework desk (adjustable height Kuru-Kuru Meka brand).

"Ph-Phew. It's hot in this room, isn't it?"

With those words, Sengoku removed her cardigan, quite suddenly.

This room? But wasn't this her room?

"If you're hot," I said, "why not turn on the air conditioner on that wall—"

"N-No! Don't you care about our planet?!"

We seemed to have a hostage situation.

With Earth as one big hostage.

"Global warming is out of control," she cautioned, "thanks to carbon dioxide… It's bad enough when carbon oxidizes, but this is dioxide!"

"O-Of course…"

Her explanation betrayed a serious lack of understanding of chemistry. Not that I can tell you why global warming is happening. If there are ice ages then the opposite must be true, and apparently they don't know for certain that carbon dioxide is the true cause.

"A-And," Sengoku went on, "we didn't always have air conditioners… 'Clear thy mind of mundane thoughts, and even fire will be a cool cucumber.'"

"Creating organic matter from fire, that's some heavy alchemy…"

It would be downright divine.

"Wh-Why not take off your hoodie, if you're feeling hot, too?" invited Sengoku.

"Huh? Me?"

"Even if you aren't, you're not allowed not to take off your hoodie."

"So it's my only option…"

What a scary planet.

Kanbaru would love this scene.

I guess it wasn't that unusual, though, for a kid in junior high to be sensitive about the environment. As her "big brother" I needed to humor her. And it was hot in here… In fact, it almost felt like a heater had been running until just a few moments ago instead of the AC.

I was wearing a sleeveless tank top under my hoodie. Since Sengoku was in a camisole, both of us were baring our upper arms.

I was one thing, but she really was just a kid not to have the slightest qualm about doing so in front of a boy.

"Now, Big Brother Koyomi, let's have some soda… There's only one cup, though."

"Why just one?!" If she'd gotten things ready, why the oversight?

"Y-You don't mind sharing, do you? We're like brother and sister, after all."

"Well, I guess not…"

Wasn't going down to the kitchen and getting another cup an option? Oh, right. She wasn't one for options.

I bet I wasn't allowed not to share.

For some reason, I was starting to feel like a captured little animal… Ordinarily, that was Sengoku.

I went ahead and took a sip of the soda.

I thought I detected a faint trace of alcohol.

"Sengoku. Is this booze?"

"Uh-uh." She shook her head. "It's just cola."

"Well, taste-wise, sure…"

"But it's extra-carbonated."

"They still make that?!"

Extra-carbonated cola, a terrifying concoction whose carbonation level was intoxicating.

And now that I looked closer, the snacks laid out were all chocolate bonbons. It was as if the idea was to get her guest drunk and unconscious.

What a devious assortment.

But I'm sure it was just a coincidence, and you could hardly expect a middle schooler to properly entertain a guest. It would be ungracious to complain. I should think of it as a chance to try something unusual.

"There's no TV in here, huh?"

"No, I don't watch much TV. It's bad for your eyes."

"......"

Said the girl with her prominent bangs—there was such a big hole in her logic that I didn't know where to begin.

Maybe she worried about her eyesight more than other people precisely because she liked to keep her bangs long.

"Then I guess you don't play video games very much, either?" I asked her. "Though nowadays, even without a TV set, there are handhelds."

"Not much… Maybe some of the popular games."

"Oh? Like what?"

"*Metal Gear.*"

"Ah…"

"On the MSX 2."

"Wh-What?!"

The MSX 2?! What kind of middle-school kid these days had one?! Sengoku was full of surprises, as always.

"It's downstairs in the living room," she said. "I wasn't really planning on it, but if you insist…"

"No, I wouldn't come over to someone's house to play a single-player game…"

"I also have a Popira 2."

"Seriously?!"

Why not a PlayStation 2…

"Anyway, Sengoku, you mentioned preparing. Did you get something ready?"

"I did!" She pulled out two disposable chopsticks, and the tip of one was painted red. "Let's play the Game of Kings."

"......"

Uhh… This was tough. How to explain.

"Sengoku… Are you sure you know what that is? It's not like the king in a deck of cards."

"I do. It's like Simon Says."

"Well…" That wasn't completely off the mark, but it was a drinking game.

"The king's word is dissolute."

"Tyrannical in its own way!" I quipped, though I was unsure if she was joking. I glanced at the chopsticks. "Well, I've never played it myself, so I don't know the details. But it's not meant for just two people."

"Why not?" Sengoku cocked her head. "I'd be fine either way. I don't mind giving orders or taking them."

"S-Sure, but how about we try something else?"

She was probably too young to understand. While her innocence was refreshing, sometimes I had trouble coping with it. I bet moms feel this way when they're asked where babies come from.

Sengoku seemed a little lost, perhaps because her plan had been dashed. Instead of giving up, however, she placed the chopsticks to the side and said, "Then why don't we play the Game of Life?"

"The Game of Life? Ah, okay."

"Life's word is absolute."

"So deep!"

Sengoku left saying she was pretty sure the board was in another room. Also: "You can't open the closet, but please be my guest otherwise. Maybe flip through that photo album."

Why did she want me to?

It was a mystery.

After a long wait, Sengoku finally returned—she seemed a little disappointed that the album was still sitting on the bookshelf, but yeah, I was probably just imagining things.

Speaking of which, the tomes lined up on those shelves were quite unique. There wasn't a single manga in sight, just rows of Iwanami paperback classics—not the average junior-high student's library. Did she want me to think she was grownup and always read such books? Some people might even wonder if she'd taken them from her father's study and put them there to impress her guest.

Besides, I could've sworn Sengoku was seriously into manga... I think I even remember her talking about the final episode of *Dodge Danpei*.

Anyway, I hadn't played the Game of Life in I forget how long. I recalled having a hard time understanding how to use promissory notes when I was a kid.

"Ah, right," I said. "Didn't we play this together at my house once?"

"Yes, I remember."

"You do?"

"In fact, I never forgot it."

"......"

I guess Sengoku had a pretty good memory. My recollections of her from back then were a bit hazy... Mostly, I just had an impression of her as a girl who liked to stare at her feet a lot.

I spun the dial.

The Game of Life was also better suited to more players, but in the end it was a game of chance—spin the dial, move your little car piece along the board, and see what kind of luck or misfortune you find. We ended up having fun.

I almost felt like a kid again.

Except...

The board was set down on the carpet, and the way Sengoku was leaning over, I kept catching suggestive glances inside her camisole. And to make matters worse, since she was sitting in front of me, I was in constant danger of seeing up her short skirt.

Honestly.

She was just a kid, but if it were anyone other than Sengoku, I might have mistaken her precarious posture as an attempt at seduction. This wasn't the first time the thought occurred to me, but she kept her guard up in entirely the wrong places... Wait, the last time I thought so, wasn't it concerning her bangs? Yet today her face was already on full display, too.

…?

Weird.

She wasn't even wearing a bra underneath her camisole.

In fact, wasn't a camisole like a piece of underwear? I wasn't entirely sure. Neither the bigger or littler of my little sisters ever wore anything so fancy.

Just jerseys and kimonos.

Not that Sengoku's honorary big brother would have untoward thoughts at the sight of her body.

You're lucky I'm such a gentleman, Sengoku.

"Ah…" she said. "You landed on the marriage square. Take a pin."

"Okay."

"If I ever get married, I hope it'll be with you, Big Brother Ko-yomi…"

"Hm? Does this game allow players to marry each other these days?"

I didn't recall such a rule.

"W-Well…no, I'm just saying, ideally."

"Huh."

Ah.

Come to think of it, when Karen and Tsukihi were little, they used to say that when they got older they were going to marry me.

What a nostalgic memory.

Sengoku wasn't as young as they were then, and she was probably just paying lip service.

"Lip service?" I asked.

Sengoku looked puzzled. "You mean, like a kiss?"

"That's not what I meant!"

"It's a little embarrassing, but if that's the kind of service you want—"

"Whoa, whoa, whoa, whoa!"

What kind of brother figure was I? That made me a straight-up pervert!

"By the way," she said, "I've been thinking."

"Yeah? What?"

"Maybe I should stop referring to you as my brother. It seems a little childish. After all, you're not really my brother."

Didn't I once have a similar conversation with Kanbaru? As far as I could recall, it hadn't ended to my liking.

I was starting to get a bad feeling, but changing the subject would be almost as awkward.

I had to play it by ear and go with the flow.

For my part, I kind of liked it that she called me "Big Brother Koyomi" like she used to.

"Well, anything's fine," I told her. "What do you want to call me?"

Sengoku gave her reply as if she'd chosen it long in advance.

"Dear."

".........."

...

Oh...

Oh, of course...

A formal term.

Nothing wrong with that.

No reason whatsoever to wonder why talking about marriage had gotten us here. My bad feelings weren't always borne out these days, eh? For a while, the probability had been a nasty one hundred percent!

"Sure, I don't mind," I said.

"Th-Then..."

For some reason, Sengoku's cheeks flushed and she seemed bashful (with her bangs pulled back, her face was surprisingly expressive) as she spoke the word.

"D-Dear..."

What a funny girl.

"Listen, Sengoku, honey..."

"H-Honey!" Her face was beet red now. She was clearly agitated. "Dear and honey... Oh...oh...oh my..."

"Huh?"

73

That was just another common term, wasn't it?

Were Sengoku and I speaking different dialects or something? Maybe I needed to seek out language-master Hachikuji.

"Anyway, Sengoku, listen. Has anything odd happened lately?"

"Wh-What do you mean?"

"Nothing, but there was that last time."

It was actually how she was dressed today that made me think of it. The Sengoku I'd met for the first time in years would have never exposed so much of her body...

Due to an aberration.

And due to human stuff.

Well, according to Oshino, her case differed from what Hanekawa, Senjogahara, Hachikuji, or I went through and shouldn't be thought of in the same way—but that didn't change the fact that she was more likely to be drawn to aberrations.

Being too vigilant was another way to have the rug pulled out from under you, but I needed to check up on her.

"No...not in particular," she said.

"I see."

"But..." Her face clouded over. "Those icky charms are still popular."

"At your school?"

"Yes, but not just mine. Among junior-high kids."

Sengoku seemed to hesitate for a moment before making her mind and speaking up.

"I think Rara... They might be up to something."

"........."

Rara was Tsukihi's nickname back in grade school—excerpted from Araragi. "They" had to mean Karen too, that is to say, both of the Fire Sisters.

Up to something.

Up to something.

Up to something!

Such an ambiguous, worrying phrase that you could interpret any way you wanted... Up to something!

Man, for a change... Be up to nothing!

"The other day," continued Sengoku, "Rara asked me about—the snake thing... Obviously I couldn't tell her the truth, and my story came out half-baked... But apparently they've been going around asking questions and looking into things."

"Things..."

I needed to learn more!

But did I really?!

Come to think of it, Karen going out today... Was it related? When it came to middle-school shenanigans, there was no way the Fire Sisters were going to keep their noses out of it...

"In other words, about those charms?" I asked Sengoku. "But they were actually bogus as curses, right? It was just that the way you tried to deal with it was mistaken."

Mistaken.

The way she tried to deal with it was—*too appropriate* and therefore mistaken.

Wasn't that the gist of it?

Or to be more precise, it was also the baneful influence of Shinobu Oshino—an ironblooded, hotblooded, yet coldblooded vampire, a legend among legends—visiting our town.

Which also meant...

With that problem resolved, middle-school kids messing around with mumbo-jumbo shouldn't have any real effect.

"Yes." Sengoku nodded. "I'm pretty sure my case was the only genuine aberration that materialized. At least I think so."

"What's the problem then?"

"Well, I doubt Rara is up in arms about the charms' effect—they probably don't believe in aberrations at all...I think."

"Yeah...you're probably right."

My sisters were fairly realistic. They might be scared of ghosts but didn't believe in them. That was their stance.

Sengoku went on.

"I think this bogus magic stuff being a fad in the first place is what they don't like... They want to find out *who's behind it,* or something."

"......"

They were trying to pinpoint the charms' source?

That seemed like a crazy idea, even for my sisters.

It was a tall order if you thought about it.

"It didn't become a fad because someone tried to make it a fad," I reasoned. "Even if they did find someone, it's not that person's responsibility at this point."

Gossip may or may not only last for seventy-five people, but by number seventy-five you'd be talking about a totally different individual. Almost like in a game of telephone.

"It's so Rara...or Fire Sisters," Sengoku said. "They're assuming that 'someone' with a 'motive' turned 'charms' into a fad..."

"It does sound typical of them..."

Oh boy.

Perhaps I needed to have a talk with Karen—it might be fine to just leave it alone, but I knew things could get dicey because the case had *a precedent* called Nadeko Sengoku.

One wrong turn...and you could end up with one foot in the grave.

Or worse—both feet.

And, if you were like me, maybe your whole head—

"B-Big Brother Koyomi?"

It must have been because I was brooding, but Sengoku called out to me, reverting to my old appellation in doing so. I shook myself out of my reverie and glanced up.

She looked upset—almost ready to cry. She was probably feeling bad that telling me had me so concerned.

She was such a decent kid.

Too bad she wasn't my real sister, I thought. If she were, we'd never ever get into scuffles.

"It's nothing, Sengoku, I'm fine," I assured her. "By the way, you know, I think it suits you."

".......?"

"Your bangs, I mean. Why don't you wear them like that outside the house, too?"

"I-I can't, I'd be embarrassed..." As if to replace the missing bangs, she brought both hands up to cover her face. "B-But if you say so...I'll try."

"Trying is a good thing."

I nodded. It was nice watching over a person's growth.

I hoped to see her through it.

"By the way, Sengoku, we're almost done with our Game of Life. What do you want to play next?"

"Twister."

"Huh, I've never heard of that one. You're gonna have to teach me."

"Of course I'll teach...you and your body."

"Ha ha ha, that sounds fun."

Still, was it just my imagination?

In her eyes that pulling back her bangs had exposed, I seemed to catch, every now and then, a brazen glint that belonged more to a rattlesnake than Sengoku.

0 0 6

Originally I had planned to stay at Sengoku's house until evening, but her mother came home unexpectedly a little after noon. Apparently there was some sort of trouble at her work. It was no business of mine. Sengoku, however, went into a panic.

"I-I kept it a secret that you were coming over," she fretted. "Oh… Oh… I'm gonna get scolded. She's gonna think I'm a pervert, dressed up like this."

I had no idea what she meant by "pervert" there, but the important point was that she had kept my coming over a secret. There was a world of difference between "not having told" and "secret," which meant that as far as Sengoku's mother was concerned, I was "a male neighbor who snuck into the house while she was away." There didn't seem to be any way I could explain, so I slipped out of the house without Mrs. Sengoku seeing me, almost like an adulterer.

Luckily, Sengoku had hidden my shoes after I'd left them at the entrance…but I had to wonder if she'd been planning for such an eventuality all along.

Hmph.

I hadn't planned on getting chased out, or running off, like that— I'd give Sengoku a call later to check up on her—but at the same time,

I couldn't shake the feeling that my purity as a boy might have been saved thanks to Mrs. Sengoku's troubles at work…

It was just a feeling, and a silly one.

Anyway, I suddenly had more free time on my hands.

I wasn't supposed to be home until evening, so I didn't want to deal with Tsukihi asking me all sorts of questions if I returned early (I wasn't in the mood to be laughed at by her once she heard why I was home). Besides, Karen probably wouldn't be back until late, and if I wanted to verify what Sengoku had said, it'd be better if I waited until both of my sisters were there…

In which case.

"I wasn't planning on calling until tomorrow…but hey."

I stopped along the side of the road, beneath a streetlamp that was serving no purpose in the middle of the day, and pulled out my cell phone.

I was dialing a junior of mine at the school I attended, Naoetsu High.

Second-year Suruga Kanbaru.

Enter, stage right!

"I hope she's not busy… I never can tell with her."

It picked up on the fourth ring.

"Suruga Kanbaru speaking," a voice came from the other end. She had a very masculine way of introducing herself. "Major armaments include an accelerator device."

"I didn't know you were a cyborg?!"

That made perfect sense!

When you thought about it, she even talked like a robot!

"Hmph. You must be my senior Araragi, judging from your voice and quipping."

"Sure…"

Why was she still relying on my voice and straight-man ways? Learn how to use the contact list on your phone already.

"Kanbaru, what do you do when someone besides me calls?"

"Heh, not to worry. Very few have this number in the first place, and I can tell them all by their voice and quipping style."

"...Do you never get to play the straight man?"

"I guess I'm queer through and through."

"Fair enough."

Well.

Despite her personality, Suruga Kanbaru was the biggest star in Naoetsu High history...a miracle sportswoman who'd led our flagging basketball team to the national finals. She was incredibly fast (rumored to run the fifty-meter dash in under five seconds) and used that speed to dominate the court and captivate crowds. Even now, after resigning as captain of the team a little early due to delicate circumstances, she was as popular as ever—and probably couldn't afford to give her number out to just anyone.

The dilemma of stardom.

Maybe I ought to understand?

But stardom aside, as you might guess from the fact that she didn't know how to use her phone's contact list, Kanbaru wasn't very good with tech. I doubted she made many calls on her end.

"Kanbaru, are you busy right now?"

"That is a vapid question. The debt of gratitude I owe you is so great that any request from you comes before all else. For instance, even if I were in the midst of a struggle to save the world, I'd rush to your side if you called for me, the world be damned."

"........."

As gallant as ever...but could she please put the world first and me second? I mean, without the world, I'd die too.

"Actually, I'm not 'calling for' you. Can I just come to you?"

"What is this?"

"Um...you're home now, aren't you?"

"Yes, ah... Just a second. I'll get naked right away."

"Why?!"

Since when is that a prerequisite for chatting?!

Who starts taking their clothes off in the middle of a call?

"What are you saying? It's none other than you that I'm conversing with. Even if we're only on the phone, simple etiquette demands that I disrobe."

"Don't make it sound like I'm the one who's clueless! And you're always looking for an excuse to strip!"

This was a new format, though.

With less and less rhyme or reason.

After Kanbaru got excited over the word "rebuff" the other day, I was seriously beginning to worry about her, but it looked like she'd gone and crossed the line.

"But," she objected, "if I don't seize every opportunity to get naked, how will I ever drive home that I'm a pervert?"

"You want to?!"

"Some heartless people out there are accusing me of being all talk and not being that pervy after all, and it's been getting on my nerves. I can't think of anything worse a person might say about me."

"Nobody's saying that!"

And, you know, don't let such a thing get on your nerves!

Save your anger for bigger stuff!

"I act like a pervert when I've never been with a man," Kanbaru admitted, "so I can't blame people for being suspicious. But it's not my fault, is it, that I don't have a partner."

"You really want me to answer that?!"

"Of course, they don't know that it's just a trifling detail and only a matter of time, since I now have a comrade as illustrious as yourself."

"Don't include me in your team of perverts!"

Especially not as some kind of forerunner!

There's not a single aspect of perversion where I come out ahead of her!

"Just keep your clothes on," I advised her.

"You wish, but aren't you underestimating my speed? I'm already naked, sir."

"Sir?!"

Too fast!!

Ah, right, during the summer she wore nothing but undies around the house... All she had to do was slip off two items, so I guess it wasn't unbelievable... Wait, she was pretty much naked before she even started!

"Kanbaru, your level of perversion is beginning to exceed what I can handle!"

"Huh, how unlike my revered senior. I'm in my own room, at home. Shouldn't I feel free to dress or undress as I see fit?"

"Hmph."

She had a point... Her house rules were her domain.

At the Araragi residence too, chilling in just our underwear after taking a bath was considered okay, and even if we didn't quite walk around in the nude, Karen and Tsukihi (and I) weren't above doing so half-naked.

"You're right, sorry... I shouldn't have said anything. It's not like you got buck-naked outside the house."

"As long as you understand," Kanbaru forgave me. "I enjoy shedding inhibitions, but outside my house? Very seldom."

"You mean there are times?!"

"For instance, at the public bath."

"Ngh..."

She was toying with me!

True, a public bath was outside the house!

"And with the basketball team..."

"You're not tricking me again. It was in the showers, during summer basketball camp, right?"

"Oh, so close. You're right about basketball camp. But I actually put together a session my first year where we were nude the entire time."

"I hope they close down the whole club!"

"Haha, come on. Obviously I'm joking. If you believe that kind of nonsense, then maybe you really do have a dirtier mind than me."

"Wh-What?!"

Ouch! Oh heavens above, punish this one for her sins!

Surprisingly, the heavens answered my prayer right away.

"U-Urk…"

I heard Kanbaru groan, and even the sound of her body sliding to the floor.

Something had happened.

"Kanbaru, what's wrong?"

"I forgot to shut the door to my room… My grandma just walked past me down the hall…"

"……"

Ah, okay.

By the way, Kanbaru lived with her grandparents, and it was just the three of them.

They'd raised her since she was a preteen like their own precious daughter. She was grandpa and grandma's special little girl.

"She looked at me like she was so disappointed and walked on without slowing her pace or saying a word…"

"Well, seeing her granddaughter talking on the phone in her birthday suit after all the loving care she lavished on you…"

Apparently, being naked in your own room wasn't their house rule, just Kanbaru's personal rule.

"Aaaa… Aaaah… I'm done for," she lamented. "How am I ever going to show my face in front of her again?"

The blow had been too much. It wasn't often I got a chance to see her in such a state—no, I couldn't see her over the phone, but I had to visit her pronto. I might never enjoy the opportunity again.

"Um, Kanbaru, I hate to bother you while you're in a state of shock, but could we get back to what we were talking about?"

"Uhh… Yes. I'm not sure I'll have anything very interesting to say now, but will you still accept me? My senior Araragi."

She really was down in the dumps.

Hang in there. Don't worry, you're super-charming right now.

"My tutoring for today got cancelled," I told her. "I promised to help you clean up your room tomorrow, but mind if I headed over today instead?"

As the former captain of the basketball team, Kanbaru tended to be thoughtful, but she was surprisingly lax when it came to her own affairs (like how she forgot to close the door just now). Despite her interest in self-discipline, she was also a slovenly mess. In short, her room was a pigsty.

It went beyond just clutter. It was so bad that if her fans ever had a peek, they might actually faint. In fact, I almost did the first time I was invited to her room (Japanese-style, large at twelve mats). Her futon hadn't been cleared away, clothes were littered all over the floor, books stood and fell in great piles, mysterious cardboard boxes hogged every corner and—worst headache of all—there was no wastebasket in the room: just plastic bag upon plastic bag of unsorted trash tumbling where they may.

It wasn't clutter, just plain filth.

Couldn't she at least take out the garbage?

As spacious as the room was, the only area left open was atop the futon. Yet pens and notebooks and other stationery had found their way under it, too. How could she sleep like that?

And so on.

Unable to relax, I'd set about cleaning up her room almost as soon as I'd arrived, and since then, it's fallen to me to clean her room twice per month.

On the fifteenth and thirtieth, that's what I did.

Every two weeks, Kanbaru meticulously—or perhaps obligingly—managed to return her room almost to its original disaster state. Anyone could make a mess, but it took a certain talent to make her kind. She could hurt herself lying around naked in that room, for real.

"Ah... Of course I don't mind," she replied. "I'm so grateful for your help, I would never presume to complain. I can adjust my schedule to fit yours, anytime."

She still sounded weak.

Long story short, Kanbaru agreed.

I said I'd be right over and hung up—depressed as she might be, it wouldn't take long for her, ever the optimist, to get back on her feet. If I didn't hurry, I'd miss my chance to witness her down in the dumps. Unlike Sengoku's house, Kanbaru's was kind of far. Speedy Kanbaru, with her under-five-seconds dash (or so-called accelerator device) could probably travel the distance in a flash, but my own legs, unfortunately, were plain average now that I was no longer a vampire. I'd swing by home to pick up the granny bike parked outside in the yard, but to avoid Tsukihi peppering me with questions, not go inside.

While I used to have two bikes, one for going to school and one for private use, my mountain bike for private use had been wrecked in a certain accident. All I had left now was the granny bike that I used to ride to and from school.

I didn't know when I was going to be able to buy a new bike.

It's not that there wasn't a particular one I wanted, but I had a feeling that even if I did buy it, it'd break (get broken) in no time...

At any rate, I took off toward Kanbaru's.

I didn't have a second to waste.

I was dying to see Miss Kanbaru down in the dumps.

I spotted something strange out of the corner of my eyes, however, that forced me to stop.

"......"

A middle schooler dressed in a jersey was walking (?) upside down on her hands on the exterior wall of some residence.

Her ponytail twitched back and forth as she moved.

It was Karen Araragi.

"......"

Handstands... She was still doing it even after grade school.

Was it to train her arms?

Yikes. Hachikuji was right.

Someone beyond a certain size doing a handstand outside of a gym felt so wrong…

She strutted—

Not noticing me, and relying solely on her arm strength, Karen leapt from the wall she was on to the next-door neighbor's wall.

"Hiya!" Sneaking up on my bike, I proceeded to lightly clothesline her across both elbows.

"A-Aaah!"

Maybe I was her better when it came to our senses of balance. Karen lost hers, even though this was hardly a low kick to the face, and tumbled off the wall.

I'd have loved to see her hit her head, frankly, but thanks to a martial artist's superior athleticism, she flipped over during the mere three-foot fall and stuck a perfect landing.

She landed facing me, so our eyes met.

"Ah, Koyomi. I thought you were a hostile."

"You have those?"

"Don't they say the moment a man steps outside his house, he has seven enemies?"

"You're not a man, you're a little girl."

"If a man has seven enemies, then a girl has seven times as many."

"Hah." In Karen's case, that was probably true. Appalled, I said, "What are you doing anyways? How long are you going to keep training my sense of shame? It's all muscle at this point. You'd have to be Ranma Saotome to traipse about doing acrobatics at your age. Don't tell me you'd turn into a man if I splashed hot water on you."

"Hyaha! How convenient, I'd only have one seventh as many enemies to deal with. Actually no, it'd be pretty boring…"

"What the hell, looking like that where people can see you… How tasteless can you be? Act a little more like a normal teenage girl. What if the neighbors start talking?"

"Huh? Am I just imagining things, or are we putting you aside here…"

"Not one bit," I shot back. And really, I had nothing on my conscience. "Besides, a handstand is one thing, but trying to travel that way is totally insane… Maybe you were light enough back in grade school, but how much do you weigh now?"

"Never ask a lady." *Heheh,* Karen put on airs. "Well, I stay as trim as I can. And if I make sure I don't put on too much muscle, my weight stays ladylike. If you ever spot a girl at the arcade playing *Dance Dance Revolution* upside down, know that it's your sister."

"That girl would be no sister of mine."

"Says the guy who used to play air hockey by himself."

"That was a long time ago…"

Anyway…

Anyway.

Anyway!

"What are you doing here?" I asked her.

"Serving. *Volunteering.*"

Karen stood up and thrust out her chest.

Her smug look was infuriating. Just the sight of it made me want to punch her.

"Idiot," I chided, "don't be saying it in English like that makes you smart. Just the other day, you thought Descartes had something to do with *à la carte.*"

"So what, they're both French."

"True."

"Anyway, why are you bothering me while we're out? We look so much alike, people will know we're related. You're embarrassing me."

"It's not like I wanted to come up and talk to you. If you don't want me to, stop behaving in ways that force me to."

To be precise, I didn't come up and talk to her so much as clothes-line her.

"Still," I said, "it's perfect timing. There's something I need to ask you."

"There's nothing I need you to ask me," Karen countered like some snotty brat.

Hup, she tilted over into another handstand—and I shoved her legs back down the other way. She landed in an upside-down crab.

Doing the crab out in public was also pretty strange.

And it was steeply angled—almost grotesquely so.

Karen's legs were way too long.

"Hey, that was dangerous," she complained upside down. She could probably hold the position for half a day.

"What's dangerous is whatever you two are up to. Tell me what you've been doing."

"I've been serving society, like I said." Karen grinned, still upside down. It was kind of a funny image. "It's got nothing to do with you, so why don't you butt out?"

"If it really doesn't, I'd be glad to…"

The charms.

I doubted Sengoku would get mixed up in it again, and the actual issue in her case had come about by chance—

Maybe I could just leave it alone.

Getting swept up in my sisters' hijinks only to be left holding the bag was the usual course of things. The royal road, so to speak.

Perhaps not seeing that yet even at this late date, Karen had the gall to say, "We're not gonna cause you trouble or anything. We're not stupid, all right?"

She lifted her palms off the ground, using her head to hold her position, and gave me a double V-sign with her free hands. And this was the girl telling me she wasn't stupid.

"Koyomi, what do you take me for?"

"I don't know. What the hell are you?"

"The slayer of marching demons," Karen replied in a sotto voice, "hell's own guard dog…Dekamaster!"

"Talk about badass…"

It was probably the first time a girl doing the crab with her head ever uttered those words.

"Super cool, perfect," she followed up with Dekablue Ranger's signature line, apparently getting into it.

There was nothing cool about the pose she was in, though.

"I'm a girl on fire!"

"Then I hope you get incinerated."

I had to hand it to her, though. Combining all those cool lines with a silly pose was a pretty good gag…

I know I could never pull it off.

Karen wasn't a musclehead for nothing.

"I see, I see," she said. "Then maybe I'll make this part of my regular routine."

"While you're down there, why not try a few more? Anything's fine, just as long as it sounds cool."

"If you want to pass, you're gonna have to defeat me first!"

"Funnier than I expected!"

"How about the opposite? You go, I'll hold the line!"

"Ahahahahaha!"

I burst out laughing.

This was a rare treat.

But, uh, oops.

I was playing with my sister and having fun, which wasn't my intention.

Despite our banter, somehow I hadn't obtained a shred of the info I was after—but as for why she was loitering around here, I could guess without her help.

Kiyokaze Public Middle School—which Senjogahara, Kanbaru, and also Hanekawa had attended—was located nearby. If Karen was investigating charms circulating among junior-high kids, this was an important area in that search.

Hm.

"Hup!" Karen made a huge performance out of straightening out of her crab pose, purposely doing another handstand (balancing on her head) before getting back up on her two feet.

A natural-born performer, she was.

Or to put it another way, a regular attention hog.

"Anyway, Koyomi, I'm kinda busy right now. I got a lot on my plate. If you wanna talk, do it with both me and Tsukihi at home tonight. Can it wait until then?"

"……"

Hm.

Well, I was in a rush, too. I wanted to get to Kanbaru's house as soon as possible.

Not stand around wasting time on my sister's antics.

I hadn't planned on talking to them until that night, anyways—and it's not like we could have a very serious discussion where we were.

"Should I really be leaving you alone?" I asked Karen just to make sure.

"Of course. The whole thing will be over soon, anyways."

"Huh…"

"No one can stand in our way, y'know?"

"I hope someone sticks a knife in your kidney."

"By the way, how was Tsukihi? She's still home, isn't she? Did you see her?"

"She was just watching TV."

But who knows what she was doing at the moment.

She'd promised she was going to mind the fort, but maybe she'd snuck out afterward as part of some Fire Sisters scheme…

Just then, a cell phone began to ring in Karen's jersey pocket.

The *Enter the Dragon* theme song.

Subtlety: not her forte.

As much as I hate to give my sister props, though, she (flat-out) refuses to decorate her phone with straps and such, and I find that pretty manly and neat (even if she's a girl).

Tsukihi's phone, on the other hand, is encrusted with that stuff.

They hadn't owned phones when they entered middle school, but my parents, unable to buck the trend (or more likely, coming to the conclusion that Karen and Tsukihi not having a means of contact was the graver risk), decided to lift the ban just this summer vacation. My sisters were already pros with the devices.

They really were good at everything.

Meanwhile, I still didn't understand half of the functions.

"Hello... Oh. Yeah—"

Ignoring the fact that her older brother was talking to her, Karen answered, turning her back to me as though to escape notice.

She began speaking in a hushed tone.

I couldn't quite hear what she was whispering. I couldn't even tell if it was some new intel related to her public service or a totally private conversation—not that I was going to eavesdrop to find out.

I'm not Tsukihi.

Karen talked for about a minute before hanging up.

Then she turned toward me.

There was a hint of seriousness in her expression.

It was a handsome look.

"Okay, Koyomi."

"Huh?"

"Everything's fine. The whole thing will be over soon."

"Oh. Uh huh..."

I could only reply vaguely.

I guess she'd received some new intel, after all?

"When we fill you in later tonight," Karen said, "it will be to regale you with our heroic deeds. Hyahaha!"

"Whatever. You're almost out of middle school and still walking around upside down, and that's what I learned to my great misfortune today."

"That'll do. Hasta la vista!"

Probably so I wouldn't interrogate her anymore, she cut our conversation short and disappeared from sight.

Incidentally, she did so by tumbling.

She vanished rolling away at a furious pace.

What a nutty, breakneck move when she wasn't working with mats or anything... Her deal seemed entirely distinct from Kanbaru's athleticism.

While Kanbaru was fast and had great reflexes, I doubted she could perform Karen's acrobatics with a straight face—in fact, Kanbaru wouldn't attempt anything so risky in the first place.

I suppose that was the difference between martial arts and competitive sports?

Ah, right, Kanbaru.

I had to get to her place, fast.

Not quite pushing my sister out of mind, but tucking her in the back, I began pedaling again.

0 0 7

Twenty minutes later.

I arrived at the samurai manor of a home where Kanbaru lived, a trip that usually took me at least thirty minutes. If I hadn't run into Karen and wasted time, I could have been there three minutes sooner.

Next to the name plate was an intercom, which seemed out of place for a traditional house. When I pressed the button, it was Kanbaru's grandmother, the woman who'd just witnessed Kanbaru's disgrace (or perversion), who answered. I'd been over plenty of times already to help clean and met Kanbaru's grandparents before, but if they knew it was me their granddaughter was talking to butt-naked on the phone, I doubt Grandma Kanbaru would have let me through the door.

—M-Ma'am…

—Thank you for being such a good boy with Suruga.

She bowed to me as she said this almost apologetically. Kanbaru, a star at school or not, was just a sweet, darling granddaughter to her… and nudity aside, the disastrous state of her ward's room couldn't have been a secret.

She had to be worried about Kanbaru.

Trusted her, perhaps, but also fretted.

……

Still, as a high school senior, it was a little embarrassing to be called a boy by someone else's grandma.

I left her behind and headed toward Kanbaru's room.

The sliding door was shut.

I could picture her hugging her knees in a little ball in the corner. This was my chance to catch her by surprise, and my heart was racing as I flung the door open without knocking.

Kanbaru was sprawled out on her futon without a single thread of clothing.

"Bfft!"

Suruga Kanbaru—a kinky girl, in others' estimation as well as her own.

Perhaps it was because she no longer had sports as an outlet that she was breaking her own record every day. Her sexual harassment was so rampant and excessive that Shinobu, Sengoku, and I, along with others, could file a class-action lawsuit.

And yet!

Believe it or not, this was the first time I'd ever seen her entirely naked!

I don't know, since June, also due to quitting the basketball team, Kanbaru was growing her hair out, which made her look a lot more feminine, so seeing her show off her bits like this…

Wait, she was lying face down!

But the line of her back was incredibly erotic!

And those shoulder blades!

Kanbaru may have retired, but an athlete at heart, she clearly hadn't been skimping on the training—her toned, compact body was too beautiful! They speak of having "legs like a gazelle," but Kanbaru was all gazelle, all over!

A Grecian statue!

Behold the beauty of the human form!

I'd noticed Kanbaru's stunningly chiseled legs, but it wasn't just her legs, her whole body was a lethal weapon!

You couldn't blame her for wanting to get naked!

It'd be a shame not to let other people see!

"……"

One caveat, though.

I said "without a single thread," but the bandage around her left arm—was still there.

"K-Kanbaru…"

It looked like she'd used the last of her strength to close the sliding door and then collapsed on the futon after her grandmother had seen her naked. I called to her though I had no idea what to say.

"Ah… Is it you?" She lifted her head up from where it was pressed into the pillow, and then—

"W-Wait, Kanbaru! Don't turn over! There'll be trouble if you did!"

Mainly for me! I might start feeling all sorts of troubled!

"Um…" *Right,* Kanbaru nodded. "You'll have to forgive the state I'm in. It's so embarrassing, being seen like this."

"Whoa…"

She was feeling embarrassed like a normal person…

But she didn't try to cover up and just lay there, limbs stretched out languidly.

The only thing she lifted was her face.

"How odd, though," she said. "The Koyomi Araragi I know is a man of impeccable character who'd never barge into a lady's room without knocking."

"I…just wanted to see you looking devastated."

"Sure, if this wretched vision satisfies you, then by all means, gaze as much as you like…"

"……"

"Don't be shy. Witness my true form… Suruga Kanbaru, laid bare."

"No…" True, she was laid as bare as the day she was born. "You know what? I'm sorry…"

I didn't think she'd look this devastated.

So swift, heaven's vengeance—I'd never thought my prayer would be answered like this.

"I apologize, Kanbaru... Let me take responsibility."

"Responsibility?" she repeated mechanically, turning to me a pair of dull, vacant eyes that resembled a dead fish's more than I ever imagined possible of her. "What responsibility?"

"I mean, I was the one you were talking to on the phone, so half of the blame for this situation falls on me." I wasn't about to tell her that I'd prayed for divine punishment.

"I don't think so," she denied.

Even in her current state, her sense of personal accountability was undiminished. You had to hand it to her. The most impeccable human being I knew was Tsubasa Hanekawa, by far, but maybe Kanbaru came in second?

"Nevertheless," she said, "if you insist on taking responsibility, I won't stop you... How, exactly, do you plan on doing so?"

"I can marry you."

"Bfft!" It was Kanbaru's turn to act shocked. "Wh-Why marriage?"

"Well, it's just the back half, but I've seen you naked."

"I think you're skipping a few steps... By that logic, how many girls would you have to marry?"

"What are you implying?!"

Scandalous.

Not that it was entirely unfounded.

"Ahaha..."

Hey—she laughed.

If only weakly, she did laugh.

Then she said, "While that's a very attractive offer, there's no need for you to take responsibility. My other dear senior would be furious if we did such a thing. In exchange, could I ask you to do me a favor?"

"Yeah, you name it. I'm your loyal slave for the day."

"Would you mind waiting out in the hall while I get dressed?"

"Ha..."

I couldn't help but laugh. A request, from Kanbaru's mouth, to be allowed to cover herself up?

It was a sublime moment, like mankind standing erect and walking on two legs for the first time.

I did as Kanbaru asked and went out into the hallway while she got dressed (Ever the jock, it only took her a couple of minutes. So she put them on as fast as she took them off). Then I finally got down to the business of cleaning up her room.

Commence mission!

First I sorted the garbage into general piles, stuffed them into huge trash bags, and set the bags out in the yard. Only the clearly useless items were sorted into trash. Objects that were less obvious were set aside for later. Since this wasn't my room, it was ultimately up to Kanbaru to decide what was necessary and what wasn't—well, most of it would get thrown out. It was just being put on hold. Awaiting due process, you could say.

Suruga Kanbaru.

She was actually well off, and actually profligate. She made senseless purchase after senseless purchase and transformed it all into trash through some marvelous magic.

In the end, nearly everything got thrown away.

Of course, that was just the groundwork.

The real tidying up still lay ahead.

Kanbaru had gotten changed only to put on hot pants and a tube top, leaving her not much less exposed than before (no wonder she was so quick, jock or not), but at least she was presentable now. Considering the state of her room, maybe she ought to have chosen something a little more protective like a jersey (the default outfit for Karen).

The funny thing, though, was that jerseys didn't suit Kanbaru. Was it because she wasn't very tall?

She did look super-cool when she dashed about in her school uniform.

Maybe it caught my attention only because I was thinking about clothes, but I discovered what appeared to be a basketball uniform in one of the heaps of trash.

The number on the back: 4.

Was that the captain's number? My knowledge of basketball was limited to *Slam Dunk*, so I wasn't sure.

"Kanbaru, what about this?"

"Hm? Oh."

By the way, she was standing out in the hallway.

Despite her athleticism, Kanbaru has a very clumsy side (She's terrible at housework. Of course, given the state of her room, this bit of parenthetical explanation is probably unnecessary) and would only get in the way during the current cleanup phase. It was somewhat thrilling to be treating a star of Kanbaru's caliber like a liability, but it was a pretty low sentiment so I kept it to myself.

"My club uniform," she said. "So that's where it went. I was wondering."

"Huh. You mean your practice uniform?"

"No, it's a souvenir from when we made it to the nationals my first year. Turn it inside out. You can see all the messages my teammates wrote."

"Is cherishing such memories a foreign concept for you?"

"I've got all the memories I need right here in my heart."

"Great line, but!"

They were here too! In physical form!

It was such a sad story that I was reminded of Hachikuji and her amnesia (even if I did make that one up).

"Back then you weren't captain yet, were you?" I asked. "I mean, you were still a freshman. How come it says '4' on the back?"

"There's no law saying only the captain can wear the number. It's conventional...but in my case, the captain let me have it for being the ace."

"I like that. You had a bighearted captain. But I don't remember this being here the last time I cleaned."

"It was hanging on the wall of our clubroom to help light a fire under the new players' feet, but I brought it home right before summer vacation."

"Huh."

"I figured it was about time for me to move on from my glory days—I retired from the team, after all. It just felt like I was throwing my weight around. Besides, the club doesn't have much of a future."

"Hmph…"

Even after quitting, Kanbaru had still been focusing a lot on the team—but I guess this was her way of making a clean break.

Maybe it was also a kind of penance for her.

The club had stayed on her mind.

"I took it off the wall without telling anyone, so it wound up becoming a police matter."

"So that's why there was a patrol car at school our last day!"

"A perfect crime. No one knows I'm the culprit yet…"

"But there's this piece of evidence!"

That said.

She'd only brought home her own clothing, so it was no big deal.

Still, given its background, we couldn't throw it away—not because the police might find it, but because it was a memento.

"You know, I don't think I ever saw you play basketball except maybe once. Hey, why don't you try it on for me?"

"If you insist." My request may have been a little insensitive since she'd already left the team, but Kanbaru consented readily. She was always generous that way. "My hair's longer now, so you probably won't get the full impression."

"It grew out super-fast, by the way…"

When we first met, her hair had been cut a little shorter than mine, even, but now there was no comparison. I had deep scars on the nape of my neck from where Shinobu had bitten me, so I kept my hair longer than normal to cover them up… But Kanbaru's was so long she could tie it back.

"You think?" she asked.

"Yeah. I've heard that hair usually grows about half an inch per month—but yours must have grown by two inches."

"Probably because I'm such a kinky girl."

"Just like that, as a statement of fact?"

I'd been thinking the same thing!

But trying not to blurt it out!

"In particular," she said, "I'm so kinky that for years I thought 'pepperoncino' was a dirty word."

"Even after you had some?!"

"I also thought mobile family rate plans were family 'rape' plans."

".........."

She really shut me up with that one.

"Wait, no," she corrected herself, "I thought a family data plan was a family dating plan."

"That's still a little too much family feeling!"

"And I used to think an exhibition game is where everyone plays naked."

"That's not a misunderstanding but a wish! Who thinks that in this day and age?!"

"Indeed. I came here in a time machine from a world that's always five seconds ahead."

"What a waste of a great invention!"

"And until recently, I thought 'bracelet' had something to do with relaxing."

"That's not even dirty!"

"I shouted it out at a game once and made a fool of myself. I can't forget the look on my teammates' faces."

"Stop! It's even worse with an example!"

"As bad as thinking a homemaker is a carpenter?"

"Help!"

Geez.

I bet I'll get along with you in our next lives, too!

"You also knocked off the Senjogahara impersonation," I pointed out.

"Hm? Oh, you mean the bangs?" she answered me absentmindedly through the sleeves of the uniform as she slipped it on. "I wasn't really trying to copy her—then again, who knows. I can't be trusted, after all."

"That's not what I meant."

"Heh. In any case, what's past is past—no need to be sensitive about it. Well, what do you think?"

"……"

It was nice of her to put on the uniform for me, but since she was only wearing hot pants and a tube top, it looked like she was naked underneath. It was pretty sexy.

There was nothing even remotely sporty about it.

Not the Kanbaru I'd been meaning to see…

Although the uniform suited her, what did that say in this instance?

"Heh." Apparently unaware of the impression she was imparting, Kanbaru smiled happily. "This reminds me of back then."

"Back then? You mean when you still played basketball?"

"No, the naked summer camp."

"You're fully aware!"

And wasn't that supposed to be a joke?!

Don't be rehashing it!

Who knows what wearing the uniform actually reminded her of, but I guess the feeling wasn't half bad because she didn't try to take it off right away.

Not that I was complaining.

It wouldn't interfere with cleaning up or anything.

"You know, Kanbaru, even if basketball is out of the question, couldn't you still play other sports despite your left arm? What about soccer?"

"I don't think there's any sport where you never use your arms. For instance, with soccer, even if you're not the goalie, you still have to use your arms for throw-ins."

"Ahh."

"Besides, I don't understand the offside rule."

As we spoke, I made another unexpected find in the same pile, right under where the uniform had been. Not that it was a rare item these days, but I didn't expect to come across one in Kanbaru's room.

"I didn't know you had a digital camera, Kanbaru." It was the newest model, too (from what I could tell): ultra-thin and ultra-light.

"Oh, I bought it just the other day."

She nodded.

Huh, it was a pretty high-tech purchase for someone who was such a klutz when it came to gadgets that she barely knew how to use her cell phone.

"I know it's unlike me," she explained, "but some photos, you don't want to send out to get developed."

"What kind of photos…"

"Self-nudes?"

I did a pratfall into the nearest trash heap.

After all the trouble I went to cleaning up.

I yelled, "You bought it just for that?! This piece of modern engineering is way too advanced for you!"

"It's not the only reason. I use it for other stuff, too."

"Like what?"

"Taking nude pics of all those freshman kitties."

"……"

She meant portraits of cats that first-years kept as pets, right? Because cats went around naked, right?

"I ask for permission first, of course, so there's nothing illegal about it."

"Kanbaru, you're not making sense. How do you get a kitty's permission? You surely mean its owner's?"

"Hm? I don't like that kind of language, it tramples on their dignity. But as for the owner, that would be me—"

"I sure love cats!" I interrupted with all I had.

The truth is, I don't.

104

They scare me.

"Hm, understood," Kanbaru said. "I'm afraid it would be a violation of privacy to show them to just anyone, but if you must, please take the memory card home. I'll take full responsibility."

"I never said I wanted to see them!"

"Heheh. No need to be shy."

Kanbaru received the digital camera from my hands.

I was wondering where it'd gone, she muttered.

Usually, a digital camera wasn't the kind of thing you misplaced... Her ability to lose things was truly epic.

USEMONOGATARI: Lose Tale.

"Since even Sengoku can't beat you when it comes to bashfulness," Kanbaru asserted, "I've arranged a little surprise for you. Wait until school starts back up to find out what it might be."

"Huh, a surprise?"

"I'll give you two hints: 'freshman' and 'breasts.'"

"......"

It sounded like something big was waiting for me next term.

I was excited already.

The next thing I spotted in the pile of trash was a manga.

This cleaning session was starting to turn into a real treasure hunt. If she had the money for a digital camera, though, why not buy a damn bookshelf? Hm, what I mistook for a comic book from the cover was actually a novel...

The Bespectacled Secretary and the Bespectacled Prince.

I could tell just from the title that it was a "boys' love" novel.

"This gets thrown away," I said. "What do you think...burnable trash?"

"It might be fiery, but it's not for burning."

Kanbaru grabbed my arm as I reached for the garbage bag.

When did she get so close?

Maybe that uniform was a +speed item.

"Rotten or not," she added, "it's quite necessary."

"It is? If it's so important to you, take better care of it. Don't you think you're being rude to the author?"

Said the guy who was about to throw it away.

True, once too many books started piling up, it was hard to know what to do with them.

"These type of books all look the same to me, though," I noted. "Can you even tell them apart when you're reading them?"

"Of course I can," replied Kanbaru. "That's as narrow-minded as saying all SF is the same. If you aren't familiar with something, you can't tell the difference. It takes knowledge, erudition, to form an accurate judgment."

"Ah. Still…" There were several other BL novels in the pile, so I compared their covers to the one in my hand. "In the end, they're all handsome, aren't they?"

"Huh?"

"Well, it's like you're into handsome men, after all. Maybe you're not really that perverted."

"Nrk?!"

Kanbaru reeled in genuine shock.

If this were a cartoon, it would be more than vertical lines on her face—the background would have turned black and white.

I guess she'd meant it: There was nothing worse you could say about her.

"Come to think of it," I pressed, "tons of girls read BL these days. It's proof that you're well-adjusted. It's normal. Perfectly normal."

"Normal?! I, the self-appointed successor to Freud, am normal?!"

She'd appointed herself…

Well, her inclination to bring any and all subjects around to sex did qualify her, maybe.

"I mean," I went on, "being into handsome men is run of the mill for girls. Wanting to see a bunch of them together is natural. It's no different from being into boy bands."

"D-Don't make such apt comparisons!"

"It's not like you love that old-people smell or are left cold if the guy doesn't weigh more than three hundred fifty pounds."

"N-No, but…"

Kanbaru was at a loss for words. She was acting suspicious.

"H-Hold on, hold on a second!" she pleaded. "Don't say that! I'm finished if my dear senior sees me that way! I'll strip! I'll strip right here!"

"Now, now, now, like you said, what's so strange about getting comfortable at home? And you only get naked outside at a public bath? And self-nudes? Why wouldn't an athlete want to see how her body is coming along? I was wrong to get on your case."

"I'm not asking for an apology! Please, just stop and listen to me!"

"Well, take today. You're not much of an exhibitionist if your family seeing you naked gets you down. I'd assumed, listening to you, that maybe you never wore anything, ever, at home! Let me just say that you're striking me as a big fish in a pond called your own little room." I was picking on her. I was practically a jock. "As you put it on the phone earlier, maybe I have the dirtier mind."

"A-Aghhhh!"

Kanbaru's eyes spun around. She seemed totally panicked.

Araragi casts Kafuddle!

"Y-You've got it wrong," she beseeched. "There just happened to be books like that where you were looking, but dig deeper and you'll find hardcore BL. Like I don't know that BL isn't all about handsome men! Please, keep searching!"

"Now, now, Kanbaru, it's not the real you if you've got to search—"

As I uttered what sounded like an admonition against the tired notion of self-discovery—

Kanbaru tackled me down.

Worse, we landed on top of the futon.

"I-In that case," she threatened, "I'll have to clear my name—through deeds!"

Even apart from her left arm, Kanbaru was too strong for me. She was better built than I was. She had me pinned tight from hip to shoulder, and I couldn't move.

"Prepare yourself!" she warned.

"Prepare for what?!"

"It's not like you haven't been deflowered already!"

"That's because I'm a boy!"

"Don't worry, it only hurts in the beginning! Soon it'll start feeling good!"

"Eeeek!"

"Mmm, you've got a fine body—my kind of muscles! So nice to the touch!"

"Eeek! Eeek! Eeek!"

"Tut! Stop squirming so much! I can't get off your underpants!"

"Aiiieeeeeeeeeeee!!"

I swore.

No matter how high I was feeling when I ran into Hachikuji, I wouldn't sexually harass her the first thing, ever again.

008

Activate skill: New chapter, reset.

Nothing to see here, move along.

"We're getting there," I said.

Kanbaru's twelve-mat room was now straightened up enough that it was starting to actually look large. All that was left to do was to return the things she'd left lying around to their original location. It was still too early to relax, but the end was at least in sight.

The perennially unmade futon was being aired out in the yard.

Additionally, the clothes (including underwear) she'd left scattered around her room after taking them off were tumbling in the washer.

"Want to take a break?" I asked.

"Good idea."

Kanbaru plopped herself down on the floor. She'd already taken the uniform off, by the way.

"Should I go make some tea?" she offered.

"No thanks, I'm not really that exhausted anyways. I just thought a breather was in order."

"Your cleaning skills really are breathtaking. Maybe I always get this room so messy because I want to see them in action."

"That's annoying. Mend your ways."

"You'll make somebody a great wife one day."

"No, thank you!"

The truth is I wasn't particularly good at cleaning up. But with a room as untidy as Kanbaru's, anybody's cleaning skills would seem impressive. It was all about the initial state.

"I wouldn't mind making you my wife," she said.

"Well, I don't think I want you as my husband…"

"I thought you were going to marry me?"

"Maybe if the roles were reversed. Either way, Senjogahara would kill you."

Heck, she'd probably kill me too.

"At any rate," remarked Kanbaru, "you and she make a lovely couple, but I can't help but feel that in the end you'll wind up married to Hanekawa."

"Don't say that!"

"And then I'll be your mistress. Maybe Sengoku will be Lady No. 3?"

"Ugh…"

What an unpleasant image of the future.

Even though it seemed impossible, a chill ran down my spine anyway.

Plus, the odds were probably on Hachikuji.

The horrifying Araragi Harem.

"C-Come on," I objected. "Eventually, I'll marry Senjogahara."

"What a pie-in-the-sky proposal, but saying it to me? How am I supposed to respond? But the truth is…" As she spoke, her expression was that of a Black Kanbaru, whom I believed had surfaced after she started hanging out with Senjogahara again. "I bet you can't refuse if I got serious."

"A-About marriage?"

"No, about an extramarital affair."

"I'd refuse!"

Probably!

Though maybe not absolutely!

"All I'm saying," she clarified, "is that your kindness makes it easy for girls to take advantage of you, so you should be careful. For now, I don't mean anything by it. I like the way our friendship is and have no desire to wreck it, but if you ever did anything to hurt her, then I just might."

"......"

No one had tried harder to wreck my relationship with Senjogahara than Kanbaru.

What was she, an enemy from the first few episodes? The kind that immediately becomes a friend?

"Actually, come to think of it," I said, "if I got married to Hanekawa she'd get killed by Senjogahara, too. I wouldn't like that. Haven't I told you? There's no one in the world I owe more to than Hanekawa."

"Hmm? Her, no..." Kanbaru seemed to hesitate for a moment. "Given their relationship, I don't think you need to worry."

"Oh, why is that?"

"They have their own thing going—not that I'm happy about it, but they seem to be satisfied so it's hardly my place to butt in."

"...? Huh."

What was that supposed to mean?

Well, whatever.

"By the way, Kanbaru. While we're taking a break, how about we try this?"

I set down a deck of *hanafuda* cards that I'd picked out of the trash and kept, thinking we might play later. It was probably the only spoils of today's treasure hunt. I'd pretended not see the "Washizu" mahjong set sitting in the same block of junk.

"Hm?"

Yet.

Kanbaru tilted her head as she took the deck from me.

"What's this?" she asked. "Some kind of card game?"

"Well yeah, sort of... But why would you not know when they were in your room?"

"Oh, *hanafuda*… I forgot about these."

Kanbaru opened up the case, removed the cards, and shuffled through them.

"I don't know the rules," she told me. "I saw it in a department store and just bought it on a whim. I looked at the pictures once and never opened the case again."

"Ah, really? I guess I'm out of luck, then. It's been a while so I felt like playing."

I don't know.

Somewhere along the line, *hanafuda* had become a minor game.

Maybe the most minor card game in the world.

Beat out by Uno, even…

It was older than the Game of Life, so maybe that was that.

"You aren't out of luck," Kanbaru said. "Just teach me. Believe it or not, I'm good at learning the rules for competitive games."

"Are you sure? The rules for *hanafuda* are pretty complicated."

"No problem. Don't lump me in with buffoons who think double-dribbling is when you dribble with two balls."

"……"

Sorry, I used to be that buffoon.

In any case, Kanbaru had pretty good grades.

I guess it was worth a shot.

It was just the two of us, so the *koi-koi* variant seemed like the best choice.

"There are a dozen suits of four cards each—pine, plum, cherry, wisteria, iris, peony, clover, eulalia, chrysanthemum, maple, willow, and paulownia—but it's probably easier to remember them by the pictures."

I offered a quick explanation and then we settled down into a game.

With stuff like this, you could explain as much as you like, but in the end you had to learn by doing. Once you got the basic combos down, the best way was just to get started.

"My senior Araragi, where did you master this pastime?"

"Hmm. I think it was at my grandma's house. There's something nice about the way the cards feel, and it's cute how small they are. But I don't have anyone to play with these days."

"Ahh." Kanbaru gave a deep nod and cast down her eyes. "Right, you have so few friends... Sorry for making you say that."

"No! That's not what I meant! No one knows the rules, that's all!"

Well.

It's true that I don't have many friends.

"Apart from girls," Kanbaru said, "the number is actually zero, isn't it?"

"Damn, that's harsh!"

"And now with Mister Oshino gone... Who am I going to picture you with when I fantasize? The prospects don't look good."

"If you're going to fantasize about that, I'm fine having zero male friends."

We started with a ten-round bout.

It was a practice game, with commentary.

By the time I, who knew the rules, easily won all ten, Kanbaru seemed to have a clear grasp of them, too.

You take a look at the eight cards in your hand and consider what combos you can make. Once the game begins, you don't focus on just your own hand but actively block your opponent from forming combos. It doesn't matter how good yours are if you're too late—when you've figured out that much, you've become a real player.

"Ah ha," Kanbaru said. "How about a real match, then? This is starting to get fun." Taking another look at the rules pamphlet included in the case, she sat up straight. "Decide who goes first by drawing a card... It even specifies, 'Refrain from rock-paper-scissors or using dice.' So old-school."

"Isn't it?"

In that regard it rivaled *Hyakunin Isshu*, the game of a hundred poems.

Of course, that one was pretty minor as well; plenty of people would probably throw their hands up in defeat if they had to play it by the official rules. *Musume fusahose*, anyone?

"I'm bad at rock-paper-scissors," confessed Kanbaru, "so I for one am glad."

"You can be bad at it?"

"You'd be surprised."

"Hmph…"

It was a sort of match, after all. Maybe she was right.

We drew cards. Kanbaru got a December, and me a September, meaning I'd go first. In *koi-koi*, though, whoever went first generally had the advantage, so I decided to let the beginner start.

I wondered if Kanbaru might not like such a handicap, but perhaps seeing it as fair sportsmanship, she accepted my offer without ado, saying, *Well then*.

"Your sisters."

"Huh?"

"Your sisters," she repeated. "Even if you don't have friends, if I recall correctly, you have two little sisters. Don't you ever play *hanafuda* with them? From what you said, it sounded like everyone in your family might know how to play."

"I have a few times, with the younger one—but when we went to grandma's, the older sister preferred to run around in the fields. In any case, we don't play like this anymore."

"I guess that's just how it goes."

"I'm sure there are brothers and sisters who do, but we aren't that close."

Besides, they were busy.

Busy playing at defenders of justice.

"I'm an only child," Kanbaru reminded me. "I don't really know what it's like to have a sister."

"It sucks, I'll tell you that much."

"Maybe an older brother. My life might have been different if I had one—and of course, I do think of you in that way."

114

"I'm honored."

"May I try calling you like you were really my brother?"

"As long as you keep it normal."

"Big Brother Koyomi…"

"……"

Shit.

Oh shit…

Maybe she was just imitating Sengoku, but it had a bigger impact than I expected. Saying it straightforwardly, with no funny business, earned her a lot of points.

"Big Brother Koyomi, it's morning! Wake up!"

"A-Ack…"

"Big brother, you're gonna be late, hurry!"

"W-Wow…"

"Big brother, you're such a meanie."

"I-I'm tingling all over."

"Big brother, would you like to have sexual—"

"And we're done."

Out of bounds.

That was close, she nearly got me.

I guess it applied to Sengoku, too, but it sounded nice and fresh because she wasn't actually my sister. That seemed to be a big part of it.

Besides, being her senior was one thing, but would I make such a great big brother for Kanbaru? Heck, that was true about being her dear senior, too.

"Okay, here we go," I said.

The game began. This time we were keeping score.

To make it interesting, we placed a little bet—it wouldn't be wholesome for high school kids to gamble, so we decided that whoever lost overall would have to do a dare.

A dare.

Well, depending on what, it might end up not being so wholesome. Worst case, betting money would be healthier…

I'm trusting you, Kanbaru!

And I don't mean that as a setup!

"………"

"………"

And so.

Ten more rounds.

This time it wasn't a practice game—

But I still won all ten.

"Umm…"

Suruga Kanbaru.

She may have been quick to learn the rules—but man, was she weak.

What was up with her? How could anyone be so unlucky?

I could see why she might be bad at rock-paper-scissors.

It wasn't classy, but when I felt curious afterwards and did a quick count, almost all of her hand consisted of "plain" cards. On top of that, she'd been dealt plains of the same suit. Three December ones in your hand? Kiss goodbye to any strategy.

Right, and when we were deciding who'd go first, she'd promptly pulled a December.

I had some experience, but it had been so long that I figured a beginner like Kanbaru would make for a good match… I was fairly stunned that it turned out so one-sided.

Not so much as a single tie.

I didn't remember for sure, but didn't the rule structure mean a significant chance of tied rounds?

Hmm…

Well, fine.

Since it was ultimately a game of luck, there were bound to be days like these. If we played again tomorrow, it might be me in Kanbaru's position. Was she born under an unlucky star, was more misfortune and heartache waiting in her future? No, I certainly thought no such thing.

Yet.

"………………………………………………………………"

....
....
....
....   ”
....

Kanbaru had grown extensively silent.

Who does for six whole lines of ellipses?!

The look in her eyes wasn't the Kanbaru I knew, either—well, she tended to look dapper, but with her hair growing out she seemed more feminine, making the distance in her eyes downright frightening.

Her cheeks were slightly puffed out, which was cute, but she did appear sullen.

The set of her mouth also seemed pretty tense.

Some people couldn't help sulking when they lost, no matter at what. So Kanbaru was Exhibit A...

Wow, she felt sore? She could be surprisingly childish at times.

"Sh-Should we get back to cleaning up?" I asked. "Maybe we've been playing too long."

"Oh ho, look who's trying to cut and run," she growled. I wasn't sure if she was talking to me or to the tatami. "I shouldn't have to tell you, but I hold you in the highest esteem."

"O-Okay."

"Indeed, my devotion to you is almost religious. When I call your name, my lips might say 'my senior Araragi,' but my heart is saying 'my savior Araragi.'"

"I wish it didn't..."

"This is rather craven of such a man, isn't it? You disappoint me. How crass to try to cut and run. Are you afraid of losing to me?"

"Actually...I just don't want to win anymore."

Kanbaru, however, refused to let me get up and demanded that I deal the cards once again.

I wondered if this was how a gambler behaved on a losing streak, but I'd never thought Kanbaru was the type to care so much about winning.

Well, I suppose she wouldn't have made it to the nationals otherwise.

If you didn't mind losing at all, you were, in a sense, sick.

But hating to lose only when you couldn't win was just the worst.

"What is this," she reprimanded. "The game isn't over yet. Are you trying to make a fool of me by quitting before we're done? It says right here in the rules, a game lasts twelve rounds. That means we still have two more hands to play. Why don't you wait until you've actually won to start congratulating yourself?"

"With the lead I've got, there's no way two rounds will be…uh, never mind."

Kanbaru glared at me so hard that I fell silent.

What else could I do? We both sat in silence as I finished dealing out eight cards each.

I started by rearranging mine so they'd be easier to play.

I still had to be friends with Kanbaru after we were done. Even if it was too late to lose the game, I could let her win the last two rounds and feel better about herself… Yet it was up to luck in the end, so losing on purpose was easier said than done.

I could play as poorly as I liked, but if my opponent didn't form combos then there was nothing I could do.

How to go about this… Oops.

"Um," I said.

"What are you waiting for? You're first."

"I've got a same-four. Sorry."

I had all four willow cards.

Making a *teshi*, or same-four. It was a special combo based on the cards in your hand upon dealing.

"It's, uh, worth six points…"

Kanbaru silently entered them on the chart we'd created on her cell phone. There was no sadistic rule that the loser of a round had to keep track. She just happened to volunteer to be the scorer at the outset and just happened to be losing every round.

Let's see. I was winning by…about fifty points?

"Now, that was a rare hand," I said. "How about we end on that note?"

"Wait, you piece of… Nkk. There's still one more round left."

She'd nearly cussed me out but cut herself off. She had great self-control but was exerting it for a pretty shabby reason.

Hey, it's only a card game.

"Relax," I told her. "Bracelet, bracelet. We're just playing."

"How do you win with an attitude like that?!"

"I'm winning, though."

"Urk."

"It's a game, so can't you at least try to enjoy it? Take Sengoku. She taught me how to play Twister, and she seemed to be having fun even though she lost to a beginner like me."

"So you don't know. You've yet to encounter the true final boss…"

"Huh? What?"

"Nothing. It's not for me to say."

Next, Kanbaru leaned over. I dealt, despite myself.

Geez, she was the type to build a fortune in sports and ruin herself at the gambling table… Oops.

I glanced down at the cards in my hand, and my eyes widened.

"Kanbaru…"

"What is it?"

"Let's decide our dares in advance."

"Well, aren't you eager. As for mine, it'll be my sexual demands— I mean, sexual commands."

"Really? You could dare me to drop dead if you like."

I countered Kanbaru's entirely unwholesome remark with a dare that couldn't be more wholesome.

"Don't ever get into gambling."

I'd been dealt another special hand.

This time it was a full-eight.

009

Don't worry, we're almost at the core part of the story.

After we were done with *hanafuda* and cleaning up, I took my leave. It was nearly evening by that point. Kanbaru's grandmother invited me to stay for dinner (like she always did. I'd accepted her offer a few times before. Her cooking was amazing), but that day I politely refused.

By the way.

While we were cleaning up, I asked Kanbaru about something that was bothering me. Namely, how she explained to her family what was up with her arm.

"I pass it off as an injury," she said. "I mean, it's not really the kind of thing I can explain."

"Hmph…and they buy it? It's not like my vampirism. All they need to do is look at your arm."

Kanbaru's left arm, possessed by an aberration, was monstrous in form.

"With Senjogahara," I pointed out, "her father knew because there wasn't any way for her to hide it…"

"My grandpa and grandma are worried, of course—but that business about my mother always stands between us. They'd never intrude where I don't want them to."

So it went.

Her mother… Right.

Kanbaru's monkey left arm was originally a memento from her mother—even if her grandparents weren't aware of that fact, if they had any inkling that it was somehow related, they probably wouldn't want to tread there.

Unless…they knew everything and were just pretending not to—that was certainly a possibility.

Either way.

I suppose it was tough for Kanbaru.

Putting aside her mother, Kanbaru looked up to her grandparents. For someone as honest as her, I doubted it was easy having to keep a secret from them.

But that responsibility, too—fell on Suruga Kanbaru.

"In any case," she said, "I only have to put up with it for a few more years."

Yes.

Kanbaru's arm would return to normal then.

Unlike my vampirism—she wouldn't have to cope with it for the rest of her life. I was sure she'd get through it, being who she was. I thought so as I stared down at my own shadow, elongated in the twilight.

Anyway.

When I got on my bike and rode through the august wooden gate of her house, I noticed a man loitering right outside.

At first glance, I thought I recognized him. But he was no acquaintance—I didn't even have to consult my memory.

He was in his late middle age and dressed in a sable black suit with a jet black tie, as if he'd just left a funeral and was in mourning. He was so obviously suspicious, and though it's a vague way to put it, he gave off the definite air of being a character.

A character. The real deal? Or some fake?

That, I couldn't decide just from looking.

He clearly seemed out of place in our town, or maybe the opposite, considering all that I've gone through lately—the exact kind of person you'd expect to find. Yes, in a nutshell…

Dubious. An ominous man.

And he was staring up at Kanbaru's house.

"Hm? Do you live here, kid?"

Given the distance, I couldn't observe him unilaterally, of course, and the man in mourning spoke to me thus as I exited the premises.

His line made me wonder if he might be a salesman, but his appearance denied it—why would one choose such baleful clothes?

I wouldn't buy a cup of coffee from such a dismal character.

"No…" I shook my head, unsure of how to react. Salesman or not, he could be the Kanbarus' guest, and I didn't want to be rude. "I don't… live here."

"Ah, my apologies. I neglected to introduce myself. You are wise to be cautious with a stranger such as myself. Treasure that wariness. My name is Kaiki."

"Kaiki?" It sounded like a word for the bizarre and mysterious, but that couldn't be it.

"Right. *Kai* as in *kaizuka*, shell heap. *Ki* as in *kareki*, withered tree."

His expression unchanging, his attitude oddly knowing yet moody, the man in mourning—Kaiki—cast me a sidelong glance.

His black hair was stiff with pomade.

There was an artificial smell about him.

I couldn't shake the feeling that I knew the man.

Whom did he resemble? If he did—then whom?

"I'm Araragi…" Since the man introduced himself, I felt obligated to at least give my last name. "Written with the characters for…"

Hmm. *A-ra-ra-gi*. The last three were easy enough, but the first was hard to explain, though not to write.

"Don't trouble yourself," the man interrupted my thoughts. "*That's a name I happened to hear very recently*," he said bafflingly. "The last character is also 'tree,' yes? While I'm withered, I suppose you're a sapling."

"……"

Did he simply mean our age difference?

His speech seemed awfully roundabout.

Well, not exactly roundabout—but almost like he was purposely talking in a way that only he understood.

"Um," I said, "if you have some business with the Kanbaru household…"

"Hmph. You're polite for a young person these days. And you're considerate. Interesting. Nonetheless, your consideration is wasted on me. I have no particular business with this household."

Nonetheless, he said. His voice was both monotone and ponderous.

"I'd heard mention that the Gaen woman's legacy resides here. Not that I had a particular course of action in mind. I simply wanted to witness the place for myself."

"Gaen?"

Wasn't that—Kanbaru's mother's maiden name? If so, was Gaen's legacy—Suruga Kanbaru?

Is that why he asked if I "live here"? But that could mean he'd visited without even knowing whether Kanbaru was a boy or a girl.

"It seems I've wasted my time, however," Kaiki said as if he'd just concluded an appraisal of some sort. "The aura is almost undetectable. Perhaps a third of what it was. Under the circumstances, I don't see the harm in leaving this alone—in fact, I have to. There's no money in it, unfortunately. This case's lesson for me is that the truth is sometimes trivial even when it is as one thought."

And on that note—

Not so much done with his business, but as if he had no business at all, he turned on his heel and walked away from Kanbaru's home—briskly, at an alarming speed despite being on foot.

"Umm…"

As for me, in contrast—I could only remain rooted in place. Not that I didn't want to move. It was more like I was reluctant to make my next move, whatever it might be.

Only after Kaiki vanished did I remember. Or rather than remember—

I made an association.

With that unpleasant aloha shirt-wearing man.

It was Mèmè Oshino who came to my mind.

Aberration expert Mèmè Oshino.

A man who'd resided in our town for a few months and left it behind.

"But he wasn't like that slacker Oshino at all—if I had to say…"

If I had to say—I could think of one other person.

His accursed figure rose up in the back of my mind.

The man whom Kaiki resembled was that fanatic—

"Guillotine Cutter…"

It was a name I didn't care to remember, nor one I should ever forget.

"Well, Oshino and Guillotine Cutter were about as different as night and day, too…"

They shared almost nothing in common, Kaiki included. In fact, it was almost weird that he reminded me of both Oshino and Guillotine Cutter.

"Should I follow him?"

Follow him—and speak to him some more?

I started working the pedals—but the handle turned in the exact opposite direction. It was like my mouth had said one thing and my heart another.

It felt like watching someone else inside my body, but I was definitely pedaling of my own volition, and was running away.

It was just a hunch…but that guy seemed like bad news.

Those mourning clothes, so baleful and dismal. But it was more than that.

He just seemed…ominous.

Like an ill omen—sinister.

"In any case, I'm going in the wrong direction…"

I was done cleaning Kanbaru's room and planned to head straight home, but the way I was facing would take me on a long detour. There was nowhere for me to stop by, either—even the bookstore was in the opposite direction. But hey, why not treat myself to a little bike ride?

Hmm...

Maybe I needed to tell Kanbaru about the guy? Judging from his final resigned remark, he probably wouldn't be coming around again—and maybe a half-baked suspicious person report would only make her anxious.

Still. It was better not to take chances—just in case.

Kanbaru was a girl, after all. She looked it a lot more these days, too.

There, settled. I'd call as soon as I got home.

I was standing on the pedals and coaxing my bike up a hill when I spotted someone else walking down the slope my way.

Her skirt was cut long enough to reach her ankles, she was wearing a long-sleeved summer sweater, and her hair was tied back at the nape of her neck. Her face was as expressionless as cast iron but also looked supremely vexed—of course, there's no need to describe her in such detail.

Hitagi Senjogahara.

My girlfriend.

"I'm running into everyone I know today..."

Was this the final episode?

Or something?

Hachikuji sightings were coincidences, and it was also by chance that I thought of visiting Sengoku and Kanbaru—and now, lo and behold, here was Senjogahara. What was up with today?

Was Hanekawa canceling at the last minute such a major event that so many encounters were required to compensate for it?

If so, she had some serious presence.

But I almost looked like some guy who went hopping about from one woman to another...which was hardly commendable.

"Hey, Senjogahara." Since it didn't seem like she'd noticed me, I called out her name and waved my hand wildly.

Her gaze was the worst, but her vision was quite good.

She must have heard me because she raised her head and glanced in my direction—before simply turning a corner and disappearing from sight.

"Wha... Hey hey hey hey!" I began pedaling at full tilt despite the incline to chase after her. "You're seriously hurting my feelings!"

I pedaled past her, pulled into her path, and blocked her way.

She—gave me such an icy stare that I felt the chill deep in my bones. Anyone who could produce such a blast of cold without chanting out loud had to be a high-tier wizard.

"Come on, S-Senjogahara..."

"I don't know any guy who'd be goofing off here when he should be studying."

"Oh, uh..." She was angry. She was definitely angry. "Y-You don't understand."

"Silence. I understand just fine. In fact, I overstand. Skipping one of my lessons is one thing, but Hanekawa's? That's just sad. I'm disappointed in you. No, I take that back. I never had enough faith in you to begin with."

"No, no, Hanekawa was busy, so she gave me the day off."

"Pathetic. I'm tired of hearing your excuses," Senjogahara cut me down.

Actually, I didn't think I made a lot of them when it came to studying.

"In the end," she accused, "you're not a man of your word. My greatest shame in life is to have had my heart stolen by trash like you."

"Geez, watch it. If I were anyone else, I'd be tempted to go jump off a bridge..."

"Hmph, worm," spat Senjogahara, thrusting her chin up like she really looked down on me. She turned her back toward my bicycle and returned to the sloping path. She'd only walked into the alley to avoid me.

It wasn't like I could just let her go, so I chased after her.

"Miss 'Gahara! Miss 'Gahara!"

"What, Churaragi?"

"Would you mind not making my name sound like Okinawa slang? My name is Araragi—and besides, that's Hachikuji's gag!"

"Sorry, a slip of the tongue."

"No, it was on purpose…"

"A slip of the hope you break your neck."

"It was on purpose!"

She didn't even turn around. She was really cross.

Honestly, I don't think she doubted that Hanekawa had cancelled our lesson. It was just that after such a show of anger, she had trouble dialing it back.

She was difficult that way.

When Tsukihi worked herself into a hysteria, it abated just as quickly—with Senjogahara, it was more deeply ingrained.

"You know, Senjogahara…"

"Ugh, some weirdo is following me."

"Who're you calling a weirdo?"

"Ugh, a weird midget is following me."

"Did you just call me a midget?!"

Damn, they'll figure out how short I am! After all the trouble I went to fudge it!

"Who cares?" she said. "When they make the anime adaptation, everyone is going to see that you're shorter than me."

"I'm against an anime! What if they ruin the original?!"

Well. It was only by a fraction of an inch, but Senjogahara was telling the truth. Which is to say that she was tall for a girl. Though not as much as Karen…

"Does everything have to be adapted?" I complained. "They act like any book would sell if it just said 'Now an Anime' on the cover, and I, for one, abhor the trend. Living in such an age, I'd love to see an original anime that's not based on anything!"

I hadn't been so upset in a long time.

All you tall guys out there would never understand!

What it's like to quietly opt for thick soles every time you buy shoes!

"Maybe your concern is misplaced," Senjogahara said. "In the anime version, they'll just cut your character."

"The protagonist?!"

"Yes… If this were *Galaxy Angel*, you'd be Tact Mayers."

"No! I demand better treatment!"

"I guess, if you'd be fine with a role like Chitose Torimaru's."

"If that's how it's gonna be, I'd rather not be included at all! Can't I at least be Normad?"

"Oh? I didn't know you were so intrigued by the mystery of corned beef cans."

"That's not what I meant!"

Did she have any sort of authority? What was she, a diva who had control over all the casting decisions, too? Dreadful.

"Now, now, Araragi, stop caterwauling. When God closes a door, he also breaks a window."

"Is that supposed to be an upside?!"

"Don't worry. You may be out, but they've added a fancy mascot to replace you."

"Clearly a merchandising ploy!"

"Besides, you're not the protagonist. Just who do you think you are?"

"Urk…" Right, I forgot. I was just the MC.

"You're not the lead, you just belong on one."

"What an attribute!"

Senjogahara was walking fast, but I was on my bike so I had no trouble keeping up. I thought about pulling around in front again, but instead of going that far I just trailed close behind her.

"Fine," I said, "if I don't need to show my face, that's okay… You'll be dancing with a blank expression during the ending song while I watch from outside the screen."

"Huh? You won't catch me dancing."

"......"

"Why should I make a fool of myself?"

".........?"

Cool!

Super-cool, Miss Hitagi!

"I'll be the one watching everyone dance," she claimed. "And after they're done, during the last splash card I say, 'No dancing in the station!'"

"Heck, I know that's from a commercial for 'Georgia' coffee, but how many people nowadays would get that reference?!"

"It'll be such a letdown if they go for a dance ending after all this buildup."

"There's no pleasing you!" Talk about greedy. She wasn't building as much as boarding things up. "Gosh, I really don't get you sometimes... Scratch that, I get you plenty."

"Are you insinuating that you have a problem with the conduct of Hitagi Senjogahara, a.k.a. 'an outpouring of nature-friendly toxic gas'?"

"That's terrible catch-copy?!"

"Maybe 'unnaturally friendly' would be better."

"Better for whom?!" And since when was she friendly, naturally or otherwise?

"Just don't get me wrong. I actually hate human scum like you, Araragi."

"Are you sure you aren't just abusing your tsundere label and baring your soul?"

"They say a woman finds happiness not by being with the man she loves but by being with a man no one loves."

"That's not quite how that expression goes!"

And a man no one loves? How would she know?!

"I was joking," she said.

"Well, as long as you're joking..."

"You're oh-so-beloved and popular with the ladies."

"......"

Sarcasm? An allusion to the nonexistent Araragi Harem?

"*Hum hum hum...*" hummed Senjogahara, phonily and without feeling. She extended one arm toward my head and proceeded to seize my skull in an iron grip. Drawing her expressionless face close, she gazed into my eyes.

Glaaare, she even mouthed a sound effect. Then she said—

"Three...no, five?"

"Wh-What?"

"The number of girls you've played with today."

"......nkk!"

Since when did she have ESP?!

Uh, but Hachikuji, Sengoku, Kanbaru—three was correct... Oh, and she was including Tsukihi and Karen!

Amazing!

"If we're being strict...six?" asked Senjogahara, cocking her head. Apparently, Kanbaru's grandma counted, too. That wasn't being strict, that was draconian. "On the basis of that estimate, I repeat: you're oh-so-beloved—and popular with the ladies."

"......"

Your blank expression scares me, okay?

Were her pupils dilated or what?

"Heheh." Senjogahara finally released her iron claw and, before I could blink, thrust the same hand into my mouth.

All four fingers, minus the thumb. Deep into my oral cavity.

"Relax, Araragi. Believe it or not, I'm pretty open-minded when it comes to two-timing."

"I-I'm knot too thyming." I couldn't even remember how to spell correctly. "The moats eye doo is the to-stroke." I meant to say something clever, but it was a fail.

"Yes. You're forever swimming the two-stroke trying not to drown in a sea of love..."

"Don't steal my joke!" I didn't need any help, but the shock did fix my spelling.

"Maybe it's a swimming pool rather than a sea? As in pooling your women?"

"You're overthinking it now," I said. I'd never use the word in that context. What a tutoring session...

"But the truth is that you're surrounded by girls," asserted Senjogahara.

"R-Really? I don't think so."

"Yet all the names in your contacts list are girls."

"Don't go poking around in people's phones without permission!"

Come to think of it...Kanbaru had said something similar.

Was it some sort of consensus? That was too sad.

"I guess it can't be helped, though," Senjogahara lamented. "Your very characterization is that you're kind to girls but cold to guys."

"Stop it! Don't spout nonsense that will demolish my reputation!"

This was slander! Pure libel!

"I bet if a guy were in trouble, Araragi, you'd tell him, 'Man, that's rough, I hope it works out for you,' and just head on home."

"Hearsay and disparagement!"

"And if the guy actually begged for help, you'd tell him, 'Uhhm, I think I'll pass.'"

"I wouldn't pass!"

"Believe it or not, I'm open-minded when it comes to two-timing."

Terrifyingly enough, before I could be cleared of her calumny, she simply repeated herself to set our conversation back on track. What was she trying to do to my image? What if people believed it?

"So," she continued, "you're free to mess around with whomever you like, however you like—but if your two-timing ever gets even a little serious, you're dead."

"......"

Good grief—it didn't sound like she was kidding, not one bit.

I understood—how serious she was being.

I didn't—as to why.

"Don't worry," she said. "I'll at least give you the time to write your last will and testament."

"That's not what's bothering me!"

"Welcome to Hitagi's Countdown Corner...four seconds remaining."

"I'm supposed to write one in four seconds?!"

"It's quite standard."

"Your standards are too harsh!"

"Rest easy, Araragi, you won't die alone—the girl will follow after you."

"Do all this dying yourself, okay?!"

"I'll also dispatch Kanbaru to make sure you're not lonely in the afterlife."

"What do you take her for?!"

"A pliant junior?"

"That's just cruel!"

"A human offering to Koyomi Araragi, then."

"She'll get sacrificed?!"

"Why not? The learned term is *hitomigoku*, which rhymes with Son Goku, the monkey king. So perfect for Kanbaru, who's a monkey."

"You know it's just her left arm that's a monkey paw, right?"

"I'm kidding. She's dear to me. Besides..." Senjogahara finally removed her fingers from my mouth. "I don't actually believe there's an afterlife."

"I see..." Well, she didn't have to tell me, I didn't suppose she would.

"I just want you to know, Araragi, what dating me entails."

"I do..." I nodded, but I hardly needed the reminder. The risk was there. Senjogahara was one big beautiful thorn. "In any case, I'm not going to cheat."

"Is that so," she said with a curt nod. She showed no expression or emotion but added, "Then we're fine. As long as you remember whose man you are—I'm good." Something in those words hinted at weakness. That was rare for her. But entirely typical, you might also say. "In my own way, I put some serious effort into being your girlfriend—if possible, I'd like to see you do the same."

"Effort…"

When was it? Hadn't Hachikuji touched on this? Staying in love—as a matter of effort. And how that wasn't insincere but rooted in good faith.

"I try, too," I replied firmly as if I were making an oath. "I've never once forgotten whose man I am."

"Is that so."

My words elicited another curt nod from her. That was all. Apparently, that was enough for her.

"By the way, Araragi, there's one last thing I want to state for the record."

"Yeah?"

"As a girl—it's quite gratifying to have a boyfriend who's popular with the ladies."

"Keep that to yourself!"

Even now, Senjogahara's expression was as stiff as a board. She had unbelievable control over her facial muscles.

In any case, it seemed like the topic was closed, so I asked her, "Were you headed somewhere?"

"I'm just on my way home after doing some shopping. Can't you tell by looking? This is what I hate about invertebrates."

"I do have a developed nervous system, thank you very much!"

Besides, how could I tell just by looking? It's not like she was carrying any shopping bags.

"Come on, get on the back," I said. "I'll take you home."

"The back?"

"Of my bike."

"Ahh…you mean that mechanical beast."

"Where were you raised, again?!"

"I'll pass. My skirt would get stuck in the wheels." True, in addition to being long, reaching down to her ankles, her skirt was also puffy and

134

flowing. "Or is this a subtle demand that I remove it in public?"

"Nope!"

Speaking of which, she basically only wore long skirts, whether it was her school uniform or everyday clothes. When she went for something shorter, like a pair of culottes, she always paired them with stockings.

She refused to expose her bare legs. I guess you could say she was being chaste? Sure, given what she'd been through, it was understandable. But still…

"Araragi." Having released enough vitriol, and feeling sated for the moment, I suppose, Senjogahara was ready to introduce a different topic. Her tone was still flat and cold, but it always was, whether she was angry or not. "Putting aside preparing for entrance exams, the culture festival is over and it's summer vacation. Don't you feel like high school will be over any day now?"

"Hm? I guess you're right." The truth is, I'd been so focused on studying that I hadn't really thought about it, but now that she mentioned it, graduation was just around the corner. "At least, I'll be able to clear the attendance requirement—I probably won't have to repeat the year."

"Too bad, that would have been funny."

"Don't see the humor in it!"

"Forgoing such a juicy gag…after so many years on air."

"We're in high school, not on a variety show!"

"When I go over my high school memories…" Senjogahara wistfully raised her chin and made as though to reminisce for a few moments before concluding, "The highpoint was eraserockey."

"You only got into it in high school?!"

Eraserockey = eraser desk hockey. In case you were wondering.

"You insult me, Araragi. In case you didn't know, I was the Eraserockey Queen."

"And the title isn't insulting for a high school girl?!"

"I practiced alone for hours after school, and my technique can't be

135

beat."

"Please, that's so depressing!"

"Of course, I didn't have anyone to play with, so I never had a real match."

"Any more and I might start crying!"

"Watch how you speak to me. Otherwise, I'll go on a violent crime spree and confess that I was influenced by your favorite manga."

"Now you're taking manga artists hostage?!"

"Eraserockey aside, I can't help but feel a little sad that once we graduate, the phrase 'seating change' will never sound so exciting again."

"Is that all high school meant to you?"

Not that I couldn't understand. More than two thirds of Senjogahara's own experience of it was characterized by nothing, literally. Nothing at all to remember in the first place—it was so light that a mere breath could blow it away.

"In fact," I said, "I can't picture you getting excited over changing seats…"

"True. Even if my seat changes, I remain the same."

"……"

As deep as it sounded, she was simply stating the obvious.

That's precisely how you've changed, Senjogahara.

But that went without saying.

"First we graduate," she went on, "then college—that is, if you get in."

"Save the commentary."

"Then we graduate from college—and become adults?"

"Adults…"

"What do you suppose the difference is between an adult and a kid?" she asked. I don't think she actually expected an answer. She seemed to be in thinking-out-loud mode.

"Who knows. I can't say I've never thought about it before…but it's the kind of question you can think about until the cows come home and still never answer."

"Here's what I think." Her tone was serious. "Children watch the movie version of *Nausicaä of the Valley of the Wind*, and adults read the manga."

"But you sounded so serious!"

"Which means I'm already an adult."

"And I'm still a kid!" Hmph. Right, Senjogahara did do a lot of reading. "Novels, comics, business books... You'll read pretty much anything, huh?"

"Yes. The only thing I don't is the room."

"That's some important reading you're forgetting!"

"I'm positively dyslexic there. I read between the lines but skip the lines." *Or just scan the footnotes,* she added.

Talk about a complicated joke. The footnotes to a mood!

"I might not be able to read the room, but I can place a pretty good chill over one," she boasted.

"Humanity has no use for your talent!"

"In the manga version of *Nausicaä*, Kushana turns out to be a surprisingly good person. I thought we were cut from the same cloth...but it turns out we'd be enemies, after all."

"I doubt either version of Kushana would want an ally like you."

"Araragi, it's about time you stopped relying on the Friday night movie slot and became an adult, too."

"You're recommending manga to a guy who's studying for entrance exams?!"

"Don't be stupid. There are far more important things in this world than some test."

"Yes, but!"

Yes, but she'd lose her top if I tried to tell her that!

Senjogahara wasn't done with *Nausicaä* yet. "Finding out that the famous line 'It's rotten. It was too soon' was correct, in that it indeed was too soon, is quite moving and makes you grow as a person...but if you've read the manga first, I wonder how you'd react to the scene in the movie?"

"I don't think I care!"

"Try to care a little. Sometimes I worry you'll never grow up."

"People keep telling me that…"

You never grow up.

A child. Yet Tsukihi had told me the exact opposite today, hadn't she?

"But yeah," I said.

"And what about you, Araragi, why are you here? This isn't your usual territory," Senjogahara changed the subject without batting an eye, ever free with her transitions.

I turned her line back on her: "Can't you tell just by looking?"

"Unfortunately," she returned my volley, "I'm not conversant in microbe behavior."

I should have known better than to get into a snarking contest with her. But microbe?

"If I were to hazard a guess, though…" she mused, "considering who I'm talking to, are you on your way home after committing some petty crime?"

"Just out for a stroll and a couple misdemeanors!"

A "petty" crime?! You're too much for me!

"I'm actually on my way home from Kanbaru's," I replied.

Mentioning that I'd gone to Sengoku's house first would only drag things out—to begin with, she and Senjogahara had yet to meet. Hm… maybe neither of them even knew the other existed.

Now wasn't the time to rectify that situation. Introducing such a scary sister to Princess Demure seemed like a bad idea.

"I see. So you committed a petty crime at Kanbaru's house."

"I did not!"

"Really? I had the distinct feeling that you saw her naked."

"I-I did not," I stuttered.

It was a total lie. But wait, it wasn't frontal!

I was merely omitting the details to keep it simple!

"I see," Senjogahara said. "Okay, you didn't go to Kanbaru's house to commit a petty crime."

"I'm glad you understand…"

"Because a sex crime is more than a misdemeanor."

"Can't you tell that I don't like thinking of my dear junior that way even if it's just talk?!"

"Seriously, though, you should see her naked at least once. Her body is like a work of art. There's nothing lewd about it, it's beautiful. Guys might have their preferences, but from a girl's perspective, she has the perfect figure."

"……"

I wanted to nod emphatically and dish about the details, but I knew better. Senjogahara might be laying a trap, so I remained silent.

But she'd seen it, too? It wasn't odd since they were both girls, but I was curious as to the circumstances… Hachikuji had been joking, and it was a secret, but Kanbaru had no-nonsense "Sapphic" feelings for Senjogahara.

Kinky. Sapphic.

Masochist. Exhibitionist.

Suruga Kanbaru. She was quality. While I'd teased her about the covers of BL novels, there was no mistaking that she was an elite-ranked pervert.

"Now that her hair's grown out," Senjogahara remarked, "she looks a lot more like a girl… All she needs to do is talk more like one, and she'll be complete."

"Not to interrupt your Suruga Kanbaru Makeover Party—but I dig the way she speaks."

"It really fills me with pride to own something so fine."

"Except you don't?!" I was afraid I'd slip up if this went on, so I decided to deflect the talk a little. "Oh, by the way, there was this weird guy outside her house."

"Huh, when did they install a mirror there?"

Senjogahara tilted her head as if she meant it—man, this girl.

"He wasn't weird so much as…ominous," I rephrased myself.

"Ominous?" Senjogahara—slowly turned toward me.

Not realizing what that meant, I continued, "He said his name was...Kaiki."

And then—my memories get cut off there.

010

When I awoke, I was being held captive.

In the ruins of the cram school, on the fourth floor. With my hands cuffed behind my back.

After checking with Senjogahara, I learned that I hadn't been unconscious for very long—maybe a few hours at most. That meant I came to late at night on July the twenty-ninth—or rather the very early hours of the thirtieth.

Hmm.

My memories may have been interrupted, but I could piece together the rest—that must have been when Senjogahara clobbered me.

Twenty wallops. Twenty, for God's sake.

I bet the first blow had already knocked me out.

Since Senjogahara didn't possess any unarmed combat skills, it seemed likely that she'd used some sort of blunt instrument. All I could say was that she'd struck without a second thought—the word "hesitation" probably didn't exist in her dictionary.

Well, this was a woman who'd had to go through hell in order to protect herself, and she must have had more trouble dragging me here than knocking me out—or so I thought as if it were someone else's business.

"Well, at least I remembered how I got kidnapped." Senjogahara was standing in front of me like nothing was amiss, so I asked her, "That still doesn't answer the question: why a kidnapping?"

"Huh? What are you talking about?"

"Who do you think you're fooling?!"

No one at all! What kind of nonsense was that?

My shouts, however, fell on deaf ears. Senjogahara simply began unwrapping the package of diapers. I felt my blood curdle.

Given what I did remember, though, I could fill in the blanks.

"That guy, Kaiki…" I said, watching closely for any sign of a change in Senjogahara's perpetually blank expression. "You know him, don't you?"

"By the way, Araragi, would you like some tea? Didn't you like that black tea with the name that sounds like a festival in Kansai?"

"If you're trying to distract me, at least try harder! You don't even have a cup, or a teapot, or hot water, or any tea!"

And it's Darjeeling! The festival is *Danjiri*, dammit!

And set up one punch line at a time, instead of three!

"I thought you'd fall for it," she argued, "since it's you."

"Just how stupid do you think I am?"

"Stupid enough to think 'amenity' is some brand of tea."

"You know, even ridicule has its limits!"

"This one, actually, isn't about stupidity, but being a chump," Senjogahara said. Her expression didn't change. "I'd appreciate your not asking why."

"If that's what's best then I won't. But I don't think it is. After all, you felt you had to go this far." To protect me—it was to protect me that Senjogahara had abducted me. "If you did, it's got to be a big deal."

"Are you sure? Even without a reason, as long as I had an excuse, kidnapping my boyfriend seems like the sort of thing I would do…"

"……"

Right. I'd realized that even as I spoke. But if I agreed now, we'd never get anywhere.

"Deishu Kaiki," Senjogahara said, looking away. "That's the man's name. Deishu as in 'mud boat.' Kaiki isn't a common name, and since you said he seemed ominous, I knew it had to be him—if any man fits that description more perfectly, I don't know him."

"......"

"Yes, just like you know nothing."

Hey. Did she have to derail the conversation to badmouth me? She really couldn't read a room. What a scary lady.

"I can't believe he's back in town," Senjogahara continued. "How odd and incomprehensible—I don't believe I even considered the possibility."

"But who is he? It's unusual for you to be so averse to someone."

"Really? Is there anyone on this planet that I'm not averse to?"

"If you're just going to keep on misrendering my meaning, this conversation won't get anywhere."

"Misrender unto me the things that are Caesar's."

"That's just theft!"

"Indeed. And Kaiki is—a swindler."

Upon reflection—

Senjogahara's acid tongue wasn't merely unchanged, but even more acidic than usual. What was going on? Right...she was having trouble broaching the subject head-on. She had to be trying to discuss something that she couldn't abide.

"Araragi, remember how you and Mister Oshino solved that issue I was dealing with?"

"Yeah."

Actually, "solve" wasn't exactly what we did, but if she was using the word, then fine. I'd only correct her on a different point: it wasn't really Oshino or I who'd done the solving but Senjogahara, herself.

"I told you, didn't I? Before you introduced me to Mister Oshino—I met five frauds."

—*So far, five people have spouted similar lines to me.*

—*All of them were frauds.*

—Are you one as well, Mister Oshino?

When she'd met Oshino for the first time, she'd said that to his face.

Five frauds.

"Kaiki was one of them—the first one."

"......"

Now I understood. No wonder Kaiki reminded me of Oshino and Guillotine Cutter.

What Senjogahara had dealt with—was a crab.

Her issue had been an aberration.

Mèmè Oshino and Guillotine Cutter held different positions and stances, and also, Oshino handled aberrations of all stripes while Guillotine Cutter was an authority on vampires only—but they were both experts in the field.

Apparently, Kaiki—Deishu Kaiki—was, too. Whether he was the real deal or a fake.

"He's a fake," the caustic Senjogahara declared. "He's a first-class fraud, though. That man brought tragedy to my entire family. He had his way with us, swindling us out of our money and vanishing without accomplishing a thing."

I recalled the man, ominous in his suit, as if dressed for mourning. Kaiki—Deishu Kaiki.

"Since he was the first—I got my hopes up," Senjogahara shared. "Having them dashed crushed my soul, but that's trivial."

"What's the...non-trivial part?"

"I," she answered me without hesitation, "don't want you to have anything to do with him, that's all."

"......"

"I refuse to be robbed, to let go of something dear to me again. That's why..." She paused solemnly. "That's why I'm going to protect you, Araragi."

She spoke as if she were making a promise to herself. I was speechless. It wasn't that she convinced me, nor did I even understand what she was saying. I felt like her argument had skipped a few steps, or perhaps what was missing was information.

Regardless—Senjogahara had let go of something precious long ago, and that experience weighed on her. Heavily.

It weighed on her, and pained her.

She, who knew nothing of hesitation and thus of regret, probably saw it as the one blot on her history. And that's why she was acting, in all earnestness, for my sake. That much seemed certain.

"Is this guy Kaiki…such a problem?" I asked her. "Why don't you want me near him?"

"He is. He's too pungent for you, Justice Man."

"Justice Man…"

What was that supposed to mean? Like I was with the Fire Sisters.

"At the very least," Senjogahara said, "until I know what Kaiki is up to—why he's back in town—be a good boy and stay here. In fact, even if he's visiting for no reason, until he's gone, I want you to stay put."

"What if Kaiki moved to our town?"

"In that case…" Apparently the possibility hadn't occurred to her, and she stopped to consider before stating, "You'll just have to live here forever."

Talk about going overboard.

"Miss 'Gahara…"

"Or," she continued, her voice extremely level, "I kill him."

"No…" Throwing words like that around didn't do.

"You're right… How about I just 'punch his ticket' then?"

"His ticket?!" A cutesy phrase didn't make it any better! It still didn't do! "Anyway, what sort of guy is this Kaiki—"

The talk was turning to violence, so I tried, tied up as I was, to obtain a little more information, when—

That was when my phone's ringtone went off, inside my jeans pocket. It was the incoming text ring.

"Can I see who it is?"

Senjogahara paused for a moment, and then, without answering, reached toward my pants and began fumbling around in my pocket.

145

"Wh-Whoa! That's a little too much fumbling! What do you think you're reaching for there?!"

"It's down deep so I'm having trouble getting it out."

"My pockets aren't that deep!"

"Right, they're as shallow as your life."

"Can't you even get my phone for me without insulting me?!"

Having insulted me, though, she did pull it out.

She held its screen up to my face.

Obviously, I couldn't read the message without working the buttons—but the sender and subject line were already displayed, and that was all I needed to see.

"From: Littler Sister / Subject: Help!"

Clink.

That very moment, the handcuffs—*the chain on the handcuffs*—just *snapped loose.*

Then, without further ado—I stood up.

"Araragi…"

Even Senjogahara looked surprised; even then, her mental composure was impeccable, and she didn't panic one bit, merely fixing a sharp gaze on me as I stood there.

"Where do you think you're going?" she asked me.

"Something's just come up. I can't play around anymore. I'm going home."

"And you think I'm letting you?"

"I'm going. It's my home."

And my family.

"I'll have you know—" Senjogahara said, "I'm not such a coward that I'd back down just because I'm facing a vampire, and I'm not kind enough to back down just because you're my boyfriend."

"I do know. That's why I love you."

"Heh," chuckled Senjogahara—like she was actually having fun. Like she couldn't be happier that she had someone on whom to sic her emotions. "If you want to pass, you'll have to defeat me first—do

146

you think you can?"

"I can and I will. That line only works on me if the other person is doing the upside-down crab. You said you want to protect me. I appreciate it, but I have things that I want to protect, too."

You aren't the only one—who's lost something precious.

"You think a little speech can persuade me?" defied Senjogahara.

"Why should I have to?"

"Really? Don't start confusing me for a reasonable woman."

"Then what about me did you fall for?" I said, returning her stare. "Would you be proud about loving a guy who'd sit on his ass now?"

"Oops… Super-cool…" murmured Senjogahara, barely audibly.

Hey, don't get back to normal all of a sudden. You're gonna make me blush.

She added, "If I were a man, I'd find you irresistible…"

"How about as a woman?!"

"Who says I don't?"

"Ah, well…"

We both fell into an uncomfortable silence amidst all the tension, but this time my phone, which Senjogahara was still gripping in her hand, rang to announce not a text but a call.

"Hello? We're busy," answered Senjogahara, annoyed by the sound perhaps, and without asking for my permission first. Her voice was impassive, and she never removed her eyes from me.

I expected her to hang up immediately—but instead, she froze. Well, not that her face could freeze any further. But somehow she appeared shaken.

Senjogahara, who didn't panic one bit when I stood up despite my restraints, felt shaken?

"N-No." Her voice was feeble, too.

I wasn't close enough to overhear, but had the other person told her something? And who was it, anyway? I'd assumed it was Tsukihi—

"I…didn't mean to. That's a misunderstanding. I never said that. Yes, uh huh—true. You're right. Wait, you don't need to. That wasn't our agreement. No, please, give me some time. Understood. I'll do exactly as you say… Is that fine?"

She hung up.

Closing her eyes, as though in resignation, she tossed the phone at me—like she was taking something out on me. Confused, I peered into her face, but as if my very gaze were irritating, she said, "You can go home."

I had no idea what had happened. I really didn't have a clue, but one thing was clear. She'd stepped out of the way and allowed me access to the door.

"I can? Are you sure?"

"You can… A-And, Araragi, um, how do I, uh…"

Bitterly, or grudgingly, like what she was about to say totally went against her will, Senjogahara, who usually spoke in such a flat and inflectionless tone, stammered out the words.

"I-I'm…I'm sor…ry!"

Whoever had called must have insisted that she apologize to me—a demand so unpalatable that fulfilling it made Senjogahara bite her bottom lip and shake with humiliation.

………

Hey, if it's that harrowing, don't bother on my account…

"Um…Miss 'Gahara? If you don't mind, who was that on the phone?"

Her answer was concise.

"Hanekawa."

011

Tsukihi had sent a message asking for help. In other words, she was in trouble.

I decided to head home immediately—by the way, when I asked Senjogahara what had happened to my bike, she told me there just happened to be a garbage pickup spot nearby, so she'd parked it there.

Such a heartless thing to do. Was the Valhalla Duo in the bicycle disposal business or what?

I asked her where the pickup spot was and wound up having to swing back there on my way home—it was pretty far out of the way, but still faster than running.

Of course, I didn't neglect to see Senjogahara home first. Even if we were fighting, she was my girlfriend.

Midnight. Dawn was still faraway.

In the afternoon, I'd had to sneak to my bike to avoid being spotted by Tsukihi, but at this hour, I had to creep in so that my parents wouldn't notice... Well, they were generally hands off with me, and maybe I didn't need to worry.

But I had to act the part. The least I could do was to appear guilty, for form's sake... Damn, that sounds so small.

Anyway, I sneaked through the front door, down the hallway, and up the stairs to my sisters' bedroom.

Karen and Tsukihi shared it.

"I didn't do anything wrong," was the first thing Karen Araragi said.

She was sitting on the bottom bunk looking sullen, her cheeks puffed out and her lips in a pout, for all the world like she was being punished for a crime she didn't commit.

Her face was slightly flushed. She seemed offended, if anything.

"What have I done to get you mad at me?" she questioned. "Tsukihi shouldn't have said anything. It's got nothing to do with you anyway so just leave me alone."

"......"

Ahh, brother and sister.

Even Senjogahara would at least have said thank you.

Do you have any clue what kind of danger I escaped to get home, Tail Head?

She'd changed from her outdoor jersey to an around-the-house jersey. She could go join Hachikuji for being such a Jersey cow. But I'd been pestering her about it for years and now wasn't the time, so I let that go.

"Karen..." said Tsukihi, sounding worried.

Tsukihi was acting pretty sheepish as far as I could tell—Karen must have given her shit for asking for my help. They almost never disagreed, but in the rare instances they did clash, just as you'd expect, it was usually the younger Tsukihi who backed down. I guess seniority ruled, and when push came to shove, it didn't matter who was the enforcer or the strategist.

Putting that aside.

"First, just tell me what's going on," I demanded. "What in the world happened after I left? I thought you were going to regale me with your heroic deeds?"

I'd read the rest of Tsukihi's message but was still in the dark. I only knew that Karen had gotten into trouble.

She wasn't injured, as far as I could tell. But with these girls, that didn't mean I could rest easy.

I urged; Karen ignored. Damn, I wanted to choke her.

"I'll ask you again, bigger sister. What happened?"

"Go...get...bent!" *Nyah,* she stuck her tongue out at me. She didn't forget to pull down the flesh under her eyes with her forefingers, either. A girl who was already in her third year of middle school!

I was so mad I raised my hand without thinking—

"Araragi."

The person who stopped me was standing by the window and leaning against the wall. It was Hanekawa.

Tsubasa Hanekawa. She'd stopped me, with a single utterance.

"Araragi," she said, "you got really mad on my behalf when my father hit me. Why would the same guy want to hit his sister?"

"......"

I had no reply. I stood still as a statue.

"I believe that corporal punishment has its place," she admitted. "If you have an explanation that would satisfy Karen, then by all means, go ahead."

"Sorry."

"Why apologize to me?"

Guided by her words, I turned toward Karen. "Sorry. I lost it." I bowed my head.

First Senjogahara, and now I had been made to apologize by Hanekawa... This wasn't a case of seniority, but the power relationship was just as clear.

That said, Senjogahara succumbing to Hanekawa surprised me. I knew my girlfriend wasn't comfortable with the class president but assumed it was just their different personalities.

But making Senjogahara issue even a stammering apology against her will when she didn't think she was at fault—that went beyond any awkwardness.

Tsubasa Hanekawa, our ridiculously brilliant classmate, not only had the best grades in our year—this one time, she also came in first for the national mock exams.

Senjogahara once referred to Hanekawa as the real deal—and a monster. I strenuously object to the addendum but agree wholeheartedly that she's the real deal.

She, alone—doesn't smell the least fake.

Hanekawa really saved me during spring vacation. I'm not exaggerating when I say that I'd be dead if not for her. I might be physically alive, but I'd have died for sure spiritually.

Calling her my savior doesn't do it justice.

She's like my second mother. Because as I see it, it wasn't that I cheated death. Thanks to her, I was reborn.

Obviously, Hanekawa is our class president (I'm the vice president, by the way—she forced me into it) and a class president among class presidents. With her glasses, braids, and neat bangs, she looked every bit the part of the model student—until the culture festival.

Afterwards…she cut her hair.

Shoulder length, with a shag to the bangs.

She also switched her glasses for contacts, and while she didn't mess with her uniform, her school-designated bag was adorned with accessories. *So what?* you might say, but it's a huge event, as if the sun suddenly rose in the west one day.

Thanks to this transformation on the part of the brightest star in Naoetsu High history, our homeroom teacher had collapsed, the head teacher for our year had been hospitalized, and the principal had penned a letter of resignation, people were rumoring in earnest.

Whether any of that was true, a hornet's nest had been dropped into our class. She hadn't dyed her hair green or gotten a tattoo, but there was a commotion like Hanekawa had turned into a delinquent overnight.

"Thought I'd change my image."

That was all she said in response to all hell breaking loose. She'd told them, and told them good. There weren't to be follow-up questions.

Actually, I knew the reason for that "image change"—or rather, I had a fair idea, nothing more, just that, which is also precisely why I couldn't ask her about it.

The other day, Tsubasa Hanekawa had suffered a broken heart.

Cutting your hair due to some romantic misfortune was no longer a thing—but Hanekawa could be an anachronistic woman that way. I doubted a haircut could wash away heartbreak, but she seemed to require such a reckoning.

Ditching the braid, getting rid of her glasses.

She didn't seem like "an obvious class president" anymore, just an ordinary girl.

Which was fine. Just fine.

It was what she'd always hoped for—she was indeed "an ordinary girl," after all, though I almost felt like she'd undergone an exorcism.

No, an exorcism wasn't it…

Maybe she'd tamed what possessed her.

That was my impression. In any case, the question was what this new Hanekawa (I say new, but it was already a month since her image change so I was pretty used to it by now) was doing in my sisters' room.

Then again, if she weren't, she wouldn't have called me at that moment. It's not like her personality had changed. She was as serious as ever, not the type to call a boy in the middle of the night—so.

I was about to ask Hanekawa why.

"Tsubasa." That was when Karen, for whom Hanekawa had just interceded, cut in. "Don't scold my brother… It was my fault just now, and if he had slapped me, I'd have slapped him back."

"Really?" Hanekawa shrugged her shoulders, jokingly it seemed. "Then I was butting in."

"Yeah, you were."

"I doubt you could slap him back, though."

"Then I'd bite him. Just so you know, I've got teeth like steel, Tsubasa."

Geez… Giving lip to her erstwhile protector was pure Karen, but when the hell did she start calling Hanekawa by her first name?

I turned toward Tsukihi.

"Don't look at me, I call her by her last name," Tsukihi tried to excuse herself.

That wasn't the point.

It's not even which name to use, I thought, you better start addressing her as "ma'am"! But that wasn't the point, either.

Partly because Hanekawa tutored me, she and my sisters were already acquainted—but when did they get so close?

"Koyomi, just listen and don't get angry. I know my brother won't get angry about such a thing," Tsukihi prefaced. "See, this time, the Fire Sisters enrolled Miss Hanekawa—"

"You did what?!" I shouted instantly.

What were they thinking?! They'd gotten Hanekawa involved!

"Araragi, don't be so loud, you'll wake your parents… And I never knew you were the type to intimidate your sisters by yelling at them."

"……nkk."

My hands were tied! I wanted Hanekawa to think I was a good boy!

"Miss Hanekawa, please don't scold Koyomi," Tsukihi pleaded, actually placing herself between me and Hanekawa. "He's just worried that we inconvenienced you."

What was with this scene where my sisters were covering for me? It seemed so unfair.

"Geez…"

After I calmed down a little, I realized something.

This morning—yesterday morning, actually, in terms of the date—Tsukihi somehow knew that my tutoring was cancelled. Figuring I must have told her when she'd woken me up, I didn't give it further thought, but that hadn't been why. She'd known beforehand that Hanekawa would have plans and that the session would be cancelled.

No wonder Tsukihi knew. She and Karen were behind it.

"Araragi, it was my own decision to help Karen and Tsukihi, so don't be mad at them. The Araragi I know would never take it out on his little sisters."

"Nrghh…" I was starting to feel manipulated. Not that I'd ever defy Hanekawa, manipulation or not.

Karen spoke next. "You know that expression, 'wings on a tiger'? This is like Feathers & the Fire Sisters."

What a clunky attempt to play on "Tsubasa Hanekawa."

Sometimes I wondered if Karen really was my sister.

"Fine, fine," I said. "I promise I won't get angry."

"And you won't tell mom and dad, either?" asked Tsukihi, pushing it knowing that Hanekawa was in their corner...

They had another thing coming if they thought I'd honor any promise I made with them. I'd break it like it was made of brittle glass.

"It's our secret," I lied. "Now hurry up and explain. What happened? What's going on?"

"*Indeed.* What *is* going on?"

I was *this* close to wringing Karen's neck. She clearly wasn't going to tell me.

I needed to ask either Tsukihi or Hanekawa, in that case... But Hanekawa was an accomplice, at most. If I wanted details, I was going to have to get them from Tsukihi.

Yeah...

I knew I'd lose my cool again dealing with one of my sisters. For now, it was better if I started with—

"Hanekawa," I said. I needed to talk to all three of them, but first, her. I pointed my thumb at the wall—in the direction of my room. "Would you come to my room for a minute?"

"Oooh, he wants to take Tsubasa to his room."

Karen was just delighted... One day, I'd kill her.

"Of course." Hanekawa stepped away from the wall. "Karen, Tsukihi, it's going to be fine. You did the right thing. Once Araragi hears what I have to say, I'm sure he'll understand. Don't worry, I'll explain everything."

"Miss Hanekawa..."

"Tsubasa..."

My sisters stared up into Hanekawa's face with twinkles in their eyes.

They seemed to trust her very much.

Maybe that was just the natural response to Hanekawa.

"But, Tsubasa, you'll be alone with Koyomi…"

Karen, shut up.

Forget about what's happening now, I worry about your future.

"Don't worry about that, either. I know I can trust your big brother," reassured Hanekawa, patting Karen, who was sitting on her bed, on the head before exiting the room first.

Seriously…there was no living up to her example.

I let out a deep sigh and called out to Karen, "Hey, biggy."

"What do you want, shorty?" she answered sulkily.

Strange… Karen returned my insult, but it seemed like her heart wasn't in it. She was lacking her usual fire. Whenever I called her that, she tended to come flying at me in a rage regardless of the situation. But she didn't even budge and just sat there with her legs crossed.

"What? Go stare at someone else," she said.

"……"

I sighed once more and told her, "I'm sure you did do the right thing. You're always right. I won't deny that. But that's all you are. You aren't always strong."

"……"

"……"

"Unless you're strong, you lose," I went on. "You do martial arts, you should understand that." I looked at Tsukihi as well. "The first requirement of justice isn't being right. It's being strong. That's why justice always prevails. It's about time you saw that. Until you do, you'll never change—you'll always be make-believe defenders of justice—"

Fakes.

I left without waiting for my sisters to reply—stepping out into the hallway and closing the door behind me.

Hanekawa was standing there, waiting. Like she had nothing to do. But she also seemed amused.

156

"I know I shouldn't say this," she said with a faint smile, "but watching you with your sisters is entertaining."

"Give me a break…"

"I think they're good kids."

"I think they're brats."

I led Hanekawa to my room. Unlike Kanbaru, I kept it in pretty good order, so I was ready for unexpected guests.

"You can sit on the bed," I offered.

"I'm not sure it's the right place to ask girls to sit."

"Huh? Why not?"

That's where Sengoku asked me to sit—in fact, I'd been told that I wasn't allowed to anywhere else. Recalling that moment, I sat in my chair.

"By the way, Hanekawa, why are you dressed in your school uniform when it's the middle of the night?" Yes, that's what she was wearing. I'd been wanting to bring it up but hadn't gotten the chance. "I know you wear your uniform even over summer vacation, but that aside…do you even own normal clothes? I don't think I've ever seen you in street clothes."

"You've seen me in my pajamas before."

"Pajamas aren't street clothes."

If we're really being picky, I'd seen her in her underwear too, but that was that, and still not street clothes. What I wanted to see was Hanekawa in a casual outfit she'd chosen for herself! Was she ever going to oblige me?!

"Today is just a coincidence, actually… This is how I happened to be dressed when I met up with your sisters earlier in the evening. Maybe I should start there?"

"Please."

"It's kind of refreshing…"

"Hm?"

"Well, the way you worry about your sisters, compared to the way you worry about me, or Senjogahara, or Mayoi, or Kanbaru, or

157

Sengoku, seems different somehow. I don't know how to put it. It's more desperate."

"Desperate…"

"You're like a different person when it comes to Karen-chan and Tsukihi-chan," Hanekawa referred to my sisters using the diminutive suffix, giggling mischievously. "You were pretty strict with them just now. They're right, but they're not strong? Are you sure that wasn't directed at yourself?"

"I hate people who're like me?"

"Not that I imagine you want to be told that. But I'm not sure that's how I'd put it. Plain 'self-hatred,' maybe?"

I sighed in response. Both because that was apparently how people saw me, and because it was true. It was a complicated sigh.

Justice Man, I'd been called by Senjogahara.

"Hanekawa. You've only known my sisters for about a month now so I don't blame you, but me, I've lived with Karen-chan for fifteen years and Tsukihi-chan for fourteen. After all that time, I can tell you—"

"Pfft… Ha ha."

I was only done prefacing what I was about to say, but something struck Hanekawa as being so funny that she burst out into laughter, so I broke off before I could get to my point.

"H-Hanekawa?"

"No, I'm sorry. But you just called them Karen-chan and Tsukihi-chan."

"…!"

What a hideous misstep! What did I just do?!

Using "chan" with them was an old habit from when we were kids. That's why I tried not to call them by name! "Bigger" and "littler" and all that was my way of playing it off!

I'd slipped up in front of Hanekawa, of all people!

"Gah… Ow, ow, ow."

"Come on, Araragi, it's no big deal. I do that with them, too, sometimes."

"N-No," I sputtered, "I was just imitating you. I was treating them like kids, rhetorically, but usually I just call them Karen and Tsukihi..."

Hanekawa gazed at me pityingly. This was so embarrassing...

"P-Putting that aside, let's get down to the business at hand, Hanekawa. It sounds like this might be time-sensitive."

"No problem," she sweetly agreed.

Stop! Your kindness hurts!

"Anyway," I continued, "I already know some of the background. They were looking for the source of these charms circulating among middle schoolers, right?"

"Oh. How do you know that?"

"Through Sengoku, actually. Unfortunately, my little sisters—"

"Karen-chan and Tsukihi-chan."

"...My little sis—"

"You mean Karen-chan and Tsukihi-chan."

Meanie Hanekawa. Maybe I was wrong, and her personality did change along with her hairstyle.

"Karen-chan and Tsukihi-chan," I relented, "are like celebrities among other middle-school kids. Sengoku hears stories about their shenanigans."

"Hmph—I see." Hanekawa seemed to believe it. "Speaking of which, Sengoku fell victim to one of those charms, didn't she?"

"She was the only one, to be precise."

"Nope, she wasn't. Just the one to suffer the worst consequences... Those charms are actually having all sorts of negative effects."

"All sorts?"

"Mostly in terms of interpersonal relationships."

....

Right. In Sengoku's case too—she wasn't the lone victim. Some relationships surrounding her had also suffered.

"When I looked into it," Hanekawa said, "the so-called charms that are popular are mostly malicious—the tendency is clear. Karen and Tsukihi's idea that someone spread them intentionally seems to have been a shot in the dark, but it didn't fall far from the mark."

She added that if it hadn't been summer break, she wouldn't have been able to investigate. True, an extended vacation was the only time for such an inquiry.

"By the way, when did you start working with them?" I asked.

"I wouldn't go so far as to say I was working with them. I just lent them a hand every now and then. But in terms of how long, I guess since the beginning of summer break."

"Huh, so..." I still hadn't asked what I really wanted to know. "You helped them. Then you must have located the culprit."

In other words...when Karen's cell phone had rung earlier, it had been Tsubasa Hanekawa, herself. No wonder my little sister had prioritized the call over me.

"It pains me when you make it sound like this is my fault," Hanekawa said.

She actually looked pained.

I didn't want to inflict any pain on her, but I had to say it. "You know, Oshino was leery about this side of you. You're too competent and can't ever not arrive at the answer..."

It had saved me. But the opposite was also true. For instance—she hadn't been able to save herself. Her own competence had stood in the way.

"True." Hanekawa wasn't denying it. She nodded, a vague smile on her lips. "But I couldn't go about it half-heartedly, either."

"Right. Just like Karen-chan, Tsukihi-chan, and I..."

Well. That ship had already sailed.

"Just like Karen-chan, Tsukihi-chan, and I have to accept our own weakness—you have to accept your own strength."

Just as fakes have to admit that they're fakes, the genuine articles have to acknowledge that they're the genuine articles. Seriously—it's not like we can cast our selves away.

"So," I asked, "Karen located the 'culprit,' went to negotiate—and *had something done to her?*"

"Correct. I was acting on my own at the time and didn't show up until later, so I never saw the 'culprit' in person... If I'd joined up with your sisters first, I might've been able to help."

"Did Karen say anything about what this 'culprit' is like?"

"Let's see..." Hanekawa shifted her weight, and the bed creaked a little. "His name is Deishu Kaiki—an ominous man, apparently."

012

Although it was only for half a day, I'd been held hostage in those ruins and was covered in dirt and grime. Right after getting the gist of the story from Hanekawa, and leaving my sisters in her care, I decided to take a bath. That might sound too relaxed, but I could tell from what I'd heard that panicking wouldn't do any good.

To be honest, I was worried that if I didn't take a short time-out, I'd wind up yelling at Karen and Tsukihi again.

Deishu Kaiki.

Ugh, of all people! Why get mixed up with a guy like him?

When I ran into him outside Kanbaru's house, he did mention that "Araragi" was a name he'd heard very recently. He was referring to Karen. Well, it wasn't a very common name, after all.

Dammit—what a coincidence.

Well, maybe it was a silver lining... I could get more info on Kaiki by talking to Senjogahara.

But he'd already gotten us into a fight. She might not be too keen on answering my questions.

By the way, after Hanekawa had finished filling me in, I'd taken the opportunity to ask her—it was thanks to her that I escaped my gruesome confinement, but what on earth did she say to Senjogahara over the phone?

"Oh, that? After Tsukihi texted you, she found it strange that you didn't reply right away, so we decided I should call. I was reluctant, considering the time, but they insisted. They might not say so, but they clearly trust their big brother."

"Yeah, I think I figured out that process. But how did you convince Senjogahara?"

None but Senjogahara.

"It wasn't hard," Hanekawa said. "As soon as I heard her voice, I more or less surmised what was going on, so I cut to the chase."

"What do you mean, cut to the chase?"

"I told her, 'If you won't listen, I'll tell Araragi that I'm in love with him.'"

"……"

Brutal. That was the biggest ace up Hanekawa's sleeve in a way.

I could hardly play the same card in negotiating with Senjogahara for info on Kaiki, so I'd just have to ask nicely—though it might not get me anywhere.

Bur first, a bath.

I washed myself carefully and submersed my body in the tub.

Clink, clink…

The handcuffs, which I was unable to remove, remained on my wrists like gaudy bracelets and lightly banged against the side of the tub.

As if timed to coincide with the sound of the cuffs—*gloompf.*

From my shadow, stretching under the bathroom's yellowish light—*gloomph*, emerged Shinobu Oshino.

It reminded me of a certain famous RPG.

Vampire A draws near!

Vampire A was looking at me.

"Um…"

Vampire A—Shinobu Oshino—spent most of her time concealed in my shadow. It was impossible to predict when she would appear, and as a result, by this point, regardless of when she happened to show, I was no longer very surprised. Still, the bath was a new one.

I suppose it was the setting, but she wasn't wearing any clothes.

A stark-naked, beautiful blond girl.

As situations go, it was supremely terrible, even criminal…but Shinobu's form was currently an eight year old's, so unlike with Kanbaru, I was unaffected by her nubile, fair skin and just felt glad that she was looking well.

Shinobu, however, flashed me a broad grin.

"Now that ye have marked me in the nude, must I become thy bride—my master?"

She spoke in a childlike voice, but pompously.

To say I was surprised would be an understatement. I nearly sank into the bathwater.

She spoke… Shinobu spoke!

"Sh-Shinobu."

"Khaha—what troubles thee? Ye look like a deer caught in the headlights. Or should I say, a vampire shot with a silver bullet? Is it so wondrous to hear me speak? Did ye presume that I had forgotten how?"

"……nkk."

Well, no. I knew she could speak. I never thought she'd forgotten. While she looked like an eight-year-old girl, and though she'd lost most of her powers, that didn't change the fact that Shinobu was actually a five-hundred-year-old vampire.

The surprising part…was talking to me. *Being so kind as to talk* to me.

Out of the blue. For no particular reason.

"Shinobu—you…"

Shinobu Oshino.

The vampire—the former vampire.

Now a pale shadow of one, the dregs of a vampire.

Unparalleled in beauty, cold as iron, and hot as blood—a monster among monsters, the king of aberrations.

Aberration slayer, they even used to call her.

She'd slain me. And I'd slain her.

That was why…ever since the end of spring break, dwelling in the ruins of the old cram school with Oshino—and sealed within my shadow now—she hadn't spoken a word to me.

Not one syllable. Not to say she was angry, or unhappy, or suffering. Nothing.

And yet here, all of a sudden?

"Hmph. I grew bored." Shinobu turned the shower spigot and poured hot water over her head. As a vampire, there was no real need for her to bathe—but she closed her eyes as if it felt nice. "I am loquacious by nature, as ye know. Just how much longer was I meant to bite my tongue? Ken as much on thy own, my master."

"……"

Ack… I was completely lost for words.

No, it wasn't that I was happy. Happiness didn't seem appropriate. But—how else could I put it?

How could I not feel happy?

Unable to think of anything appropriate to say, I went for: "Thanks."

"Eh? For what?"

Shinobu closed the spigot and glared at me, the water dripping off her body. Despite her childlike appearance, she was still a vampire, and her gaze remained as sharp as ever. It seemed even more bitter and piercing now than when she'd simply stared at me in silence.

"Oh—uh, I mean, this thing…" I hurriedly held up the cuffs and the broken chain. "You helped me snap it, didn't you?"

Right after Tsukihi texted me.

Obviously, I hadn't done it with my own strength—no matter how urgent the situation, I couldn't have summoned enough adrenaline to break through steel. It had to have been Shinobu's doing, from within my shadow.

"Did I? Khaha. I forget. In any case, thy taste in jewelry is atrocious. Come."

Shinobu reached her tiny hand toward my wrists. This time she destroyed not merely the chain but the cuffs themselves, tearing them like a couple of plump doughnuts.

Her love for Mister Donuts was no secret.

Before I even had time to register shock, Shinobu tossed both of the cuffs into her mouth and chomped and smacked.

She may have lost most of her power—but she was still every inch the vampire, free from the slightest ounce of logic or reserve.

The same Shinobu that I remembered.

It was oddly comforting.

"Save thy thanks. I do as I please—before, now, and always. 'Twas pure serendipity that my deed accorded with thy wishes in this, my master."

"Um, Shinobu—"

"My hair!" she cut me off before I could finish. She pointed toward her golden locks. "My hair."

"Wh-What about your hair?"

"Ye may wash my hair. I wish to try this 'shampoo' as a lark. I have been watching from thy shadow for some time, and it always strikes me as diverting."

"I'm allowed to…touch you?"

"How else will ye wash my hair?"

"Okay…I'll include a conditioning treatment."

I got out of the tub. I was naked too, of course, but in Shinobu's case I didn't feel very embarrassed—I had little shame left to hide from her eyes.

I cupped shampoo in my hand and passed my fingers through her hair.

It felt as I remembered—like a clear stream.

"I haven't seen you without your helmet and goggles in a while," I said.

"Ha! I am done with that."

"You are?"

"'Twas lame. Unfashionable."

"......"

I thought it had suited her. I suppose it was Oshino's taste, and maybe she was never happy with it.

I worked her small head up into a lather (as a vampire, she equaled her image of herself, or in other words, didn't get dirty, so I easily worked up a vigorous, frothing lather) and said, once again, "Um—"

"Shush," Shinobu interrupted me again.

"......"

"Save thy breath. I shall not pardon thee—nor do I suppose ye'll pardon me." She spoke facing forward, staring at the mirror affixed to the wall, at her absent reflection. "So be it. We shall not forgive each other—so it shall be. We must not wash away the past. Still we may accost each other."

"......"

"I have pondered the matter carefully these three or four months, and that is the conclusion I have reached—how do ye like it, my master?"

Shinobu closed her eyes, annoyed by the shampoo suds that hung down her face.

"I didn't know you were bothering to think about it," I said.

"Ye seem to have given it consideration as well—I would know, conversant with thy shadow as I am."

"Haha."

I reached over Shinobu's head to turn the shower spigot and began rinsing her hair. Next I began applying the hair treatment. She had an impressive amount of hair, so I had to use ample conditioner.

"It's not as if I can hold a grudge forever," she remarked. "I am not so petty... Besides, I have something important to communicate that cannot be left unspoken."

"Yeah?"

"While I do fancy Pon de Ring doughnuts—I much more favor the golden chocolate flavor. Know as much if ye would purchase two."

"Of course..."

Well. She was a blonde vampire, after all—I guess "golden" suited her.

"Handle the rest yourself," I said, getting back into the tub.

"The Cinderswarm Bee," Shinobu uttered right then. "A giant hornet aberration."

"Huh?" Hornet—Class Insecta, Order Hymenoptera, Family Vespidae?

"The particular variety is not found in my homeland so I know not the details, but they say that among bees—nay, among insects—nay, among all organisms, no stronger fighting regiments exist. In collective warfare, at least, none other compare. They are social, yet viciously fierce and aggressive."

Though perhaps less so than vampires, Shinobu added.

"Wait…don't tell me—"

That way of speaking, which reminded me so much of *that dude*.

"It is the aberration," she confirmed, "currently afflicting thy dear, giant younger sister."

"'Giant' seems like a bit much…"

After all, Shinobu was even larger in her true form. If I recalled correctly, adult Shinobu was nearly six feet tall.

"I give thee fair notice that none of this is my own knowledge—I may be the aberration slayer, but even I am not familiar with all such creatures. Besides, I specialize in devouring. I don't concern myself with the names of my vittles—only with their taste."

"So then…"

"Aye. This information is courtesy of that brat."

As a vampire, Shinobu generally declined to distinguish one human from the next. The person she bothered to call a "brat"—was Mèmè Oshino.

"Do ye have any notion of how it felt for one such as myself?" complained Shinobu, grimacing. "Forced to give ear while that piddling excuse of a man expostulated incessantly, day in and day out, regardless of any personage but himself, and always with the most trivial of stories about aberrations?"

"……"

That did suck. I always wondered how Oshino and Shinobu passed the time when it was just the two of them—I guess now I had my answer.

"The Cinderswarm Bee was just one of the countless arcana he blabbered on about. If I am not mistaken…it is an aberration hailing from the Muromachi period. The long and short of it is that it is a contagion of unknown cause."

An infectious disease. That was the truth of the matter. But the illness was interpreted as the work of an aberration. While that belief was in error, the important point was that it was *thought of in such a way*.

From there, aberrations bubbled out.

Just as the vampire phenomenon ultimately owed to a hematological affliction…

"The contagion causes a fever severe enough to immobilize its victim and eventually runs to death. In fact, several hundred perished—it was some time before a renowned shaman of the time was able to quell the outbreak—or so, I've heard, records an old chronicle. *It was as if, stung by an untouchable bee, one's body were enveloped in fire.* Something to that effect."

"……"

Karen—was just being brave, like always, and though I sadly hadn't even noticed, she was physically exhausted.

Wracked by a fever so high it was like burning. Enveloped in fire.

She was feeling hot.

The long and short of it was that she was sick.

That was why she'd been sitting on the bed. That was why her cheeks were so flushed—not because she was cross. And the only reason she didn't fly at me in a rage was that she could barely move.

Until I came home—she was asleep. Or more like passed out.

If not, Tsukihi probably wouldn't have been able to send for my help in the first place—now I understood what Hanekawa meant when

170

she said, "I doubt you could slap him back, though."

She knew how sick Karen was, that she was exhausted.

"Tsk. No wonder Hanekawa protected her. But you know, Karen had it coming."

"Had it coming?"

"The chickens came home to roost. Or maybe that should be 'roast'?"

"Roast chicken?" Shinobu narrowed her eyes and shrugged her shoulders. "Thou art harsh on thy kinswomen... Not that it astonishes me at this point, as I have been watching thee from the galleys for some time now. Still, not to copy a phrase from the former class president, but I never knew."

"Former?"

Hanekawa was still class president. Did Shinobu think the title referred to fashion choices?

"I don't think I'm particularly harsh," I retorted. "Anyway, it's hard to tell from just Hanekawa's account, but it sounds like this Kaiki guy *infected my sister with an aberration's poison.*" Like with an illness... Karen had caught an aberration. "Not that I know if the toxin is from this Cinderswarm Bee aberration or if such a thing is even possible."

"Perhaps. Such things are known to be," Shinobu said. "But if thy tsundere maiden is to be believed, this Kaiki is a fake and a swindler, is he not?"

"True," I agreed. Still...tsundere maiden?

Being in my shadow, Shinobu experienced everything that I did... She'd think that about Senjogahara. But thinking of Senjogahara as a run-of-the-mill tsundere amounted to a massive misunderstanding of human culture.

"Of course," Shinobu cautioned, "being a fake does not preclude him from using true arts—the counterfeit often rings truer than the real."

"Wise words." I nodded. That hit home with me. "You can be suspect as an expert and still be an authentic swindler."

The culprit was suspect? So much for bad jokes.

"Suspect…" Shinobu looked thoughtful. "If that is so, he might turn out to be more perilous than an authentic expert. Unleashing an aberration without the skills to control it seems devious, even by my standards. Speaking of suspect—I doubt he's even human."

"……"

"If our actions define us, he seems an aberration, himself."

An aberration, himself. What exactly did that mean? What was our definition?

"Well, I'll try asking Senjogahara," I said. "I mean, what else can I do? The problem right now is the bigger—I guess there's no point in playing games with you, the problem right now is Karen-chan. We have to find some way to alleviate her symptoms."

Apparently, Hanekawa had taken Karen to the hospital first.

They had applied the most reasonable measures in the world for a person with a high fever—but it hadn't helped. Even if Hanekawa had lost her memory of it for a while, she had some experience with aberrations—and was probably able to deduce that something wasn't quite right.

"In that sense," I observed, "Karen was right to choose to call Hanekawa after whatever happened. It was better than calling me, at least, like Tsukihi did."

"Hmph. But if not for the former class president, thy sister would have likely never arrived at this Kaiki, no?"

"Well, no…"

When you put it that way, Hanekawa really went around starting fires so she could put them out… She always had the perfect response to any problem, but without her the problem might have never occurred in the first place.

During the incident with Shinobu, Hanekawa saved me. I was grateful to her, from the bottom of my heart, but if you thought about it, she was also partly responsible for my encounter with Shinobu.

The real deal.

172

Strong. Just, and also strong.

"The fever medicine isn't doing anything," I said, "and strangely, as painful as the fever is, her mind still seems to be lucid. My parents still think she just has one of those summertime colds."

Maybe thanks to her everyday behavior? It was anything but exemplary, actually. But she could be glib.

"Shinobu. Can you—eat Karen's illness?"

As a vampire, she ate aberrations.

That's what she kindly did—with Hanekawa's cat.

Well, "kindly" wasn't right—in the end, Shinobu Oshino had simply had dinner.

"Unfortunately," she said, shaking her head, "an illness is merely the effect—I could consume the hornet itself, and happily so, but I cannot devour the effects of its sting. Just as I can partake in an apple, but not the human sensation that it tastes delicious. The aberration is now past. The symptoms before us would not be disposed by consuming the hornet now."

"I see. That make sense. Well, did Oshino say anything about how to deal with this Cinderswarm Bee?"

"Who knows? I have a feeling he may have, but his vociferations were always so rambling."

Shinobu rinsed the last of the conditioner from her hair and slipped into the tub. It was a standard household bath, not large enough for two, but being child-sized she managed to just barely squeeze in.

It certainly wasn't because I'm short!

"Come to think of it, I hadn't taken a bath in some time…khaha."

"Is that true?"

"Mm-hm. It has been four hundred years."

"What a timeframe."

That was incredible. Well, during spring break, when I was a vampire, I didn't need to wash, either—it was no use applying human standards.

Be that as it may…

This was my first time taking a bath with Shinobu, obviously. I'd never even dreamed that such a day would come.

Was "moving" the word?

Sitting face to face with her like this was also a first—over spring break, I'd lacked the mental composure.

I stared at Shinobu, moved.

"What are ye gawking at? I had no idea ye were a genuine pervert who grew liver-veined at the sight of a naked little girl."

"No, that's not why."

"Ha. The way ye ogle me has actually given me some funny notions."

"Um?"

"No, no, 'tis nothing. But what if, for instance, I started to shriek so loud that everyone in the house could hear? Such notions."

"Ack!"

Shinobu grinned from ear to ear. What a sick imagination!

But she did know that this sort of thing was taboo? Shit, did Oshino teach her? What an unnecessarily elite education!

"Yet if ye were to prepare a large tribute of doughnuts in requisition for my silence, I may be willing to boot a bargain."

"Go ahead, scream..." I acted unfazed and even sat up straight. Dirty threats weren't going to work on me. "You and I are joined at the hip—as long as you're stuck in my shadow, you'll pay for it. At the very least, you'll never have Mister Donuts again."

"Khaha! Well played. Ye have grown, my master—"

"Hey, Koyomi, how long are you gonna stay in there? I thought you wanted my story next..."

The glass door suddenly burst open and Tsukihi poked her head in.

At some point she had come downstairs. Entered the changing room. And opened the glass door.

"Umm..."

Now, let's set out the situation!

Place: Bath!

Cast: Koyomi, Shinobu, Tsukihi!

Synopsis: Koyomi (a high school senior) and Shinobu (blonde, looks like an eight year old) are discovered taking a bath together by Tsukihi (little sister)!

So straightforward!

No need to set anything out!

"……"

Tsukihi—gently closed the glass door and strode away, without saying a word.

"……?"

What was she planning to do? Hell, whatever she was planning, I was lucky she'd walked away. Quick, before she gets back—

But.

Not even ten seconds had passed before Tsukihi returned. She threw the door open with a bang.

"Huh?" Tsukihi blinked in confusion. "Koyomi, what happened to that girl?"

There was no one in the bath other than me. Shinobu had returned to my shadow just in time.

"What girl? What the hell," I chided. "We're in the middle of a serious situation here, don't talk nonsense, you idiot."

What kept my voice from cracking as I spoke, of course, was the sight of a kitchen knife in Tsukihi's right hand.

A carving knife. Apparently she'd gone to the kitchen.

No wonder I was as cool as ice. Despite the hot bath, my guts had frozen over.

"Huh…I guess I was seeing things," muttered Tsukihi.

"You definitely were. There's no flat-chested eight-year-old girl with dazzling blond hair, translucent white skin, and a pompous, archaic way of speaking here, move along."

"Hmm. I see…" Tsukihi crossed her arms, baffled.

Watch the tip of that knife!

By the way, she was holding a lid to a soup pot in her other hand.

Good to see she wasn't neglecting defense.

"Fine, I guess... But Koyomi, this is some long bath you're taking. When do you plan on finishing?"

"Ah..." Washing Shinobu's hair meant I'd taken twice as long as usual. "I'll be out soon. Go wait in the living room."

"Okay!"

"And would you mind knocking next time?"

"What? I don't remember you ever asking me to. You think you're so mature now? Just because you've gotten all muscled lately, don't go getting full of yourself!"

With that weird rant, Tsukihi exited the changing room. She'd left the glass door open, so I got out of the tub to shut it.

"Khaha!"

When I turned around, Shinobu was back in the tub. Since she was alone this time, she was resting her legs on the opposite rim, elegantly enough.

"That was alarming. Quite the hellcat thy sister is."

"Give me a break..."

Hey, I was astonished too. Who immediately ran to the kitchen to grab a knife?

Thanks to Shinobu quickly slipping back into my shadow, we were able to dodge the bullet. If she'd tarried another second, we'd have had a bloodbath.

At least the cleanup would have been easy.

I pushed Shinobu's legs out of the way and stepped back into the crammed tub, sitting across from her again.

"By the by, I don't believe the brat ever broached this subject—in fact, I imagine he intentionally avoided it..." An impish, perhaps evil, expression flitted across Shinobu's face—that gruesome smile of hers. "When will ye expire, I wonder?"

"What do you mean?" I didn't understand what she was asking, or why. When would I die? How would anyone know?

"Well, that is to say... Ye may now be nearly human, but there is still *a bit* of vampire left, is there not? What will that mean in terms of thy lifespan?"

"Huh…"

I see. I hadn't thought about that. Or rather—I'd been trying not to?

I said "the rest of my life" fairly often—but how many years did "the rest" actually refer to?

"Thy intensity may have reverted to a human's, but thy lifespan may yet be a vampire's—seeing that ye have retained a decent regenerative factor. Since thou will not be prone to illness or injury, an untimely demise seems unlikely, at least. Like a hermit wizard, or like me—ye might persist for four centuries, if not five."

"……"

"Thy paramour, friends, juniors, and sisters—they will all pass, quenched in death, while we two remain. Whatever bonds ye build, time will see them rust and crumble."

This was no hypothetical musing. Nor, certainly, lighthearted banter.

She spoke as if she were prophesizing the future.

Almost as if—she were recounting her own experience.

She stretched her legs out in the tub—as though to kick my belly.

Not sated with kicking—

Grind, grind.

She ground her heel—hard.

She might call me "master," but she was just as domineering as ever.

"How does it feel? Even ye must be thought-sick at the prospect." An inviting and befuddling lilt—as though to seduce me, domineeringly indeed, she said, "Yet I have a proposition for thee. Why not slay me and return at last to a human without disclaimer?"

"Get serious," I brushed off her falsely casual offer. I made my refusal clear. "Your conclusion still stands. I won't forgive you, and you won't forgive me, period. That conversation is already over—there's nothing more to discuss. We live, until we die."

Take it as—my sincerity.

Take it as my resolution.

Take it as my atonement.

If you never forgive me, I'm okay with it.

Because—I don't want to be forgiven.

"Hm, as ye wish."

Shinobu laughed. Just as she used to back then—it was a thoroughly gruesome laugh.

"Pray, then, that I do not cut thy throat while ye sleep, my master. I merely live out my years, and have no care. I shall kill time in thy shadow for now—but I do not crave amity. Grow careless, and I shall kill thee."

And so, having gone down a slippery slope—

Shinobu and I reconciled.

013

When comparing the two Araragi sisters—the Fire Sisters—Karen, the enforcer, can't help but stand out, but lest that lead you astray, allow me to dispel any mistaken notion that Tsukihi is less of a handful as a sister.

As the earlier incident with the knife indicates, Tsukihi is just as hazardous. Don't find her endearing just because she asked for my help. The truth is that she employs Karen's cockier personality as a clever shield for her own actions. If Tsukihi seems less objectionable, then you have fallen into her trap.

In that sense, a show-off like Karen is easier to manage, while Tsukihi, no less of a fool, yet a smart fool, is almost impossible to handle.

Take the sunflower bed episode. In a way, she is even more aggressive than Karen.

I have another example from the past.

The Tsukihi Files: Part II.

Back when Karen and Tsukihi were still in grade school—as was I.

Come to think of it, Tsukihi and Sengoku may have been in the same class at the time. If so, Sengoku probably remembers the story as well.

Karen got herself into some kind of trouble—this was when they still worked separately, before people took to calling them the Fire

Sisters.

Whatever trouble this was, Karen couldn't get out of it, and to save her, Tsukihi jumped off the roof of the school building without a second thought.

What could result in such a deed?

I wondered, too, at the time, but only Karen and Tsukihi know the reason—actually, considering whom we're discussing, perhaps they don't remember.

Whether it was luck or careful planning, Tsukihi happened to land on the canopy of a truck parked below (like in some kung-fu movie), sparing her life (naturally, she broke several bones, and her body is covered with multiple so-called battle wounds, just ordinary scars). In any case, thanks to that leap, her previous reputation as a quiet girl who likes to play indoors vanished like so much mist.

What I found most perplexing is that not a single one of her friends stopped coming over to play.

At any rate.

Tsukihi is extreme, and hiding her extremism is almost second nature to her. The corollary is that she has the ability to throw herself, intentionally and whenever she chooses, into a rage that is no mere bout of hysteria.

Intentionally running amok. What could be more dangerous?

Her hysteric fits aren't the problem. It's the genuine fury—Tsukihi's true persona—that lies behind them.

But back to the matter at hand.

Once Shinobu returned to my shadow, I got out of the tub, dried myself off, and headed to the living room with just a towel wrapped around my waist. There was no reason to get dressed just to hear what Tsukihi had to say. I couldn't shake the feeling that I was forgetting something, but I had business to attend to.

In the living room, Tsukihi was plopped down on the sofa. The knife…she had apparently returned to the kitchen.

"Where's the bigger sister?" I asked, sitting down across from

Tsukihi.

"Mm." She nodded. "Miss Hanekawa is looking after her."

Hanekawa…

That was what I'd forgotten. What was I doing dressed like this with her under the same roof? I was forfeiting my right to needle Kanbaru.

"Still, even if I want to change, my clothes are in my room… I guess it's fine since she's upstairs."

I'd ask Tsukihi to bring me down a set later. There, problem solved.

This was the twenty-first century where you didn't run half-naked into a female classmate even in a slapstick comedy.

"All right," I said, "time to fill me in on the details."

"Okay. But first, make me one promise."

"You're not in a position to make demands."

"I'm your little sister, that's my position."

"And in my position as your big brother, I refuse."

We glared at each other. We always ended up arguing if we weren't careful.

"Fine, I withdraw my request," Tsukihi folded first after three minutes of silence. This was actually rare—usually I was the one who backed down. She really had to be feeling out of her depths this time around. In that case…

"Well, what were you going to demand?"

"That you not get angry with Karen."

"Fat chance."

"That you can be angry at me, but not Karen."

"I'll scold you both."

"How about…you can be angry at Karen, but not me?"

"I'm angry already! Just tell me and get it off your chest."

"Is that supposed to sound cool? I thought you promised Miss Hanekawa you wouldn't get angry," Tsukihi pouted.

Dummy. That was only for Hanekawa's sake, needless to say.

Despite her sullen attitude, Tsukihi turned her drooping eyes my way. This is just my own prejudice, but people with drooping eyes, not just Tsukihi, always look to me like they're plotting something.

She said, "Just because you're a genius who's good at everything, that doesn't give you the right to make fun of me and Karen, okay?"

"How about I agree to put up with all the annoying shit you say. There's your terms. Now talk. How did all of this get started in the first place? I can't even figure that out."

"Huh, even a modern-day Renaissance man like you?"

"......"

Oh boy. I was already beginning to lose it.

"How much did Miss Hanekawa tell you?" she cut to the chase with perfect timing. If this was her way of bargaining, she was actually pretty good at it.

"I heard most of it, but Hanekawa is an outsider in all of this. I haven't heard any of the inside story yet. And besides—I can't act until I hear what you two have to say."

Plus, Hanekawa being Hanekawa, I suspected that she was hiding something because it made Karen and Tsukihi look bad.

If Hanekawa wanted, she could easily keep me from noticing that she was holding back. She must have purposely dropped hints to prompt me to ask my sisters.

What a stance she was taking. Neutral, but one misstep and she'd be a friend to neither party.

She was like a double agent.

She did look up to Mèmè Oshino, and I suppose that was his M.O., after all.

"Can't act, huh? Mostly, Karen and I start acting before we've even begun to think. I guess Karen this time around is a good example."

"I bet."

"Koyomi… Is there anything you regret?"

"Regret? Of course. Is any human being free of it?" Though maybe some people never repented. That was human, too.

"You know what? I don't really regret things much."

"I bet. You two don't really seem like the type."

"But that's exactly why—" Tsukihi inserted a pause. "Sometimes I regret not having regretted it at the time."

"......"

"So much for that," she said before falling silent.

She dared to fall silent.

....

"Are you trying to get me to wring your neck?" I asked her.

"No, that's not it..."

"Then hurry up and get to the point."

"Ah, that reminds me. I have something interesting to tell you."

"Interesting?"

"You know how my catchphrase is 'I'm dagnabbit mad'? That actually started out as 'a bit mad' for me, so it doesn't mean that I'm really that angry despite how it sounds."

"I never even knew that was your catchphrase!"

"How could you not? I'm dagnabbit mad!"

"You're clearly more than just a little angry!" Color me dagnabbit surprised—she wasn't making any sense. "Look, no more tricks. Stop trying to change the subject."

"Ah... I was just testing you."

"Then I was testing you for testing me. Now hurry up and get to the point."

"B-Before that, could you tell me about a time you regretted something? I wanna hear about you, too."

"Huh?"

"It'd be a waste to just tell you. This way, it would be like we're sharing secrets. Like late at night, during a school trip."

"You idiot." But even if I thought—okay, said—that Tsukihi was an idiot, maybe it was part of my duty as a big brother to humor her childish whims. Besides, I felt like I might blow my fuse if I didn't play along a little. "Well, let's see, something I regret... It's hard to come up with on the spot."

There was plenty of material. Too much, really.

For instance, Shinobu Oshino.

Everything relating to her. The vampire stuff.

But…even if I were to tell my sisters, now didn't seem like the time. It was a bit too heavy for the situation at hand.

Tsukihi seemed to mistake my reluctance for stalling. "There has to be something," she prodded.

"Uhh, this is so out of the blue…. Be a little more specific about the kind of story you want to hear."

"Just something a little embarrassing. Right, like…why you don't have any friends."

"I do now!"

"Really? How many?"

"Did you just ask? Get ready to be surprised!"

Hanekawa was a friend. Kanbaru…was my junior, but also a friend. Hachikuji was totally my friend.

Sengoku…a friend, too. Well, we got along really well, but maybe she didn't think of me that way… Maybe she just felt she had to talk to me because I was her friend's (Tsukihi's) brother. Yeah, as gratifying as it felt to be called her big brother, I needed to get out of that zone. Still, I wasn't wrong to see her as a friend.

Senjogahara…was my girlfriend. In terms of this discussion, I didn't see any reason not to count her, though.

"Five!"

"You got me, I really am surprised." Tsukihi seemed taken aback, so much so that her drooping eyes arched up. "Poor Koyomi…you're going to die lonely."

"What a thing to say to your brother!" Tsk, jerk sister. "Anyway, if you want to know why I didn't have friends before… Well, back in the day, I used to think they'd lower my intensity as—"

"No, I've heard enough embarrassing stuff for one day… I'm sorry for asking."

"Don't apologize yet! I haven't said anything embarrassing!"

"Please, no, don't put yourself through any more of this! Really, it's over!"

"But it isn't!" Why was she trying so hard to stop me? There were tears in her eyes!

"Not having any friends is one thing, but you take it to a whole new level… You don't even realize you have a problem. It's too sad."

W-Was it? Was I just not self-aware?

"If you ever get in a car accident and die, I'll make sure the funeral is family only," my sister promised. "Otherwise, everyone will find out how lonely you were."

"Excuse me if I don't find that very comforting!"

"As for your wedding… Well, someone with no friends doesn't have to worry about marriage."

"Aaaah!"

Tsukihi's words were so overwhelming that I couldn't find the words for a comeback. All I could do was shout.

"But Koyomi, isn't it actually harder not to make friends?"

"Thank you for your elite advice!" Seriously, that hurt! "You know what, I'm not like you guys, I don't want to be part of some in-crowd. I aim to be a mysterious character about whom everybody says, 'Hey, what do you think he does when he's alone?'"

"But the thing is that nobody, let alone everybody, bothers to say that about you. And 'when he's alone'? You're always alone."

"Well, who are you to talk? How many friends do you have?"

"Huh?" Tsukihi blinked. "I'm not sure you can call them 'friends' while there's still few enough to count."

"……"

Let me have a few of yours, I thought for real.

"Isn't 'friends' supposed to be like an uncountable plural?" remarked Tsukihi.

"You…have a point."

"So isn't it a little weird to be counting them on your fingers?"

"You're the one who asked!"

While we went on like this—

"Araragi, we can hear you up on the second floor—it sounds like you're just making small talk, so maybe keep it down a little?"

The door swung open and Hanekawa entered the living room.

At some point (as I continued to quip), I must have gotten quite loud.

"Oh, sorry. I will."

As I said so—

Crap.

I remembered.

I was sitting on the sofa talking to my sister with nothing but a towel around my waist. Worse, I had gotten so wrapped up in arguing with her that I was leaning forward, and the towel had come askew.

In the next instant, I realized three things.

One: That even Hanekawa screams on occasion.

Two: That her scream is loud enough to fill our home.

And three: That my parents are preternaturally sound sleepers.

014

Let me spend some time on Karen Araragi's story.

A word of caution, however. The following is a recreation, based solely on a combination of what Hanekawa and Tsukihi told me, and may differ slightly from actual events.

In any case, it's not as if the narrative perspective has suddenly shifted, so please relax.

While Hitagi Senjogahara still held me captive, Karen Araragi, dressed in her usual sports jersey, visited a certain karaoke place located near her school, Tsuganoki Second.

At this point she had already pinpointed the "culprit" behind the charms circulating among junior-high students.

Technically, Hanekawa had. Grateful for her help as Karen was, by now all the blood had rushed to her head, and that fact was far from her mind.

Nor was she thinking about Hanekawa's advice "not to do anything until I get there." It had gone in one ear and out the other.

Hanekawa admitted her mistake—it was careless of her not to foresee that Karen might go alone. As for me, I blamed Karen for making Hanekawa commit such a blunder. It was just plain wrong to betray Hanekawa's trust like that.

Could Tsukihi have stopped Karen before anything happened? No, I doubted it.

All Tsukihi ever did was rile Karen up. The brain had no interest in reining in the brawn's excesses.

"Welcome, young lady. My name is Kaiki. As in *kaizuka*, shell heap, and *kareki*, withered tree. What might yours be?"

"I'm Karen Araragi," my sister introduced herself, loud and clear, to a man who was dressed in a black suit as if in mourning as he sat waiting in a private karaoke room. "Take the 'hill' radical and add 'possible' for the first character of Araragi. 'Good good' for 'rara,' and finally 'tree' as in *wakaki*, young sapling. 'Fire' and 'compassion' for Karen."

"An excellent name. You should thank your parents." The man's ponderous speech was devoid of feeling.

Karen began to feel nervous.

She summoned her courage quickly, however, and closed the door. The two of them were now—alone in a cramped room.

Usually, that was a highly risky situation, but Karen didn't think so. She even believed that she had the advantage on such a field.

Was she stupid? A rhetorical question.

"Well, which are you here for?" the man asked. "Do you want me to teach you a charm, or remove one? The former will cost you ten thousand yen. The latter, double that."

"Neither. I came here to give you a wallop," Karen said.

Judging by her words, she was feeling pretty confident. The truth, however, was that she wasn't.

She sensed it. She hadn't trained for nothing, wasn't a martial artist for nothing.

It was impossible to miss—the ominousness that was Deishu Kaiki. There was no telling *what he might do to her*.

Her body sensed it. But at this point, she still didn't think she'd screwed up—and didn't regret coming alone.

Because she's stupid. Or if you ask me, fake.

She couldn't recognize real danger.

"A wallop. A-ha. In other words, this is a trap. You sent a lying email to lure me here. I see, very clever—but I have a sneaking suspicion this maneuver was not of your own contriving. Someone as brash as you could not ferret me out."

"Yeah…"

"So whose scheme—no, I suppose you wouldn't tell me. But few are capable of such a feat. Only someone fairly unconventional could force this encounter. To arrive at me, and not the other way around? No kid in junior high has the caliber to pull it off."

The caliber. Well, he had a point. Hanekawa, who'd arrived at him, was in high school, not middle school. But in terms of caliber, she was hardly just a kid in high school.

If only she'd been there. It'd have played out very differently, no doubt.

Not even Oshino liked to face Hanekawa one on one.

Gulp, Karen swallowed a host of words along with her saliva.

Then—

"You've been causing a lot of trouble. I don't have to explain how, do I?" she accused.

"What trouble? I simply sell you children the goods you seek. You alone are accountable for what you do with them."

"Accountable?" Karen curled her lip. She wasn't so naive as to find that word choice palatable. "Look who's talking. Get real. You've been wreaking havoc, turning friends against each other. What are you up to?"

"Up to, eh? A profound question." Kaiki nodded quietly.

Karen wasn't expecting that response. A petty scoundrel who slinked around spreading rumors of dire curses to bilk middle schoolers out of their money would immediately panic when confronted and fall on his knees blubbering for forgiveness—that had been her assumption.

That was her conception of evil, after all.

That evil could be strong, and resilient…was unthinkable.

"Unfortunately," Kaiki lamented, "I only have a shallow answer to your profound question. It's for money, of course."

"M-Money?"

"Yes. My objective is to obtain notes issued by the Bank of Japan, nothing more—money is everything in this world. You seem to have come here out of some mistaken sense of justice—a pity, really. You could have easily charged your client a hundred thousand yen," Kaiki appraised like it was the most natural thing to do. "The lesson you should take home from this is that it never pays to work for free."

"Wh-Who said anything about a client?" Karen put on a show of bravery to hold on to her courage. "I'm not doing this because anybody asked."

"I see. Then you should have waited until somebody did."

"Even then, I wouldn't take their money."

"Ah, youth. I can't say that I'm envious, however," Kaiki said.

He seemed more ominous with every passing minute. It was as if their confined quarters were accelerating the process. The air grew thicker and thicker with it.

"What's wrong? You're trembling, Araragi."

"I'm not trembling! If I look like I am, then I'm rumbling."

"How delightful to meet a girl with such cataclysmic sensibilities." *Ah yes, to be young*, Kaiki added. He glanced at Karen appraisingly. "Regardless, I suggest that, next time, you think before you act. Not doing so halves your charms. The lesson to take home from this case, Araragi, is to think before you feel. Now, I've answered your question. I have explained myself, I believe. Your turn—what is your objective?"

"I already told you. I'm here to wallop you."

"Is that all?"

"And to feed you my boot."

"Violence?"

"Force. And I'm going to put an end to what you're doing. You've got some nerve plying your filthy trade among middle schoolers. You call yourself an adult?"

"Indeed. And I can't help it if my trade seems filthy. After all…" said

Kaiki, almost proudly, "I am a swindler."

"......"

Appalled as she was, Karen denounced him again.

"Against middle school kids? Aren't you embarrassed?"

"Not particularly. Children are simply easier targets to deceive. But Araragi, neither punches nor kicks will be enough to stop me. It would be more expedient to come back with cash. My target in this endeavor is three million yen. It has taken me over two months to lay the foundation for this project. I seek at least that amount in profits for my troubles. However—if you insist, I will not be unreasonable. Pay me half of that sum, and I will gladly depart."

"You punk..."

"That's a rather cheap word."

Kaiki smiled a little.

What did he find so funny?

Was it a sneer? A grimace?

Karen wondered aloud. "You call yourself human?"

"My apologies, but that is precisely what I am. Just a human—willing to dedicate his life to a precious cause. You fill your heart through good deeds, while I fill my wallet through bad. Are we so different?"

"Wh-What?"

"Exactly, it's not different at all. Perhaps what you're doing makes lives better for some—but I stimulate our capitalist economy by squandering the money I earn, which has the same effect. The lesson for you to take home from this: just as there is no issue that is immune to justice, there is no issue that is immune to money."

"Nrk..."

"My 'victims' would certainly agree with that assessment. They all paid me. Which is to say, they recognized the monetary value of our transaction. And this is no less true of you, Araragi. Or did you not pay money for that jersey you are wearing?"

"L-Leave my jersey out of this!"

Karen was incensed.

She was certainly silly to feel that way on behalf of her jersey.

But that was when she decided that the time for talk was over. When it came to verbal exchanges, without her sister, Karen was at a disadvantage. She could count on one hand the number of times she'd defeated an older opponent through logic.

"Make your decision," she said. "Do you want me to punch you, or—"

"I don't want to be punched. Nor kicked. Therefore…"

Kaiki moved—unexpectedly.

For some reason, despite her martial arts training, Karen failed to react. It wasn't as if she'd let her guard down or wasn't prepared to strike—

"I present you with this bee," the man announced.

He didn't rush her. Rather, it seemed as if he were trying to slip his body past Karen, who was still standing by the door to block his way.

He wasn't interested in a fight, but rather, flight.

He'd been summoned and trapped. Ready to do business but called out instead, and cornered, he was turning tail.

That was all. Put into words, his move couldn't be shabbier. However…

Tup.

As he slipped past Karen, he extended the index finger of his left hand—

He stung with his forefinger.

A gentle poke—to her forehead.

"…? …nkk? …nkk?!"

Karen gasped once, twice, three times in surprise.

The first gasp was when his finger stabbed her forehead.

He could have punched her in the face. If Kaiki had made a fist and swung with all his strength instead of tapping lightly, even Karen, with all of her training, would not have fared well for the blow.

The second gasp was in bewilderment. Why hadn't he punched her?

And the third gasp.

"…………nkk!!"

It was from a sudden wave of nausea that brought her to her knees. Fatigue. Malaise. And most of all…

Her body was on fire.

The heat. It was burning her. Like she'd hurled herself into a furnace and real flames.

"Gah…ah, ahh?"

Her throat felt so scorched that she couldn't piece together any words.

Gazing down at her, Kaiki said, "I see the effect was immediate. You must be very susceptible to belief. The lesson for you to take home from this is to assume that everyone you meet is a swindler. Do not trust so easily. Did you think that I would beg for forgiveness? If so, you are a fool. If you wish me to mend my ways, then bring money. My starting price is now ten million yen."

Karen could hear him. She was fully conscious. But her body—wouldn't listen. Not her arms, legs, or head, nor her eyes, ears, or mouth were functional.

"Wh-What did you…do?"

What had been done to her?

What…done?

What…done… What…done?

What—stung?

"What did you—do to me?"

"Something very bad. And not for free. I expect to be paid."

Kaiki reached into Karen's jersey pocket and took out her wallet as she crouched helplessly. She could do nothing but watch as he began rifling through it without permission.

No, not even watch. Her vision was hazy.

"Four thousand yen… That will have to do. Consider my lecture a gratuity. I'll leave the spare change so that you have enough to get home… Oh? You have a bus pass. Then you don't need your change."

Karen heard jingling. Kaiki was scooping out the coins.

"That's an additional 627 yen… Hmph, not much. This point card doesn't have your name on it. I'll take it, too."

Kaiki set Karen's wallet, now practically empty, on the table.

"The poison will settle soon, and you should be able to move again. I suggest you use your cell phone to call for help—in the meantime, I'll beat a hasty retreat. Of course, I plan to continue my entrepreneurial efforts. In the future, however, perhaps I should avoid meeting customers directly. Most edifying. Farewell."

With that, he opened the door and stepped outside—without a second glance at Karen, who now lay crumpled on the floor.

Karen—Karen Araragi.

Still her stubborn self, it was some time before she called for help.

015

For now, I decided to send Hanekawa on her way before my parents got up. We'd relied on her too much already to call it "a helping hand"—besides, it was getting to be late. I'd see her home part of the way on my bike.

Obviously, riding two to a bike was out of the question. Hanekawa was a stickler for traffic regulations. She'd never allow it unless it was an absolute emergency.

Not that I had any ulterior motives! Please, why would I want her to hug me from behind?

"I'm sorry for all the hassle," I thanked her. "I'll take care of it from here."

"Yes, of course."

Hanekawa and I made conversation as we walked.

Come to think of it, we hadn't talked like this in a while—though I saw her all the time since she was my tutor.

We couldn't chat while I was studying.

"It might be better if I stopped lending a hand," Hanekawa said. "It doesn't seem like any good would come of it. I've already done all I can."

"Yeah…probably." It killed me not to be able to contradict her.

Hanekawa was just, and strong.

But maybe too just, and too strong.

Without due caution, and even with it, she risked uprooting the entire garden.

"Araragi, are you angry?"

Our gait was almost the same, so we could walk side by side even if I didn't try to match my pace to hers.

"Angry at what?" I asked, pushing my bike beside her.

"Come on. I mean what happened with Karen and Tsukihi. After all, I'm the one who arrived at the culprit. Then that happened to Karen. Are you angry?"

"If I was, it would be at those two. There's no reason for me to be angry at you… You know what, I'm not angry, but I have a complaint. Next time you decide to help the Fire Sisters, please come talk to me first."

"But if I did, you'd get just as angry. Besides, if I want to be friends with Karen and Tsukihi, isn't that my business?"

"Certainly." Even if it was bad business for me. Ah, well. There was no point in getting into that now. Spilled milk.

"Right," said Hanekawa. She bashfully drew her student diary from the breast pocket of her uniform. "Still, as a way of apologizing for keeping everything with Karen and Tsukihi a secret, allow me to present you, sir, with this ticket."

With that ostentatious preamble, she neatly tore a blank page from the diary without using a ruler or folding the edge (how did she do that?) and handed it to me.

I turned over the page—ticket?—but there was nothing written on the back, either. What the hell? Was it a metaphor or something? The ticket to the future is always blank?

Did that make her Rem Saverem? What a moving finale that was! Love and peace!

That probably wasn't it, so I asked, "What's this?"

Hanekawa was even more bashful now. "That ticket authorizes the bearer to touch my breasts at any time and place of his choosing. Take it."

"Ack! Are you serious?!" My hand shook as I gripped the piece of paper—correction, the deluxe ticket.

"Yes, I'm serious. If you ever use it, though, I'll despise you forever."

"Then what's the point?!"

I ripped it up and tossed it away.

Hanekawa laughed lightheartedly.

Uhh… She was making fun of me.

I'm pretty sure she'd never have made a joke like that back in the day.

I take back what I said earlier. Or rather, I underline it.

She'd changed.

Probably—for the better.

"Would you rather it was a ticket to receive a pair of my underwear at any time and place of your choosing?" she asked me.

"Wouldn't you despise me forever if I used that ticket?"

"Of course."

"Then you can keep that one, too… How about a ticket to ask for your skirt at any time and place of my choosing."

"That ticket doesn't exist," Hanekawa shot down my proposal.

Too bad. I thought it was a pretty clever idea, if I do say so myself. Even if a skirt wasn't as electrifying as a pair of panties, maybe I wouldn't be despised, and I'd still obtain a piece of Hanekawa's clothing. And if I had her skirt, I'd also get to see her in her underwear (whereas if I received the underwear, I'd miss out on that visual pleasure!).

"Anyway, putting myself aside, Araragi… Maybe you shouldn't pick on Karen and Tsukihi so much."

"Don't worry—you can rest easy on that count, as well. It's not like they were just acting selfishly. I understand that."

"You're right. I don't mean to bring up 'hating people who're like you' again, but those two do resemble you."

"I suppose you aren't talking about our appearances?"

Well, we did have very similar facial features. It was easiest to no-

197

tice in photographs. Incidentally, the quickest way to tell us apart is by looking at the eyes.

"Nope, on the inside," replied Hanekawa. "Not that I'm one to talk, I suppose."

"True… But we're siblings. It's a bit different in your case."

"Mister Oshino…" Hanekawa suddenly brought up Aloha Shirts. "What do you suppose he's doing now?"

"Who knows? But I'm sure he's looking down at us from wherever he is," I said, treating him as if he were dead. Actually, Oshino being who he is, he'd die rather than watch over us. "I bet he'd be able to solve Karen's problem in no time… From what Shinobu tells me, this Cinderswarm Bee is a pretty low-level aberration."

"Shinobu? Cinderswarm Bee?"

"Ah." I hadn't brought that up yet. I quickly filled Hanekawa in on the progress I made with Shinobu, and what she told me about the aberration responsible for Karen's fever.

"I see." Hanekawa apparently put the pieces together from my simple explanation. She was as smart as ever. "The Cinderswarm Bee—doesn't sound too difficult. It seems minor, at least. But you made up with Shinobu? That's good to hear."

"Well, it's not bad," I said, glancing down at my shadow. There was no sign of Shinobu at the moment, but I guess that didn't surprise me. Unless I dragged her out, Shinobu would never appear in Hanekawa's presence.

"I don't know about taking a bath together…"

"Why did I tell you that?!"

Why was I always shooting myself in the foot? I had to learn to be more careful about what I said to Hanekawa.

"So, Araragi, are you going to start calling Shinobu by her true name now? The one from back when she was a vampire?"

"Her true name…"

"You know. Kissshot Acerolaorion Sata Andagi."

"Not exactly!"

It did sound a bit similar!

I was impressed that anyone could couple Shinobu's true name with an Okinawan snack!

Hanekawa the funny woman!

Churaragi and Sata Andagi, what a nifty team!

At any rate...

"I don't think so," I answered. "She's lost that name forever—Shinobu Oshino is her true name now. And I've decided never to call her by that other name again. Regardless of whether we make up or fall further apart, nothing will steer me from that resolution."

"Hmph. Well, Mister Oshino only went away because he decided he could leave Shinobu up to you now. Really, I thought you'd make up right after the culture festival."

"Then I guess we've been keeping everyone waiting. You could say I was being neglectful."

"You're not neglectful. I would know," Hanekawa said smoothly.

Indeed.

She seemed to think of me more than anyone else did.

Even when she'd lost her memory, she'd kept me in mind.

"You know everything," I told her, my heart full.

"I don't know everything. I only know what I know," she replied.

It was our usual back-and-forth.

"Araragi, do you want to hear a scary story?"

"A scary story? Like what?"

"Like, say, you look at your phone and there's a missed call from Senjogahara. She's left a message. It says, 'Call me back as soon as you get this.'"

"What's so scary about that? I'd just call her back."

"The message is dated yesterday."

"That's terrifying!!"

Whatever the message's content, I'd be too scared to return the call!

"Just kidding," Hanekawa said. "That was just small talk."

"S-Small talk. You startled me. It felt real."

"Why would I know if you didn't know about it yourself? You see, I don't really know everything. Anyway, the scary story I wanted to tell is actually about Shinobu."

"......"

"The hardest part of a fight is after making up—make sure you don't forget that."

Believe me, I hadn't. That statement barely merited a nod, which was all the more reason to give one.

"All right," Hanekawa said, satisfied with my response. Not touching on that subject any further, she returned to our previous topic. "About what we were saying. Even if Mister Oshino were still around, he might have ignored Karen's case. He could be pretty cold when it came to people getting themselves into trouble."

"That's a good point..."

If Oshino did "save" someone—it was because that person was a "victim" in every way. Pretty much the only one among us whom he accorded such treatment was Sengoku—true, it was possible that he was just a pedo.

Even then, he wouldn't help Karen.

There's nothing remotely "Lolita" about her. I mean, she's taller than I am, even if that's shorter than Oshino.

"You're right," I said. "In Karen's case, he'd flat-out refuse or it'd be: 'I'm not saving you. You're gonna go and get saved on your own, missy.'"

"That was really good..." Hanekawa enthusiastically ventured off the subject again.

I had no idea how many times I'd been made to hear that line.

"Araragi, you never told me you were good at impressions."

"I wouldn't say I'm good at them..."

"Do another one. This time, Senjogahara."

"No. Why do I have to?"

"Do it."

"No."

"Do it."

"…"

I couldn't refuse a third request. Not when it was Hanekawa making it, at least. I didn't know why she was insisting, though.

"My my, Araragi, what a lavish waste of time it is tutoring you. If I were to put a price on my loss, it'd probably come to around two hundred million yen. You hear me? It'd take someone like you two hundred million years to earn that much."

"I don't know if that was a good impression or not, but Senjogahara must have said something terrible to you…"

Hanekawa looked aghast. Spot-on or not, I guess my impression came off a little too real.

"Okay, do Mayoi next."

"Let's see…" I was Hanekawa's jester, at her beck and call. "S-Stop it, Mister Araragi! Away with your hands! If you're not moved by that emotional appeal, I'll just have to appeal to the law instead!"

"Just what have you been doing to Mayoi? Away with your hands?"

"Me and my big mouth again!"

When was I going to stop putting my foot in it? I really did have the intellect of an invertebrate!

Hanekawa glared at me.

My eyes jerked around like they were doing the underwater backstroke.

"S-Sorry, a slip of the tongue," I said.

"What did you really mean to say?"

"Away with your hams…"

I was now some weirdo who force-fed a little girl. I imagined myself running around, defying Hachikuji's wishes and putting food in her stomach. What a surreal image.

I was doomed.

"Fine… Do Kanbaru next."

"My senior Hanekawa, you are truly a sight to behold. The gods themselves must have come down from the heavens to bless you. I am but a worm at your feet…heh. Having been born into the same era as greatness such as yourself, I swear never to avert my eyes from that fact. You remain, forever, my shining beacon to follow."

"……"

"Wait, I was really proud of that one."

"Kanbaru has never said anything like that to me…"

"Huh?"

"I admit she's very polite, but a bombastic phrase like 'the gods themselves must have' doesn't sound like her."

"Oops."

Kanbaru wasn't like that with everyone. I never knew.

I thought she used that kind of language with all her respected elders and seniors, but did she only speak that way to me?

That was a lot of pressure…

What exactly did she see in me that was so worthwhile?

"Okay, last one. Do an impression of me."

"These breasts are yours, Araragi. Feel free to touch them anytime you like."

"I never said that!" yelled Hanekawa.

I got scolded by Miss Hanekawa!

I felt like jumping off a bridge.

"B-But you said something like that…"

"It wasn't like that at all. And besides, you were a gentleman and ripped that ticket up. When you did, I felt all tingly about you for a second."

"What?!"

And the points I scored were now void?

What an unfortunate development.

An absolute tragedy.

"So if I hadn't overstepped," I moped, "I'd have been allowed to fondle your breasts as a reward for doing impressions… Oh God."

"There would have been no such reward."

"You know, you shouldn't tease me this way. What if I wind up committing a sex crime thanks to having to repress myself? Take stock,

Hanekawa. Only you can prevent that."

"You do realize that fantasizing about groping me is already dangerously close to sex crime territory."

"Ludicrous… Since when is love a crime?"

"Leave that word alone."

Hanekawa grew even angrier.

I guess I was being pretty inappropriate.

"Fine then," I said. "As a compromise, can I at least fondle your upper arm?"

"Huh? Why my upper arm?"

"I have heard tell that upper arms feel like breasts."

"That's just silly…" Hanekawa looked exasperated. "I mean, I don't think it's even that close."

"Oh? Really?"

Then it was just an urban legend.

Mere superstition, or wishful thinking.

"Yes," Hanekawa confirmed. "They're not similar at all, at least not when I feel my own."

"You've been feeling up your breasts?!"

"No, wait! Don't get the wrong idea, I mean like in the bath!"

"The bath—so when you're completely naked?!"

"I do have to wash my own body. What's so strange about that?!"

"Hanekawa! What were you thinking?! You should have said something. You know you can rely on me. I'd totally wash your body for you!"

"I don't know what to make of you!"

Hanekawa seemed flustered. How cute of her.

Hm, she nodded. "Okay, how about this," she said.

"How about what?"

"If you get into college on your first attempt, I'll let you fondle my breasts as much as you like."

"Uh."

I froze. Hanekawa fidgeted bashfully.

"Y-You're not fooling me this time," I warned. "You'll let me fondle them as much as I like, but if I do, you'll despise me forever, right?"

"Nope. In fact, I'll be visibly glad and strike a sexy reaction pose, like Miss Machiko. I'll say, 'Maicchingu!' just like her."

"You, of all people?!"

She'd go that far?! With the pose, too?!

I'd pay two hundred million yen to see that!

"Your studies have been coming along pretty well so far," she explained, "but I'm afraid you might start to hit a wall soon. When that time comes, don't you think a reward—or rather, a return on your efforts—would help keep you motivated?"

"W-Well, yeah…"

"I'm willing to do whatever it takes to help you get into your first pick. My breasts, my upper arms, I'll let you do whatever you like with all the soft parts of my body."

"H-Holy…" I was awestruck. All the soft parts? "So I could even do something like lick your eyeballs?!"

"I'm starting to suspect you have some very unusual fetishes…"

"I-I do? You mean licking a girl's eyeballs isn't something that every red-blooded guy fantasizes about?"

"It sounds to me more like something a big-name serial killer might fantasize about… But yeah, I wouldn't mind."

"You wouldn't?!"

"But you've got to choose. You can either lick my eyeballs, or all the other soft parts of my body. It's one or the other."

"O-One or the other…"

Talk about a tough decision.

Wait a sec! The answer was obvious!

"I'm gonna lick your eyeballs!!"

"Understood…" Hanekawa seemed awestruck as she nodded. "But only if you get into your college."

"……"

Honestly, though.

Did she think my chances of getting in were so low that she had to mortgage her body?

Have you ever heard anything so sad?

Even for a joke, it was harsh.

"Do you feel motivated to study now?" she asked me.

"I want to crawl into a hole…"

"Ahahaha."

She laughed at me, too.

But as long as Hanekawa was enjoying herself, I didn't really mind.

Heh. Besides, even if I did get into college, I'd never have the guts to accept my reward.

"So," I said, "we were talking about boobs."

"We were talking about Mister Oshino."

"Sorry, a slip of the tongue."

"That might catch on, actually. I'll have to give it a try sometime…"

Hachikuji was taking the world by storm.

"Mister Oshino probably wouldn't have helped Karen…but what about you, Araragi? Are you going to? Maybe not?"

"Of course I'll help her. But I won't be doing it for her," I replied. "And I sure as hell won't be doing it for the sake of justice."

"Then what will you be doing it for?"

"Nothing, really. That's just the rules. When your little sister is in trouble, a big brother helps her out. Ask anyone, they'll say the same."

No, that wasn't entirely true. It wouldn't elicit any such declaration in the first place.

"I'm relieved to hear that," Hanekawa said.

"What's that supposed to mean? You thought I'd just abandon my sister?"

"I thought you might." Hanekawa didn't outright negate my flippant rejoinder. "You're very strict with them. Besides," she added firmly, "what happened this time was their fault."

"……"

"That's why maybe you'd choose not to act."

Of course. Hanekawa was exceptional—she excelled at most everything, more than most anyone. And she had a great personality. Fair and aboveboard. She made the right call whatever the situation. Plus, she always thought of others and never put herself first.

However.

For instance, the time when I became a vampire—

She'd been very solicitous and gone to great lengths for me. At some points she even made almost unbelievable sacrifices for my sake.

But never, once—did she offer any words of pity.

As if to say—the hellish spring break I was going through was, strictly speaking, my own fault.

She had comforted me, protected me, and saved me. But she most certainly had not sympathized with me.

She had indulged every care I might have need of. But never once had she been indulgent.

"I'm not as steadfast as you...or Oshino," I admitted. "I'll do what I can—and whatever I can't do, of course, I won't."

"I see." Hanekawa nodded. "Well, I think this is far enough."

Her house was still nowhere in sight—but this was as far I would accompany her.

We had our respective domains.

The sun had yet to rise, though. The dangers of walking alone at night had little to do with distance.

"You should ride home," I suggested. "You can borrow my bike."

"Are you sure? Because I'd take you up on that."

In place of an answer, I simply turned the handle her way.

"In that case, thank you." Hanekawa held down her skirt and hoisted herself onto the bike. The length of her skirt gave even Senjogahara a run for her money, so there was nothing to see.

Not that I was hoping for anything racy.

Just knowing that Hanekawa was straddling the saddle of my bicycle was satisfaction enough... Wait, that's more perverted!

Hrm...maybe I really do have unusual fetishes.

Senjogahara didn't seem to care, though.

"I'll return it tomorrow," Hanekawa promised.

"Okay."

"And make sure you settle this today. You have to start studying for your exams again tomorrow. It's great that you're thinking about your responsibilities as a brother, but don't forget about your responsibilities as a high school student."

With that final bit of advice, Hanekawa slowly worked the pedals homeward.

She rode standing up on them.

016

I watched Hanekawa until she disappeared from sight. Then I traced back our route and went straight up to my sisters' room—Tsukihi had already fallen asleep, exhausted. She was only fourteen, an age where it was still hard to stay up all night—she'd probably been forcing herself to stay awake. I'd asked her everything she could tell me, anyways. She could rest for now.

Karen, on the other hand, had been asleep, albeit fitfully, nearly the entire time from when I was released from captivity to when I came home—she didn't seem to be able to sleep now. Between that and the high fever, she had to be suffering.

Not wanting to disturb Tsukihi, I moved Karen to my room. I carried her in my arms like a princess and set her down on my bed.

"Argh, Koyomi, you're making too big a deal out of this. This is why I didn't want to tell you. Everyone should have kept their mouths shut. It's just a little fever, what's the big deal?"

"Silence. Just be a good patient and do as I say. Are you hungry? How about some canned peaches?"

"No appetite."

"I see... Do you want me to let down your hair?"

"Run me a bath. I'm all sweaty."

"What about your hair…"

"Do whatever you like."

Karen lifted her head up slightly and tilted her ponytail toward me. It may have seemed like she was just being lazy—but the truth was, even such a small movement probably pained her.

Earlier, when I lifted her up—her body felt like it was burning up.

An inferno. The Cinderswarm Bee.

Karen had stopped trying to act tough, I guess because her condition was out in the open. Not that she'd let go of her last reserves of stubbornness.

"A bath is out of the question," I said, setting the hairband by the bedside, "but I can wipe you down if you like."

"Yeah… Please. Not that I'm thrilled."

Although her speech was clear, talking seemed like a chore for her—perhaps her body wasn't responding properly to her commands.

Or to her stubbornness, as the case may be.

"Tsukihi just wiped me down a little while ago, but I'm already drenched…though I guess a little while ago is already yesterday."

"I guess it is. Well, get undressed," I said, leaving Karen in my room while I went downstairs to the bathroom. I wet a towel, and then went to the kitchen to heat the towel up in the microwave. I figured it would be better if the towel was a little warm.

When I got back to my room, Karen was still wearing her jersey.

"Hey, I told you to take off your clothes."

"I'm sorry…"

"Huh?"

"I'm too tired. Can you take them off for me? Then wipe me down and get me dressed."

"Son of a…"

She just didn't do cute.

Where the hell did the image of the "little sister" in manga and anime come from anyway? I guess it ultimately had to do with the observer—anything could be cute if you were ready to see it that way.

Maybe there was a demand for Karen's recalcitrance, too.

For my own part, I'd rather pass. But I could be nice if she was sick.

I did as Karen said, removing her jersey and rolling up the t-shirt she was wearing underneath. Although her body wasn't tempered to the same ascetic level as Kanbaru's (I never dreamed I would use the word "ascetic" in conjunction with Kanbaru), it was still quite toned. I began wiping her down carefully.

"Nggh," Karen groaned. "My own brother is / seeing me with no clothes on / how embarrassing."

"Why are you talking in haiku?"

"To hide how embarrassed I am."

"Says the girl who dances around the house half-naked after a shower."

"That's not dancing... I was doing aerobics."

"Well, you can dance by yourself during the anime ending."

"If I'm gonna dance, it won't be just for the ending song... It'll be the whole thirty minutes."

"That might be a little too avant-garde..."

The funny thing is, I was completely fine seeing my sister naked. It affected me even less than when Shinobu had been naked.

I guess when your genes are so similar, the brain's response just shuts off subconsciously... If not, siblings probably wouldn't be able to live under the same roof.

"Aghh," Karen groaned again. What a crybaby.

"I'm wiping your back. Roll over."

"I can't, it's too hard. Roll me over."

"Tsk..." After I was finished with her back, I stripped her lower half and wiped her legs down. Obviously, I avoided the inside of her underpants. Either Tsukihi or my mom would have to take care of that.

"Damn," muttered Karen. "I can't believe I screwed up like this."

"Huh?"

"Even I know that being strong is more important than being right, you didn't have to tell me that..." vented Karen as I wiped her down.

"But it's not like I can just snap my fingers and become strong all of a sudden."

I don't know if it was the hot towel, but I was starting to feel like a massage therapist.

"What am I supposed to do—ignore all the injustice I see until I become stronger? Justice runs in my veins, and I can't stand by while evil is afoot."

"From where I'm standing, it seems like you just want to cause a ruckus."

"Yeah, well, from where you're standing, it's all make-believe... But," said Karen, biting her lip plaintively, "that guy doesn't play by the rules."

"......"

By "that guy," she meant Deishu Kaiki. The ominous man in the suit, dressed as if in mourning. "It doesn't make sense—how can someone just make me sick? It's weird, it isn't right. Like something out of a melodrama."

"A melodrama?" I wasn't sure what she meant by that. I continued wiping the underside of her foot as I spoke. "Anyway, I'll figure something out. You forget about all this and just rest easy. Leave the rest to me."

"I can't rest easy. The truth is I'm in a lot of pain."

"Well, then rest hard. Either way, there's no need to worry. I'll have you as good as new in no time."

"How? The medicine isn't working."

"......"

I still hadn't told her—about aberrations. Apparently, Hanekawa had managed to finesse that part, too.

It was as I had discussed with Hachikuji, Sengoku, and Kanbaru. Better not to speak of that stuff if you didn't have to—about aberrations or about Shinobu.

Or Deishu Kaiki.

If this could be settled without getting Karen and Tsukihi involved any further—then it was better not to involve them. They were responsible for what had happened, sure. But they weren't accountable. Not in my mind.

They were still children.

They were fakes.

"From where you're standing, this is all make-believe," Karen spooled back our conversation. Maybe she wasn't talking to me, and it was more like the fever speaking. "Still…Kaiki."

"Hm?"

"Deishu Kaiki. You heard from Tsukihi, didn't you? Why he's pushing this mumbo-jumbo occult stuff—those charms—to middle schoolers?"

"……"

"Yeah. For money." Desihu Kaiki, swindler, fake expert. Karen spit her words out with contempt. "He instills malice and anxiety and then takes advantage of the situation to trick people out of their money. In exchange for nothing. Ten thou, twenty thou. That's what he said. He's taking that kind of money from middle-school kids. I thought he'd feel ashamed when I called him out for it, but you know what he said? He wasn't even shy about it. Children are easier to deceive."

"Easier to deceive…"

"Tsukihi's friend, that girl Sengoku? She was really tightlipped about it, but I got the impression you helped her out a lot. But she was lucky. There are other kids who went to Kaiki for help, not knowing he was the source of the rumors, and got arrested for shoplifting trying to steal the money he asked for. Could you really forgive something like that? Could you look one of those kids in the eye and say, 'Sorry, can't help you, I'm not strong enough yet?'"

Karen said that as if one of those kids were in front of her right now. As if here was where she had to stand tall and pass her test.

"Kaiki said that money is everything. That sounds like something some villain in a manga would say. I never thought I'd hear a line like that in real life. I mean, money is important, but there's lots of other important things as well. Like love!"

Wow! We agreed.

My sister and I actually agreed on something.

I spoke up. "Money isn't everything—it's just almost everything!"

"……"

Never mind, I guess we didn't agree after all.

"Koyomi," Karen said. "Tsukihi and I are doing what we believe in. We're not gonna learn the hard way, or whatever. If the same thing happens again, we'll do the exact same thing, no two questions about it."

"……"

"I may have lost in terms of the outcome, but I haven't lost in spirit. Next time I'll win. I won't give up until I win. And even if I'm not going to win, I still won't give up. It's not…the outcome that matters, right?"

"You mean, you may have lost the match, but you've won our hearts? That doesn't sound like much of a warrior's code."

"That's not quite it—but I'll say, it's far from it."

"So it's totally not it."

"You can lose the match and lose people's hearts—but if you don't lose to yourself, then you haven't really lost. There, that's my warrior's code."

"Okay… But as long as you follow that motto, people around you are going to suffer. That's why…" If that was how she felt, then I'd use her own words against her. "That's why—you never grow up."

"I'm already grown-up… Just look at these tits."

"What am I supposed to see? They're not even half as big as Hanekawa's."

"Wha? Are hers really that…"

Yes. Yes, they were.

She looked much more slender in her clothes than she was.

"Hanekawa's the real deal," I said. "I don't think I need to tell you that, though."

"……"

"Honestly, for my own part, I don't really like you guys and Hanekawa getting friendly…but it's a good opportunity. You could learn a lot from her." I know I had. Since meeting Hanekawa—I'd changed. "If you don't want me to grow up without you, you'd better start growing up too."

"I never said that… Did Tsukihi?"

"Her opinion is your opinion. She's the strategist."

"Ugh. True."

Karen began squirming and groaning.

"Don't move," I ordered, "it's hard to wipe you down."

"That's enough, already, I feel much better now."

"I've come this far, there's no need to get shy now."

"Well, don't blame me if you get sick, too."

"Huh…"

Huh? If I get sick, too? My hand froze mid-wipe—I had an idea.

"O-One sec," I said, setting aside the almost cold towel and stepping out into the hallway.

Tsukihi was asleep, and it would probably still be a little while until my parents woke up. But just to be safe, I headed to the downstairs bathroom and locked the door behind me.

"Shinobu," I called to my shadow.

"What now?"

She hadn't emerged. It was just her voice, but that was fine. It was all I needed.

"'Tis nearly time for my slumber. I may have lost my pith, but I am still a creature of the night. And I hate to be roused as much as ever."

"Okay, then let me ask you just one thing." It was the idea that Karen's words had put in my head. "My sister's *illness*—is there a way to give it to me?"

"Hrm?"

"I say illness, but basically it's an aberration's poison—it was deposited in her willfully in the first place. In that case, couldn't we transpose the toxin one more time, from her to me?"

"You wish to shoulder her illness? Hmm…"

215

Shinobu seemed to be considering the matter—in my shadow.

Perhaps she was thinking of what Oshino had told her—even if she couldn't fiddle around in her brain anymore.

"Well…thy constitution is still partially vampiric. 'Tis unlikely the rankle of a creature such as the Cinderswarm Bee would raise your temperature very much—"

"Right?"

Vampires belonged on a different plane from other aberrations and stood virtually unopposed, unless it was something like Hanekawa's cat—in fact, even the cat had only proved formidable thanks to targeting an exceptional host, namely Hanekawa.

Regardless of what type of aberration the Cinderswarm Bee was, it basically couldn't hold a candle to the might of a vampire. A bee sting did little against a demon.

"In that regard," Shinobu said, "absorbing the Cinderswarm Bee's rankle is an excellent idea. If I cannot eat the poison, why not absorb it? Thy notion has merit. But since we do not know by what means Kaiki inflicted the poison upon thy sister, we shall need to rely upon a method of our own to transfer it."

"What? You mean you know a way?"

"I may. Yet…frankly, I do not recommend it. Well, it is not that I would not… I merely balk at the thought."

"You mean it's risky. I understand."

"No, not risky, exactly… It may be no more than an urban legend. I believe the brat was talking about something entirely unrelated when he mentioned it."

"You don't seem very enthusiastic about this. It's not like you. I'll do it, whatever it is, as long as it's not something weird like sucking her blood."

"Like sucking her blood… Hmm, well, who is to say? I know not whether this is something ye would consider acceptable."

"I have no idea what it is, but I'm pretty sure I'll find it acceptable. If we don't do something, the Cinderswarm Bee could kill her, right?

And even if it won't kill her, if there's some way to ease her suffering, we should try, whatever it is."

"True," agreed Shinobu. However, she still seemed hesitant. I had to badger her until she said, "Fine, do as ye like," and finally shared the method.

I returned to my room.

"Koyomi… If you were going to the bathroom or wherever, you could have at least dressed me first," Karen said as soon as I entered the room.

"Karen-chan," I called to her, ignoring her (very justified) complaint.

Feeling in a rush due to the circumstances, I'd accidentally uttered her name. But that was that. I followed up with—

"We're going to kiss now."

017

In the end, I wasn't able to absorb all of the aberration's, the Cinderswarm Bee's, poison. Maybe half—or even just a third. That was all.

Which was unfortunate, I guess. But at least it was enough to lower Karen's fever somewhat—from over 104 degrees down to about 101. That might not seem like much, but it made a huge difference for her.

In fact, she was feeling so much better that, up until a moment ago, she had been making a big ruckus. "My first kiss! I can't believe you stole my first kiss! I was saving it for Mizudori!!"

By the way, Mizudori is Karen's boyfriend. That's his last name. I haven't met him yet and don't know his first, but apparently he's a cute younger boy.

While we're on the topic, Tsukihi's boyfriend is named Rosokuzawa (I don't know his first name either, nor have I come face to face with him). Supposedly he's a dashing older boy—the polar opposite of Mizudori—so I guess the two sisters have very different tastes in men.

In any case, Karen had worn herself out and was asleep. I guess the treatment had its intended effect.

Afterwards, Shinobu said, "Spreading a cold through a kiss, or giving a cold to someone else to get better, does not even rise to the level of an urban legend. But be it mouth to mouth or indirect kissing, it takes a charm to beat a charm." She added as though she was fed up, "Thou art less a vampire than a demon. Or should I say, a devil."

Hmph. For the first time in ages, I'd made my sister cry.

....

It served her right, the idiot!

It was the morning of July thirtieth. After putting Karen to sleep, I waited until it was past nine and got on my way, leaving a note for Tsukihi to "stay put at home with Karen for today."

Since I'd lent my bike to Hanekawa, I walked. Destination—Senjogahara's house.

Along the way, I spotted Hachikuji.

As usual, she was plodding along with a massive knapsack strapped to her back—what did she cram into that bag, anyways? I liked to imagine that it was full of heavy dumbbells, and she was using it to beef up.

In any case, I must have really been in luck to run into her two days in a row. Probability-wise, that seemed even less likely than running into her twice on the same day. I'm not sure I could keep treating her as a lucky charm, though. After all, I'd run into some pretty bad luck the day before.

In any case, was this area actually part of her territory, too? Unless she was branching out? Was she making a map of the neighborhood or something? Who did she think she was, Tadataka Ino?

"Hey, Hachikuji," I just greeted her normally. I'd learned my lesson the hard way with Kanbaru.

"......"

Hachikuji had a very dissatisfied look on her face.

"H-Hachikuji?"

"Oh...it's Mister Araragi."

"Come on, don't pronounce it right!"

What happened to our routine?!

Don't just change things up!

"Mister Araragi, that was such a boring hello. You've really come down in the world. Did something happen?"

"Why so maligning?!"

The look in her eyes!

It wasn't cold so much as incisive!

Even Senjogahara didn't glare at me like that!

I had to object. "I thought you didn't like it when I harassed you!"

"I was signaling for you to step it up. How could you stop just because you were told to? Tsk, you've fumbled a great pass."

"That was an overly complex cue!"

"I feel like I've been told a long joke with a flubbed punch line."

"Is it that bad?!"

"Besides, 'maligning' is too fancy a word for you. Maybe if you misspelled it…"

"So malighning!"

"An easy way to remember how to spell that one: associate it with 'malignant,'" Hachikuji gave me a gratuitous lesson.

Then she turned her back to me, forlornly, and began trudging away.

Leaving me in her wake.

Well, she wasn't going to.

"Hey, Hachikuji. Wait."

"Go away. The friend I knew is dead and gone… When you take the sexual harassment out of Araragi, all that's left are the fleas."

"There were no fleas to begin with!"

"I don't even want to look at you anymore. Get lost."

"Don't say that! Senjogahara has at least a hundred times, but when you do, I really want to disappear!"

"Strange, I told you to scram, and yet you're still here… Can't you even manage that much?"

"I wish I could start over from my last save!"

I pulled up beside her.

Although Hachikuji still looked dissatisfied (It didn't seem like she was doing a bit. The girl was hard to understand at times), she finally sighed after a while and turned to face me.

"So, what happened?" she asked. "You certainly seem to be in serious mode today, unlike yesterday."

"Serious mode… Yeah, I guess."

The day before, I'd been heading to Sengoku's house just to hang out.

Senjogahara—was scarier. Who knew what she'd been up to after we parted.

"A lot happened," I said.

"Oh. I won't press you for details."

Hachikuji nodded. She could be considerate when it came to boundaries, like no other grade schooler.

"But, Mister Araragi, I'm a little worried that you look a bit under the weather."

"Huh? I do?"

"Are you feeling all right?"

"Hmm…" Although I'd absorbed half of Karen's illness, I didn't think it had affected me enough to be visible. But maybe since this was Hachikuji—*she could tell?* "Apparently it's called the Cinderswarm Bee. It's a very different kind of aberration than your snail… Still, it's a pain in the neck."

"I see—what a bother." Hachikuji crossed her arms and frowned like she was genuinely bothered. "But I'm sure you'll be fine. You've dealt with these things plenty of times."

"I hope you're right. Nothing seems to be going smoothly, so far. Not that I ever handled it smoothly before. I always mess up."

Griping to someone younger than me seemed lame, but I'd have pretty much no one else's ear on the topic, so I went ahead.

"You see, my sisters are such idiots."

"Even bigger idiots than you, Mister Araragi?"

"Hey, what's with that premise?!"

Yup, this was how it ought to be. It was too stupid to discuss seriously.

"What they say is right," I conceded, "and I want to respect that— but they're too simpleminded. What they want to do is right, but they

222

don't know how to go about it. At least, that's how I see it."

"Isn't that what people always say about you, Mister Araragi?"

"Hrm…"

True, Oshino and Hanekawa criticized me in similar ways. In my case, I tended to be told that a pretty solution wasn't always right, but it meant essentially the same thing.

"Plus, if you weren't that kind of person," added Hachikuji, "I wouldn't be here strolling down the street so fancy-free. Maybe there are a lot of people out there who were helped by your sisters, too."

"………"

There were.

A lot of them, no doubt.

How else to make sense of my sisters' ridiculous reputation?

Their charisma skill was rooted in results—at the very least, the pair were more popular than I was.

Loved, even.

What more could you ask for?

Wasn't that sufficient proof?

Hachikuji made a persuasive point, and yet—

"They're such brats," I said. "They don't listen to anyone. I have to try to wrap this all up while they're still stuck at home, behaving…"

The fact that the aberration was this Cinderswarm Bee was in a sense a lucky break. It was forcing Karen to stay at home and be mature.

Mature…

"Hachikuji, when does a person grow up?"

"Not while they're still asking," nailed Hachikuji, the fifth-grader. "The age of majority in Japan is twenty now, but it depends on the times. Back in the day, girls used to get married when they were fairly young. It was like all men were pedophiles."

"That's unsettling."

"All the warlords were into BL."

"That's even more unsettling."

"The biggest historical battles were all just lovers' spats, maybe?

Social studies textbooks become so much more interesting then."

"I don't even want to think about that."

"Nobunaga, Hideyoshi, and Ieyasu were in a love triangle!"

"That totally subverts Japanese history."

I suppose that was one aspect of war. Neither society nor the world ever changed. What a poignant reality.

"Subverted or reversed, reality is reality," Hachikuji said. "They call it the Warring States period, but that should be 'Rawring' instead."

"I don't know... I'm not sure everyone would agree that it was so great."

"Well, it depends on what your idea of paradise is. Me, I picture a drink bar with free refills."

"Why?!"

Such an intense longing for free refills... Not that it didn't make any sense. When I was a kid, it did offer its sense of wonder.

"Mister Araragi, what do you picture when you hear the word 'paradise'?"

"I don't know... Clouds and angels?"

"Hmph."

"If I had to say, then Hanekawa."

"Is that because of all the obscene thoughts you're harboring for her?"

"They're not all obscene!"

What a rude thing to say.

In any case, that was my image.

It was Senjogahara, by the way, when I pictured hell.

That kind of went without saying.

Hell hath no fury like her every whim.

"Some people would say you're a grownup if you've started working, but you can grow up without ever working," opined Hachikuji.

"You mean growing up is just part of getting older."

"By the way, do you have any vocation in mind, Mister Araragi?"

"Sorry, I haven't thought that far ahead..."

"That doesn't sound very mature."

"......"

Hmm. Maybe so.

"A job where I hold Hanekawa's breasts so they don't spill out would be great," I stated.

"How did you ever say that with a straight face?"

"Seriously, who the hell invented the bra? I don't know how much money the bastards made, but thanks to them I'm out of a job."

"Please calm down. That career option never existed in the first place."

"How about what we said once? A job fondling your breasts all day until they get bigger would be quite acceptable to me."

"I would fear for their shape... Besides, are you even aware that your fantasies are leaking out?"

"Uh oh."

"Zip your lips."

"They don't come with such a convenient feature."

"Then staple your lips."

"I'm having a flashback!"

Ah, by the way, Hachikuji mumbled as if she'd just remembered something. "After we said goodbye yesterday, I passed a group of freshmen girls from your school who must have stayed behind for extracurricular activities. They were gossiping about it."

"About what?"

"Apparently, there's a rumor that a third-year called Araragi can make your breasts super big by fondling them."

"......"

I think I knew who might have started that rumor.

A certain second-year who ran like the wind.

Talk about a nasty surprise. I'm sure she meant well, but it was plain harassment.

Now I was scared to go back to school!

"Mister Araragi, returning to our discussion, I heard this joke."

"What kind of joke?"

"A bachelor is asked by his mother, 'When are you going to get married?' 'Very soon,' he promises, 'I'm just waiting for the girl to turn sixteen.'"

"That's not funny!"

What a point to return to.

Why were we discussing that, anyway? That was just going off-topic.

"Well," I said, "maybe there's no point telling girls in junior high to grow up. Age-wise, they're kids, after all."

Unlike Shinobu.

Glancing down at my shadow, where she was probably asleep, I had that thought.

"That's it," Hachikuji agreed. "How could middle schoolers not be kids? The problem is not knowing that they're children."

"Ooh."

Hachikuji was on to something. She could be very good at catching things that I missed.

Maybe that was it, and the issue was self-awareness.

"Still," Hachikuji said, "it might beat adults who don't see themselves as adults."

"Yeah, grownups who think of themselves as kids are the worst."

Not that they were uncommon. A few of my teachers fit that bill.

"By the way, Hachikuji, which do you consider yourself?"

"I have the body of a child and the mind of an adult."

"Like Detective Conan!"

"Speaking of detectives…"

Hachikuji was about to go off topic again, but I didn't stop her. We were getting close to Senjogahara's place, but we had enough time for one more round.

"Lately standard mysteries have been getting popular again, as opposed to newfangled ones."

"You actually know and care about that sort of trend? Well, fine.

'Standard'? Standard or not, isn't the whole mystery genre in decline?"

"What are you saying? Even if mystery novels aren't big anymore, the mystery genre is going strong. Procedural dramas, mystery manga, whodunit games—the category is alive and kicking. All of those are pretty popular."

"……"

That was true.

On TV, mysteries regularly cornered prime time. Even the repeats were on round the clock.

Why was it that only the novels had gone out of style?

It had become like a traditional art form.

"I guess people just don't read as much as they used to?" I hypothesized. "But then cell phone novels are all the rage." Though I wasn't very good at using mine and hadn't read any. "Still, I haven't heard anything about mysteries being mainstream in that world."

"They say the number of words people will read in their lifetimes is set. However many hundreds of millions that is."

"Oh yeah?"

Yet another bit of odd trivia.

You had to wonder just what kind of books Hachikuji read.

"And so," she continued, "exhausting that amount through emails and the internet, people read less."

"Do you think that's true?"

"I highly doubt it," Hachikuji withdrew her theory (well, probably not hers) without protest. "Mystery novels aren't popular simply because they're getting trite."

"Is that your own view this time?"

"I'm contrite that they're trite… Ahahaha!"

"That wasn't so clever that you should be laughing hard at your own pun!"

"It was different back in the day, but you can't compete with the kinds of images and directing you get in other media. The main weapon left to novels is identification. Being a novel and not relying on visuals makes it easier to step into someone's shoes. But you don't want to be identifying with any character in a mystery. The whole selling point is that you never know whom to trust."

"Hmm, you may be on to something."

"Which is why mystery novels are now a minor genre. They're even less popular than *hanafuda*."

"Huh?" Now that was a comparison that piqued my interest. "You know how to play *hanafuda*?"

Hachikuji nodded. "Because of my name, I always liked the *hachi-hachi* variant."

"At last, I've found you!" My soulmate! I wanted to play right now! "Ah…but we don't have a deck! Dammit! When I try to play *hanafuda*, no one knows the rules, and when I find someone who does, no one has a deck!"

"Well, I can't imagine anyone happening to have one on hand."

"No, from now on, I'm going to carry one with me," I vowed. "The next time I run into you, we'll have a *hanafuda* tournament!"

"Mister Araragi… For some reason you seem to be under the impression that you mustn't meet me except by accident, but we could just make an appointment, you know? Why not pick a date and place?"

"Uh…that's so formal, I'd feel shy!"

"Are you actually blushing?"

Hachikuji shrank back. Unmistakably, as the tide ebbs.

N-No, it was an expression of my love for *hanafuda*, not Hachikuji… Wait, did I love *hanafuda* that much? I couldn't help but suspect that a total dearth of opponents was inflating my interest in the game.

The only combo anyone seemed to know was boar-deer-butterfly.

"I bet Sengoku doesn't even know that the game exists. Ugh… Why can't somebody put out a hit manga about *hanafuda*?"

"Aren't you being a little over-dramatic? Plenty of people know how to play."

"Maybe, but I never seem to meet any of them."

"I've heard that it's relatively popular in Okinawa."

"Is that true?"

"Only relatively speaking, though."

"I see… It wouldn't be worth moving there, then…"

"Are you really that crazy for it? Well, I guess it rivals mahjong in having a strong gambling element."

"Gambling element?"

"Which is also to say a strong affinity with illegality."

"Hrmm."

I see.

Recalling the Washizu mahjong tiles that I had found in the same area as the *hanafuda* deck in Kanbaru's room, I gave a deep nod. It was quite true. In fact, even for regular playing cards, young people of my generation did shy away from poker, blackjack, baccarat, and other typical gambling games.

The temperature difference between people who understood the game and those who didn't was severe, so to speak.

Gambling element, huh?

"Anyway, what were we talking about, Hachihachiji?"

"Where did that one temple go?"

"Oops, I didn't even notice. Anyway, what were we talking about, Hachikuji?"

"About how much you love panties."

"I'm pretty sure that was yesterday."

"Not panties… Then do you mean mysteries?"

"Don't pair those two things. Anyway, you were saying that mystery novels aren't big anymore but that the genre itself is going strong—and standard setups are on the rise. But I'm not sure exactly what you mean by a non-standard mystery."

"If the catchphrase is, 'The killer is not in this room!' then it probably isn't standard."

"Definitely not!"

"How about, 'This case is clothes!'"

"That would be pretty niche!"

"'QUod Erat…S. T. I. O. N!'"

"The demonstration is intentionally lacking!"

When you went that far, a certain catchphrase was inevitable.

It's no mystery.

"Anyway, Hachikuji, we still haven't gotten to your point, have we?"

"No. If it's a mystery, someone gets killed, and the killer is revealed, but in a lot of the cases, the culprit ends up having a really sad motive. Something about that feels like it lacks closure. You're left not quite sure who was the bad guy… Though reality is like that, too, and I should find that interesting."

"Well, dramatically, when a good person gets killed and the killer is a bad person, we don't have much of a twist—though with period pieces and such, that actually works better, so I don't know. Still, no matter who the villain is, he'd have some reason or other, wouldn't he."

Deishu Kaiki.

His reason—was money.

Money, the be-all and end-all.

"Hm? Oh—sorry, Hachihachiji…"

"You're forgetting a temple again."

"A-Ah, sorry, Hachishichiji…"

"Is a temple disappearing every time you say my name?!"

"Hachirokuji. We're almost at Senjogahara's house, so I'm going to have to say goodbye."

"Hmm? Right, yes. Right, your friend doesn't like me very much."

Hachikuji halted and turned around.

She had no destination in the first place.

"Mister Araragi, farewell."

"You too."

We waved at each other and parted ways.

Thank goodness I'd run into Hachikuji to make the trip interesting, I thought idly as I watched her receding figure—however.

At the time, I didn't know what would beset the amiable girl named Mayoi Hachikuji—

No, I mean, just in the sense of actually not knowing.

Hachikuji was a mystery, in her own way—what did she do while she was alone, or rather, when she wasn't out for a walk?

018

The wood-and-mortar Tamikura Apartments, Room 201. Hitagi Senjogahara's place of residence.

I hadn't called in advance, deliberately showing up without an appointment. Proof of my resolve.

There was no fancy device like an intercom for these apartments. I made a backward fist and knocked on Senjogahara's door.

No answer—I knocked again.

Still no answer.

This time I gave the knob a try. It was unlocked.

How careless could you be?

While Hitagi Senjogahara was a wall of iron when it came to her up-close and personal defenses, in general her long-range defense had more holes than a block of Swiss cheese.

As for the woman herself—

"……"

She was sitting in the modest apartment room—sharpening pencils.

She seemed to be absorbed in the task.

A state of perfect Zen.

She didn't even notice me.

Obviously there was nothing particularly odd about a high-school senior sharpening pencils—it was a normal part of keeping one's stationery in order. But a glance at the massive pile (of about a hundred?) next to the newspaper she was working over made it clear that something was amiss.

If I were to make a comparison…she resembled a warrior preparing her weapons for battle.

"Err…Miss 'Gahara?"

"Araragi, I want to know…"

I was wrong about not having been noticed. She just hadn't bothered to look in my direction—my visit, it seemed, was less pressing than sharpening those pencils.

Still gazing at the tip of the one she'd just sharpened, she said, "If a hundred sharpened pencils that you happened to have on you impaled a third party, that would qualify as an accident, yes?"

"It would be an incident!"

And how!

The local news section would be all over the Pencil Murder!

"Heh," she said. "Then I'll use that very sheet of newspaper to sharpen my next batch of pencils."

"Calm down, Senjogahara! Despite the smug look on your face, that wasn't such a clever joke!"

Don't waste your precious store of smiles on it!

You only crack a smile an average of five times per day!

The box-cutter—probably the same one she'd thrust into my mouth—had turned pitch-black with lead. She turned it slowly in my direction, the blade glittering in the light.

A black sheen.

"Take your shoes off and come in, Araragi. Don't worry, I won't kidnap you again."

"All right…"

Closing the door behind me and turning the lock, which Senjogahara had left undone, I took off my shoes and stepped into the tatami room. Since it was only six mats, I didn't even have to take a look around to see that she was alone.

"Where's your dad?"

Senjogahara lived together with her father, just the two of them. He didn't seem to be in the bathroom (I'd overhear the water running), so he wasn't home.

He was a bigwig at some foreign multinational. I already knew he hardly made it home most days, but today was Sunday—I guess with the massive debt he was shouldering, weekends were not a luxury he could afford.

"My father's at work," confirmed Senjogahara. "He's on-site right now…well, posted overseas. But the timing works out great. I wouldn't want to kidnap him too."

"……"

But she'd kidnap her boyfriend.

You latent criminal.

"Well, I guess you became an actual criminal the moment you kidnapped me… Anyway, if I asked you why you were arming yourself, would you tell me?"

"Ask away. Like they say, there's no such thing as a stupid question, and it would be more stupid to be Araragi."

"Don't paste my name into an adage! Especially not like that! It's stupid to 'be Araragi'?!"

"I was just telling you not to be shy."

"I can tell you're lying!"

Anyway.

I sat across from Senjogahara on the other side of the newspaper. It was piled high with pencil shavings.

"I'm going to settle things with Kaiki," she said. "Since you refused my protection, the only option remaining is to go on the offensive."

"Abducting isn't protecting." Well, I did know that she'd been protecting me, in her own way—and I might have never refused if it hadn't been for Tsukihi's text. "If that's what it was, though, want to give kidnapping another try?"

"I already told you that I wouldn't do it again."

"All right. By the way, I talked to Hanekawa after that—"

"Huh? Did Mistress Hane... No, uh, did she say anything about me?"

"Were you just about to call her Mistress Hanekawa?"

"I-I wasn't! There is no bullying at our school."

"You're being bullied?! You?!"

Well, the "model student prone to illness" façade that camouflaged Senjogahara's wall of iron worked on our other classmates but no longer meant anything to Hanekawa... She wouldn't just be understanding with Senjogahara all the time.

Hanekawa was a good person, but that meant she was willing to forgive wickedness, not overlook it.

"Senjogahara, you've shown your true colors so she's going to get on your case, but don't call it bullying, it makes her look bad."

"When did I ever call it that? It's because I like doing it that she lets me polish her shoes every morning!"

"Why are you so servile with her?!"

One hundredth! Show me just a hundredth of that deference!

"Anyway...so you're going to meet Kaiki?" I asked.

"Yes. But don't worry. I plan to settle this with words, if at all possible."

"Says the lady with the full arsenal of pencils... Thank goodness I showed up. But Senjogahara? Does that mean you know where Kaiki is?"

"I had a business card." Senjogahara reached into her bag and pulled out an aged scrap of paper. "He gave this to me a long time ago. It's a miracle that I hadn't torn it up and thrown it away. It's only got a cell phone number listed...but luckily he still uses the same number."

"Hmm... Let me see that for a second."

It was a simple business card. The only things on it were the name Deishu Kaiki, its reading in phonetic letters, and, as Senjogahara said, a cell phone number.

Wait, no. There was one more thing, a job title.

—*Ghostbuster.*

"Senjogahara, I know it's one of the worst things I could say, but wasn't it your own fault if you were taken in by this?"

"That's the trap. It's hard to believe that someone who'd go for such a silly title is actually a fraud."

"Maybe…"

True, I actually heard somewhere that one of the techniques used in cons was to intentionally come off as phony.

Appearing overtly phony made the target assume the opposite— since anything that sounded so fake couldn't actually be fake. Usually, it would just arouse suspicion, but maybe the tactic did work better on overcautious marks.

"If you're going to say that, Mister Oshino was about as suspicious as they come," Senjogahara pointed out. "Compared to him, even Kaiki is a respectable adult."

"Yeah, a Hawaiian shirt versus a suit…"

They did have a few points in common. It's not like Oshino was just volunteering his services, either… In fact, in my case, he asked for five million yen.

Not that I thought the price was high, considering.

"So then, Senjogahara, you called this number—and spoke to Kaiki?"

"Yes. He doesn't seem to have changed at all—dreary as a swamp. I haven't just been twiddling my thumbs since your release. Sure, I was in a bit of a funk after Hanekawa scolded me, but that only lasted for about five hours."

"Five hours?!"

Senjogahara could be skittish about the strangest things. Hanekawa really was her nemesis.

Having been lured out by Karen's fake message (which actually must have been Hanekawa's doing), Kaiki would be wary of using his cell phone for business purposes. But it seemed he hadn't disposed of the phone, itself, so far. Taking into account the age of the business card as well, it was more than mere luck but a miracle that Senjogahara had been able to contact him.

But did the miracle favor us?

"Then by my calculation," I said, "you made the call not long before I got here."

"Very astute. Not everyone can perform single-digit addition in their heads."

"Do you have to make fun of me all the time?!"

"When does it get difficult for you? Multiplication?"

"I'm good all around at math!"

"Wow. Are you bragging?"

"Nkk…"

Maybe I was! So?!

"Hah," snorted Senjogahara. "Says the man who latched on to Fleming's left-hand rule so hard he didn't even know Fleming's right-hand rule existed until just the other day. You, brag? That's preposterous. Oh, I'm sorry, I didn't mean to use such a big word."

"Hey, I might be especially bad at physics and modern Japanese, but what's so wrong with knowing what I'm good at?!"

"Yes, yes, of course, of course. You're blameless, and I'm always to blame."

"But you are! You totally are."

"And? What did you want to ask me based on the conclusion you derived from your differential and integral calculus? You came here motivated by a mathematical understanding that the roots are inverse and absolute, didn't you?"

"There's something seriously wrong with you as a person!"

"As a person, perhaps, but not as a beautiful woman."

"As anything!"

Geez. Sometimes I had to wonder why I was dating her.

Um, I loved her, didn't I… Remind me, what exactly about her?

Since she'd prompted me—I seized the opportunity and did ask her.

"Is it all right if I come with you? If you're going to settle things with Kaiki—I want to join you."

"I'm willing to pretend I didn't hear anything." I know I should have seen it coming, but her response was as cold as ice, her tone even drier than usual. "This is what they mean by a dog that licks the hand that feeds it…"

"I know I should be angry that you're comparing your boyfriend to a dog, but I'm such a comedian I can't help but quip: That just means it likes you."

Not even biting the hand that feeds it.

I was the one getting licked here.

How confusing.

"If you don't want to die," Senjogahara warned, "take back what you just said."

"It's my sister. Kaiki has done something to her." I didn't take back my words and instead buttressed them. "He hit her with some kind of weird aberration, the Cinderswarm Bee, and she's got a burning fever. I managed to neutralize it somewhat by absorbing half of it, but there's no saying how it might progress."

"You absorbed half of the aberration? Are you all right?"

Senjogahara's face remained expressionless, but she seemed to be showing genuine concern for my wellbeing. One of the occasional displays of humanity from my girlfriend.

I've rarely seen her direct such feelings to anyone but myself. It was a limited-offer humanity, conditions may apply.

"Yeah," I answered, "thanks to my vampiric healing. I wouldn't say I'm in tip-top shape, though."

I felt a little sluggish—hot.

I was hardly burning up, but I might be standing too close to a heated brand.

"I see," Senjogahara noted. "Then it's too late for you to turn back—not that I suppose you would if your sister is involved."

"It's not just my sister."

"Huh?"

"You are, too," I said, looking straight at Senjogahara. "You were about to do something stupid for my sake—like face Kaiki alone. Right?"

"It's not only for your sake. Kaiki is…just something that I need to settle."

Senjogahara—had once lost something dear to her.

"I can't forget about it, can't just leave it alone—I need to bring it to an end. If I don't, I won't be able to move forward. So much so that if Kaiki hadn't returned to this town—I'd have gone looking for him instead."

"It's that important to you?" I was intimidated by her determination, but I had to ask. "Wasn't it supposed to be—trivial?"

"I was just tsundering."

"Tsundering…"

Now it was even functioning as a verb… Honestly, it sounded scarily German to me.

"So, what… Are you planning to get revenge on all five of the frauds?" I asked. "That's over now—isn't it? Aren't there other things you need to settle?"

"Don't be silly. They might have been con artists, but I'm not interested in playing the victim, as Mister Oshino would put it. They betrayed me, but it's not like they forced me to rely on them, and I wouldn't hold such an unreasonable grudge. I'm not that kind of…that kind of… Okay, let's put my personality aside, but I don't plan on getting it all wrong."

"……"

So there was a problem with her personality.

She was aware of it.

"But Kaiki is different," she said.

"How so?"

"He ushered my parents' divorce," Senjogahara remarked without feeling. If she'd put any in her voice—it wasn't hard to imagine how it might have sounded. "Obviously, I can't lay all the blame at his feet, and I won't—but he made a plaything out of my family. I can't forgive him for that. If I forgave him for it—I wouldn't be myself anymore."

"……"

Senjogahara's father and mother divorced by mutual agreement—late last year, I believe. It was around that time that she moved out of the house she'd lived in for many years and into these ramshackle apartments.

Since then…she hadn't seen her mother—not even once.

"Even if it weren't for Kaiki, I'm pretty sure my parents would have gotten divorced. Our family would have split up. My mother leaving—that was my fault, I think. But, Araragi, just because the outcome might have been the same, do you think I can forgive someone causing it out of malice? Just because it would have happened sooner or later anyways, is malice forgivable?"

"Malice…"

"I should have a monopoly on malice."

"Well, I dunno about that, but…"

The charms that Kaiki was circulating must have affected the relationships of other people in Sengoku's life.

Either for better or for worse.

It would be simple to say that any relationship that ended up crumbling thanks to such hocus-pocus would have crumbled anyway. But there was something wrong with that simplification.

By that logic, what else could you say? If a person was dying, was it all right to kill that person? If a thing was going to disappear—you could eradicate it?

If it was fake, it had no right to exist?

Where did it end?

"Out of greed—Kaiki used my encounter with the crab to make my family fall apart. Since it was going to anyway."

"……"

"Maybe you were secondary to me in all this. Protecting you was a convenient pretext—it's really just my resentment for Kaiki that's driving me."

"Pretext…"

"I was tsundering," Senjogahara said—very quietly. "Don't misunderstand, Araragi. None of this was for your sake."

"I…doubt that, I think."

I say this with conviction—with unfortunate conviction.

The crab that Senjogahara encountered.

~~An event that occurred while she'd been possessed by it.~~

Back then, she *probably hadn't even been able to hate Deishu Kaiki.* Because that's the kind of aberration the crab was.

That had to be Senjogahara's regret.

Deishu Kaiki, the ominous Deishu Kaiki—she hadn't been able to hate him in real time.

That was Hitagi Senjogahara's regret.

That she couldn't hate him as it happened—unlike Karen and Tsukihi Araragi, who did out of a shallow sense of justice.

In truth, she should have been angry—like a child. Like a child who'd just lost her mother.

"But in that case, there's one thing I still don't understand. Kaiki is supposed to be a fake and swindler, right? But from what you're saying—it sounds like he was able to spot your crab aberration."

Just like he had managed to infect Karen with this Cinderswarm Bee.

Wouldn't that mean…Kaiki was actually the real deal?

"Who knows?" Senjogahara said. "But a fake with powers surpassing the real deal is also more dangerous than the real deal—though at the time I thought he was nothing but a quack. Thinking back, he may have been feigning incompetence. Just in order to squeeze more money from my father."

"Now he's hitting up junior-high kids for their milk money… My sisters were trying to stop him when he got Karen."

"I see. So your sister is a Justice Man, too."

"Yikes, that name…"

"Well, she's a girl so maybe Justice Woman."

"You know, your coinage sounds even crappier than you think."

"The Fire Sisters of Tsuganoki Second Middle School… I heard some of the rumors."

"Right, you did." In Senjogahara's case, it was more like gathering intel than getting wind of gossip.

"Like brother, like sister—you badmouth them a lot, and that makes sense. Justice types tend to be incompatible."

"Don't flatter them… They're make-believe defenders of justice. As for me, I never thought of myself as an agent of justice. We're more like a bunch of kids squabbling over who gets to play in a vacant lot."

In that sense, wondering if it was "hating people who're like me" or "self-hatred" was overblown.

It was just siblings fighting, nothing special.

"Araragi, let me say for the record that justice won't work against this ominous fellow—not as far as I can tell. Let me be blunt. You and your justice might be potent against hypocrites, but it's weak against really bad people."

"I keep telling you, justice isn't my thing…"

My sisters were, at least, right. I wasn't even that.

I could make it pretty—but not right.

Shinobu had been a victim of that very shortcoming.

There was a long line of mistakes leading up to where I was today.

"Still," I said, "I can't just stand by while you turn into a criminal."

"My plan isn't to commit a crime. It's to mete out punishment."

"Modern society would view it as one and the same."

If she'd been born in mythical times, people might have handed down tales of some seriously heroic deeds… Without a doubt, she'd been born into the wrong era.

Either that, or the wrong world.

But I, for one, was grateful—that she'd been born into this world and this era. I felt truly grateful to have met her.

"Senjogahara, maybe you don't realize this, but I love you. If you did turn to crime and were sent to prison, I would visit you every day—but if possible, could we always be together? At times I wonder why I'm dating you—but I love you so much, I don't need any reason."

It goes without saying—but the list of things I want to protect includes you, Senjogahara.

"If we're going, let's go together," I insisted. "Protect me—and I'll protect you."

"Dammit...that sounded insanely cool." Senjogahara's face remained stiff and expressionless, but her shoulders were trembling from whatever she was feeling. Was that a genuine reaction? "If I were a man, your runaway manliness would make me so mad with jealousy that I'd murder you."

"You're scaring me!"

"Luckily I'm a woman, so I can just be attracted to you instead."

With that—Senjogahara pushed over the pile of pencils by her side.

"Okay, Araragi. We'll do it your way."

"You mean you'll take me to see Kaiki?"

"Yes." Senjogahara nodded. "But in exchange, I have one request."

"A request?"

"If 'request' sounds too mushy for your tastes, then call it a condition—a prerequisite for bringing you to Kaiki. Well?"

Her tone was testing, but there was only one way I could answer.

"Go on. Whatever the request, or however many, I accept."

"I only have one." *Araragi,* she called my name gently. "I'm meeting Kaiki—in order to turn a page. Just like when Mistress—I mean, Hanekawa cut her hair."

"Hold on, you did it again. I can't possibly let it slide."

"I'm not being threatened!"

"You're being threatened?! By Hanekawa?!"

"It's only normal to kneel for her, wherever we are!"

"Wherever, you say?!"

"Yes, just like when Hanekawa cut her hair," Senjogahara reprised, ignoring my interjection and reverting to her usual tone, "and was able to move forward—I plan to face Kaiki and make a break with my past."

The past. Senjogahara's past.

Did that mean middle school? Her first year of high school? Her second year?

Or…some other time?

She declared, "I, too, am ready to move forward."

"……"

She was already facing forward. I considered saying as much—but it would have been superfluous. Besides, maybe facing forward and moving forward—were two different things.

"Okay, so, what's your request?" I asked her. "What do I have to do for you to take me with you?"

"I'm not ready to tell you yet."

"It's something you can't even tell me?"

"You're going to listen to any request, right?"

"Well, sure…"

But it was scary.

I wasn't going to back out of it—but that was scary.

Like signing on the dotted line of an unfilled contract.

After all, it was Senjogahara I was dealing with!

"Once we're through with Kaiki—however that turns out—I'll tell you."

"Why not now, then?"

"If I told you, it wouldn't be foreshadowing."

"Foreshadowing!"

"Yes. You die, and forever regretting that I didn't voice the request now, I live out my life alone."

"So I die in this plot line?!"

"Yes, and in the climactic scene, the telescope you gave me on my birthday comes into play as a key item."

"I can't think of any situation where it would! Forget about foreshadowing or whatever, just tell me now!"

"Fine, forget the whole thing."

"....."

If she was going to be like that, I had no choice. Senjogahara drove a cutthroat bargain as usual.

I nodded. "All right—understood."

"Ah. Then let's go." Senjogahara returned my nod, her face as blank as ever. "We'll protect each other."

019

That morning, Senjogahara had phoned Kaiki, not as a client but as a past victim, in order to request a meeting—I suppose you might say a confrontation. When you thought about it though, it had been a bit of a gamble to begin with, since there was no way of knowing whether Kaiki would even pick up.

But in that wager, it seemed Senjogahara had prevailed.

As well as in the conversation that followed.

The result was—that they were now scheduled to meet in the afternoon. The other party, i.e., Kaiki, had accepted Senjogahara's demand without objections.

Things had gone almost too smoothly, it was unsettling.

Unsettling—and ominous. Anyway…

"The meeting is scheduled for five p.m."

"I see—in that case, I'm going to head home first," I said. "There might be more I could learn from my sisters. Karen is still laid up, but Tsukihi should probably be awake by now."

"Fine. Come back here in the afternoon, then."

"Okay… Don't go running off without me."

"Of course I won't. Have I ever lied to you before?"

"……"

Lying was all she did. She could play a ballad on a lie detector.

"I'm tired of lies, but they won't leave me alone," she said.

"I guess it's all in the phrasing...and when I think about it, that makes zero sense."

She was tired of lies? Then just tell the truth.

"Relax," she counseled. "This is all about having you hear out my request—I might lie, but I'm promising you."

"I see... Fine, then."

"Heh, it's called negotiating."

"......"

Promising and negotiating were two very different things...

"I'm a little sleepy anyway," she said.

"Ah. That's right, you were up all night."

All night. Sharpening pencils.

Except for the five hours, of course, when she was too depressed because Hanekawa had scolded her.

Senjogahara's face was still as passive as cast iron, but under the circumstances I'm sure she must have been tired. It was impossible to tell just by looking at her.

"You were up all night too, Araragi, even if you were unconscious for some of that time. I don't think you want to face a conman like Kaiki while you're half-asleep—instead of talking to your sisters, wouldn't it be better if you took a nap?"

"Well... When it comes to lack of sleep, I cope pretty well. Because of the vampirism."

"Still, get some rest. There's no guarantee you'll get any sleep tonight, either."

With that chilling piece of advice to chew on—I headed home. However our confrontation with Kaiki might play out, I probably needed to be in good shape going in. To be prepared, so that whatever scars remained afterward, there would at least be no regrets.

At the same time, I was telling the truth when I said I wanted to hear what Karen and Tsukihi had to say—no, maybe I should talk to

Hanekawa again? I could head over to her house and get my bike back at the same time—but we'd already caused her enough trouble.

It was better not to get her any more involved—though perhaps that was just me being overprotective when it came to Hanekawa.

She was a good person—they didn't come any better—but was never overprotective, not of anyone. You could say she valued personal responsibility for what it was worth.

Actually…she was too callous about herself.

Now that she'd cut her hair and decided to move forward, it would be nice if that side of her changed as well… But I was probably speaking out of turn.

I was going to take college entrance exams. I had made the decision in June.

Beginning to study for exams in June of my senior year—you couldn't dally more than I had. Normally, I'd have to resign myself to taking a year out.

I was only able to give it a try thanks to Senjogahara and Hanekawa's finely geared tutoring—as for their own studies, Senjogahara had some of the top marks in our year and would be getting into college on a recommendation (By the way, I'm hoping to get into the same school as her. The order of this explanation got flipped, but basically, I started studying for exams because I want to join her there), whereas Hanekawa, who had *the* top marks, wasn't planning on applying to any university, truth be told.

The top of her year. Actually, if we're being honest, one of the smartest people in the world.

The whole faculty had high hopes for her—but Hanekawa had chosen not to choose a college for herself.

The only ones who knew so far were me and Kanbaru—I suppose it was also possible that Senjogahara had heard it straight from Hanekawa, but I hadn't said anything.

I couldn't blab about it.

If people found out, an uproar would overtake Naoetsu High, the likes of which no haircuts, contact lenses, accessories, or bags could ever prepare us for—classes would be suspended, and the school would be boarded up until further notice. After all, it was said that if you added up the IQs of everyone else at our school, it still wouldn't be equal to Hanekawa's—well, I'm fully aware you can't do that with IQs, but the difference between Hanekawa and the rest of us was so great that it surpassed the bounds of common sense.

I knew, without a shadow of a doubt, that I'd never meet another person in my life as great as Hanekawa—but perhaps that was why passing up an obvious choice like going to college made sense for her.

Even if it made sense, it was still unexpected.

As for what she was planning to do instead of going to college, when you put it into words, it sounded incredibly banal—she was going to travel.

One long journey, around the world.

She had already worked out a complete multi-year plan as to her itinerary—in that sense, she was a typical model student.

"So whether I get into college or not," I'd asked her when I found out, "once we graduate I guess I won't be able to see you anymore?"

It was right after summer vacation started—we were studying in the library. I tried to sound casual, but that probably just made it seem more awkward.

"That's not true," Hanekawa replied with a bashful smile. "All you have to do is call for me, and wherever I am in the world, I'll come running. We mean a lot to each other."

"Okay, if you ever need anything, you can call me, too. I don't care if I'm in the middle of midterm exams, wherever you are in the world, I'll come running."

"Ahaha. Say that again after you actually get in."

Which is how the conversation ended.

I couldn't help but wonder how her life might be turning out if she'd never met me—and had never gotten involved with aberrations.

If she hadn't come to know the demon.

If she had never known that cat.

Her life probably would have never gotten thrown so far off track—not after all the time where staying on the straight and narrow was her only goal in life.

The real deal that she was.

"Yeah, I'll leave her alone…"

I'd reached the decision by the time I arrived home.

I figured Hanekawa had probably told me everything that I needed to know, and even if there was more, if she found out Senjogahara and I were going to go meet with Kaiki in the afternoon, she might ask to come with us.

I couldn't get her involved to such an extent. I didn't want to.

If I could—I'd have preferred to go alone.

Of course, Senjogahara had likewise tried to keep me from going with her, so I guess my behavior was contradictory.

I just had to resign myself to contradiction.

Because that's the kind of person I am.

"Koyomi!"

Tsukihi was standing near the front door. Noticing me, she'd yelled my name.

"Ah…you're up. Good mor—"

"Karen's gone!" she cut me off with a plaintive cry. "Wh-When I woke up just now, I couldn't find her anywhere—she's still sick!"

"Calm down, Tsukihi-chan," I accidentally called my agitated sister by her name and grabbed her shoulders. She seemed like she might run off, at any moment, so I forced her to face in my direction. "Did you check my room? I put her to sleep in there."

"Of course I did! Why are you wasting time with stupid questions?!" Tsukihi was getting hysterical. She was on the verge of tears. "H-Her shoes are gone, too—and it looks like she changed."

"……kk!"

Perhaps absorbing half of Karen's fever had been a mistake. Even if she wasn't well yet, she was feeling well enough to be able to leave the house.

She'd just pretended to feel worn out and to fall asleep.

Then, after she saw me leave, she slipped out the door?

Damn, the kid was a handful!

"Mom and dad think it's just Karen up to one of her usual stunts—obviously I can't tell them the truth. Koyomi, what am I gonna—"

"Calm down. Think. Do you have any idea where she might have gone?"

"No…" The strength drained from Tsukihi's body. She seemed to wilt. It was almost like—she'd lost half of herself. "She'd probably try to go wherever Kaiki is… But we don't know where that is."

"Are you saying…Karen does know?"

"I don't think so. He already slipped through her hands once."

"……"

Karen. That bumblehead.

It meant she, herself, didn't have any idea where she was going—the idiot! She couldn't stomach just waiting around, even if she had no clue, and so she bolted out of the house determined to do something?!

Stop faking it, for goodness' sake!

"I'll go look for her," I said. "I'm sure she hasn't gone far—she couldn't have. You wait here."

"What? I wanna go look for her, too."

I figured as much. She was probably just about to leave when I got home. But…

"Even if you find Karen, chances are she'll persuade you to join her," I tried to reason with Tsukihi. "If things get any more complicated than they are already, I'm not sure I'll be able to handle it."

"You really don't trust us, do you…"

She was half laughing and half crying.

Of course I didn't trust them. Day after day, they were all wrong. Or too right.

"Trust, no," I told Tsukihi. "But I do worry about you guys."

"……"

"But more than that, I'm angry!"

How many times did I have to say it?! Frustrated, I removed my hands from Tsukihi's shoulder and turned on my heel—heading out the gate and onto the street. And then I started to think.

What to do? Where to look?

If Karen didn't have a destination in mind, all I could do was wander around and hope for the best—she was the worst kind of missing person.

Unlike Senjogahara, Karen had no way of contacting Kaiki directly—even if she did, Kaiki wouldn't agree to meet her.

It was a good thing I had lent Hanekawa my bicycle. If not, Karen would have almost certainly taken it without asking. Being on foot rather than on a bike made for a big difference in her movement radius—unless she got on a bus, in which case I was screwed. Unlike me, my sisters had bus passes.

Think.

If I were Karen, what would I do?

She's not in her best shape, but she has something she needs to do. Other people want to stop her, but she can't quit...

"First, she'd try to put some distance between herself and the house—because if we found her, we'd bring her back. That's step one. But what next? What next...what next..."

What would Karen do next?

Gah, how would I know what an idiot was thinking?! Maybe she'd just gone to the store!

I gave up on that approach...but maybe she'd use her new phone she was so proud of to contact Hanekawa—sneakily, before even leaving the house?

No, I doubted it.

Karen and Tsukihi had kept it a secret that Hanekawa was helping them. They'd asked Hanekawa to keep quiet about it too. That meant they felt guilty, and Karen could at least guess that if she contacted Hanekawa now, it would get back to me. Ah, but then a knucklehead might make the call without bothering to think…

I could try calling Karen's cell, but there was no way she'd pick up… The GPS feature on her phone could track her down, but I'd need to ask my parents.

Under the circumstances, I couldn't go to them for help.

Besides, she might have switched off her phone—

"Will ye shut up?"

I couldn't stop fretting, my thoughts all over the place, but in the middle of my panic, a voice spoke to me—abruptly, from the shadows.

From my shadow.

Before I even registered the fact…Shinobu Oshino was standing by my side.

It was like she had appeared even before she appeared.

She was wearing a kiddie dress that was whiter than a real one ever could be. It was tunic length and of a different design than the one she'd worn in the cram school ruins. No leggings.

For shoes, she was wearing mules over bare feet. The mules were also nearly translucent in their whiteness.

As for her helmet… She was skipping it—just as she'd said. Her blond hair was magnificently exposed.

She was staring at me with drowsy eyes.

"I cannot sleep amidst this clamor. Has it never occurred to thee? We are bound through thy shadow, and any vexation on thy part is imparted to me. To be forced to share in insufferable panic when one does not feel agitated is the worst, I say. Show some consideration and try to control thy madness…though I suppose 'tis impossible of one such as thee."

"Shinobu… Do you know what's going on?"

"More or less. These kinswomen of thine are foolhardy enough to give thee a run for thy money—ahhhhh." Shinobu released a huge yawn, showing me her canines—her fangs. "Hrm, come to think of it, ye came seeking for me as well, when I went lost. Ah, such fond memories."

"Would it be all right…if I asked you to help?"

"Kakak," cackled Shinobu, in vampiric fashion. "Unfortunately, I am not in a position to deny thee—our relationship as master and slave may be complex, but in power ye exceed me. I told thee, long ago, did I not, that the vampire's bond is a bond of the soul? If ye command I cannot but obey, however much I dislike the task."

"It's not a command. I'm in no position to be giving you orders."

"Then I refuse, ye dunce," spat Shinobu. "I am willing to help, but I do not wish to make the offer. That would be shameful. That is why I am telling thee to word it as a command, for appearance's sake. Can't ye even brain that much? Why else would I interrupt my slumber and show up at an opportune moment, if not to aid thee?"

"You're more than a little tsundere, too…"

I couldn't help but grimace at Shinobu's words. When did she get so tinted by our world, anyways? After living for five centuries, five months was all it took for her to adopt our mores? This had to be more of Oshino's elite schooling at work.

What was that aloha guy thinking?

"Fine then, it's an order. Where is she? Find Karen for me."

"Ah, woe is me, what a calamity, to be forced to obey such a lowly human. But if ye insist on being a tyrant, I suppose I have no choice. Hmph. How would ye ever manage without me? Dear dear, how adorable."

Khaha, Shinobu laughed again and then pointed her thumb.

"Thy sisterling's blood is similar in composition, so I can sniff out her general direction. Hmph. It seems she hasn't roamed far, after all."

020

Apparently Karen had been trying to catch a bus after all—she was probably planning to head toward the school she attended, Tsuganoki Second MS. I found her sitting on a bench inside the kiosk at her usual bus stop, the one closest to our house.

No, not sitting on the bench, sprawled across it. She'd run out of strength before she had a chance to board.

It was a Sunday, nearly afternoon—not many folks were looking to catch a bus at such a time in our country town. Karen had the kiosk all to herself.

Dressed in her jersey, she was slumped across the bench. Her breathing seemed regular. Resting—but not asleep.

I felt like a fool for running for three minutes straight at Shinobu's urging—then again, the inside of the kiosk was a blind spot. If it wasn't for her, I might never have noticed. Without accounting for the fact that Karen might be feeling weak, I'd have glanced at the stop from afar and continued on my way.

"What's up, kiss monster…"

Karen glanced up at me listlessly before dragging herself into a sitting position. She seemed to have worked up a fair amount of sweat again, as well. After all the trouble I'd gone to in order to lower her fever, she seemed to have stoked it back up by traipsing around outside.

Cinderswarm Bee or not, her temperature was still too high for her to leave the house. Even if she was clearheaded—her body couldn't keep pace. She may as well have been in a regular stupor.

"Let's go home," I said.

"You go home. Leave me alone."

"If you insist on being difficult, I might have to kiss you again."

"Don't you understand? My precious virtue is gone, now... I've nothing left to fear."

"I wouldn't be so sure. You don't know what true fear is."

"The only one who will be experiencing true fear—is you." Karen staggered slowly to her feet. "Don't even think about trying to stop me."

"Whether I stop you or not... I mean, I am going to stop you. But where do you think you're going? You don't even know where Kaiki is, do you?"

"But I'm going to go find out. I can't just sit around!"

Karen's hair was still down from before. She hooked it back with a practiced move, using a rubber band from around her wrist to tie it into a single lock. It was the same ponytail she always wore. She looked cooler than she should.

"So what do you plan to do, if not sit around?" I asked her.

"I plan to search, to find, and to wallop."

"You sound like you were born before the Christian era."

"A fist to the eye, and a fist to the tooth."

"The more you talk, the dumber you sound."

"I already told you what that man did to me. Do you know how disheartening it feels?"

"And I already told you, leave the rest to me."

"But I never agreed."

"Come on. You should be at home now, resting."

"That's the kind of thing a complete stranger might say. You're my brother. You should be saying something like, 'Don't give up, go get 'em, you got this.'"

"Do you really think I would ever say something so irresponsible? Mom and dad have real hopes for you, unlike me. You're supposed to be the good kid. Can't you just stick to normal bratty pranks? They're willing to overlook most stuff. So don't be crossing a line."

"You're turning yourself around now, so it's fine."

"They won't even let me go to a cram school."

"But you're actually…"

Karen started to speak—and then stumbled on her feet. Was she having trouble standing up straight?

It was mostly willpower that was propping her up. No—even her willpower was probably exhausted at this point. So what was it, then?

Her sense of duty? Her stubbornness? Her pride? Or perhaps…

It was conviction.

"……"

Whatever it was, if she couldn't stand, I'd just carry her home on my back. And this time I'd tie her to the bed so she couldn't escape.

"Words won't get us anywhere," Karen beat me to the punch right when I was about to bring the conversation to a close. "You're not interested in anything I have to say in the first place."

"I'll listen later. Maybe as I peel you an apple while I sit by your bedside."

"Ha."

Karen raised her arms and closed her hands into fists. She dropped her hips and bent her knees slightly.

She'd been swaying unsteadily until moments ago but snapped out of it in a flash—her back was erect as a steel column.

She wasn't defending herself.

Karen turned toward me—aggressively.

"Come to think of it, it's been a while since we've had a serious fight."

"Don't flatter yourself. I was never serious about any of our fights. You're just my little sister," I shot back, still not taking a fighting stance. I was on my guard, however. "So you've gotten stronger, big whoop.

What use is that going to do you now? This isn't some dojo. Besides, you're hardly in your normal condition at the moment."

"My condition? Ah, that's right, my condition isn't normal," Karen agreed, nodding. "My head feels fuzzy. And I'm hot all over like my body is on fire. It feels like my clothes might burst into flames from the heat. My joints are heavy, and every time I take a step I feel like I might fall—I can't even see you straight, it's like my eyes are parched. If I so much as blinked, they might never open again."

"……"

"In other words, I'm in my best condition."

She edged toward me—still in her fighting stance. Before I knew, she'd closed the distance between us until she was near enough to land a punch.

"You know, you're pretty slick," I said. "If you weren't my sister, I might have a crush on you."

"And if you weren't my brother, I might have gone easy on you."

Too bad—Karen took a swing.

It wasn't hard to see the punch coming. She wasn't even on the rebound from her illness, she was still as sick as a dog. I blocked it—and then twisted her wrist.

Back and up.

The next instant—I was soaring through space.

"!"

I didn't even have the time to register my surprise. Forget about a scream, the best I could manage was an exclamation mark—before crashing, supine, onto the asphalt.

The asphalt. It's not a comfortable surface for the human back.

I was ready to scream now.

"G—ahhh!"

"Too bad this isn't some dojo, Koyomi. That wouldn't have hurt so bad on the mats. In our style, we start learning throws after the first stripe. Did I forget to mention that?"

"……nkk!"

You've got to be kidding me. Since when were there throws in ka-rate? Apparently there were a lot of things I didn't know about in this world.

And it seemed Karen could move just fine. I hadn't been expecting that.

"Thanks—that really opened my eyes," she said.

By that, I guess she didn't mean recognizing the error of her ways and feeling penitent. Moving around had quite literally woken her up and cleared the cobwebs from her brain. She slowly stretched herself out.

"Let's see…twenty minutes until the next bus. Do you want me to call you an ambulance in the meantime?"

"Don't make me laugh. The only one who'll be getting in an ambu-lance is you," I retorted, struggling back to my feet.

The wind had been knocked out of me when I landed on the ground, so I was breathing heavy. But that didn't matter. There was no need for me to catch my breath.

Stare straight ahead.

At your sister.

Your little sister, who's ill.

"You're kidding," she marveled. "How are you standing? That throw could have killed you—in fact, the instructor told me I should never use that technique outside the dojo, under any circumstances."

"Then I hope they kick you out."

"Just stay out of my way!"

I didn't see the next punch coming. Not that the punch itself was any faster. She hadn't purposely slowed her earlier attack to set up the throw.

This time, however…she added in a feint. It made a big difference.

The first strike was full force.

But the second strike—was a doozy.

"Ack… Ng—nghh!"

Karen landed five punches to my torso before I hit the asphalt again.

I had failed to block a single one.

It was a total onslaught, a barrage of fists.

"By the way, Koyomi. Don't you think the phrase 'my body is on fire' sounds kind of dirty?!"

"No, I don't!"

"It sounds almost like 'my body is for hire.'"

"You sound like a friend of mine from school!"

"A friend?! Who?!"

"I'm talking about the biggest pervert I know!" I shouted angrily.

Kanbaru would be over the moon if she could hear me. While I was still shouting, Karen tried to land a kick. This time I caught her by the ankle—yes! I was still the stronger one, and her wrist was one thing, but there was no way she could throw me while I was holding her ankle!

Unfortunately.

Karen had two legs.

I never saw it coming. Using the ankle I was gripping as a fulcrum, she swung her other leg up to kick me hard in the side.

This hurt.

After all, she was taller than me and had just put her whole weight into the kick—I think I felt my organs flatten. But I didn't let go—at least, not until she landed the same fiendish attack three more times.

No good, I wasn't going to be able to ride this beating out.

I didn't have a vampire's constitution anymore. To be honest, purely in terms of how it felt to me, Karen seemed a notch above the likes of Guillotine Cutter.

"Ahem, master…"

As I released Karen's leg, I heard a voice coming from the ground—no, not from the ground. From my shadow, which was cast across the ground.

In other words…from Shinobu Oshino.

It was just her voice. And it seemed like I was the only one who could hear it—Karen didn't react.

"Did I tell thee earlier? Just as thy vexation and panic are conveyed to me in a most direct manner, with the same intensity, so is thy pain."

"Just try to endure it a little longer," I spoke to my shadow.

I was talking to the ground, so from Karen's point of view, I was the sort of person you'd steer clear of—unless she thought I was starting to get delirious from all the pain.

"Command, and I shall step in."

"I'm fine, I don't need your help."

"At this rate, I might whether ye order it or not."

"Then my order is for you to stay out of this."

"Ye gall my patience."

"I'll stroke your head later, I promise."

Stroking her head—was a ritual for pledging absolute obedience. When I washed her hair yesterday, the intent was partly symbolic.

"The head is not enough," Shinobu said. "I demand a stronger ritual."

"A stronger ritual?"

"Yes, something which argues greater devotion."

"Huh, I didn't know. What kind of ritual is this?"

"Instead of stroking my head, ye stroke my chest."

"Why didn't you tell me when you were still in adult form?!"

I struggled to my feet, nearly in tears—the third attack wasn't accompanied by words.

Karen's punch simply came at me.

Just endure it a little longer. That's what I told Shinobu, but "a little longer" was pretty vague. For now, what she had to endure was another ten punches.

I endured it too, of course.

I endured the unendurable and suffered the insufferable.

Karen really had gotten stronger. I was practically no match for her as I was. Vampiric or not, I can't believe I was ever arrogant enough to think I might kill her by accident if we fought. She'd progressed so far while I was avoiding our squabbles? How could she have gotten so strong in a matter of mere months?

Who was this instructor of hers, Grand Elder Goro? Did she drink the Ultra Divine Water or something?

Believe me, I wasn't trying to be suave. I wasn't letting her hit me because she was a girl, or my sister, or whatever—though I was faring so poorly that an excuse would have served nicely. There wasn't even an opening for me to launch a counterattack. Talk about unfair... Was she an original character introduced in the anime, or what? It was a whole different worldview.

Maybe being sick meant that Karen's brakes had stopped working as well, because her assault showed no signs of slowing down.

However...

"This is getting ridiculous," she said, pausing momentarily when she saw that I still wasn't collapsing. "I bet my hand hurts more from punching you."

"Don't be stupid, I'm the one getting hit. Obviously I'm in more pain."

Geez. If it wasn't for my lingering vampirism's healing factor, I'd be dead by now—no joke.

"You know you can't beat me, Koyomi."

"And you know you can't beat me, Karen."

I could feel myself bleeding all over—I'd let Shinobu drink it afterward as a peace offering.

In fact, if I didn't boost my healing skill that way, I'd have to check into a hospital.

"If you wanna give up, you better do it now, Koyomi."

"Isn't it a little late for that line?"

"My hands hurt."

So I'm done punching you, Karen said—before coming at me again. This time with a leg sweep.

I'd expected her to use her legs next, so I was able to avoid it by jumping backward—but I wasn't able to dodge the follow-up attack.

She brought her other leg up high—and brought it crashing down heel first.

A *naeryeo chagi*.

What the hell was up with her karate school?!

"Nrgh…kk!"

I raised both my hands in a cross above my head to block—but my sister was the musclehead. There was no way it was going to be enough to stop her kick.

In fact, I was probably about to have the bones in my arms shattered.

What kind of a technique is that to use against an amateur, I thought, but oddly, while the force hit me like a ton of bricks, and I felt like I was about to be squashed from the force, it didn't knock me over.

What? Was she holding back?

Unless…

"Hmph! Not bad! But…that was just another feint!"

Even as she spoke, her leg, which had swung low from the axe kick, now came slicing up, toes aiming for my jaw—but she had another thing coming if she thought a flashy move like that was going to connect. I swayed my upper body back just enough to evade it. But she hadn't meant the move as a strike.

Karen kicked her other leg up as though to chase the first—tossing her whole body up into the air.

She supported herself on her palms.

A handstand.

"Hup!"

With her legs spread open in a straight split like a bamboo-copter, she began to spin.

"Ngh…rrk!"

Somehow I managed to block with my arms—if you could call it blocking. I wasn't guarding myself, I was having my arms pulverized.

It felt like I was being beaten with a baseball bat.

I think she spun about five times—in other words, she kicked my arms ten times. I couldn't even feel them anymore. How could she generate so much force standing upside down?

Didn't I know the attack from some fighting game?

It wasn't karate, it was capoeira!

"Y-You…"

After being kicked again and again, I tried to grab one of Karen's legs. She had messed up this time—she underestimated me if she thought such an acrobatic maneuver would finish me. Now was my chance to counterattack—only…

As if she'd been waiting for me to reach out, and as if to shake it off, she sank toward the ground.

Sinking, and momentarily lying on the ground from her handstand position without losing any momentum as if the asphalt were slippery ice, she kept spinning on her back like she was breakdancing—speeding up, if anything, and sweeping at my legs again. The kicks were so sharp they were like a scythe.

Circular motion. Torque.

Unable to utilize her full strength due to her illness, her strategy seemed to be to take advantage of the laws of inertia and centrifugal force—and it was proving extremely effective.

I was so focused on guarding my upper body that my shins were wide open. My knees crumpled from the kicks—which looked to be Karen's aim all along.

She stuck her palms against the asphalt again.

Raised herself into another handstand.

And then pushed, leaping into the air using just her arms.

Shit! All that time spent training upside down was paying off!

While I was busy gawking, Karen's long legs, which she'd just employed as a scythe, turned into a pair of scissors that clutched my head where her meaty thighs joined. She immediately bent one knee, locking my head in place.

With my face smothered against her jersey's crotch, I couldn't breathe. But that was only for a moment.

Karen spun her arms in mid-air, hard, like a screw—the momentum whipped her whole body around.

Her twist—*yanked me off* the ground.

Through sheer force—she uprooted me.

A-Another throw?

A neck throw—using her legs?!

Karen had taken mine out in advance, and I was powerless to resist the completely unexpected maneuver. Before I had time to say "impossible," the world grew blurry.

I was soaring through space once more.

Karen released her leg hook on my head halfway through, allowing me to somehow avoid landing headfirst (I'm pretty sure this was another "never use under any circumstances outside of the dojo" technique. It reminded me of something out of Muscle Man wrestling but was probably an ancient martial art move)—but there was no way I was going to make a clean landing.

I hit the ground hard, striking my hips on the pavement.

I seized up—white pain wracking my body.

Karen, meanwhile, had landed perfectly, just as you would expect. She was already launching a follow-up strike—she'd used her legs like a scythe and a pair of scissors, and this time they lashed out like a whip.

I instantly grabbed a stone and lugged it at Karen—not just one, either. I threw one each with both of my hands!

A big boy throwing stones at a middle-school girl.

None other than me.

"I don't think so!"

Hollering, Karen didn't even slow as the missiles approached—she deflected the arc of her kick and knocked away the two stones that were hurtling toward her.

No—not knocked away. She smashed them into smithereens.

H-Her kicks can shatter stone mid-air?!

That was a metal bat she was swinging!

"Geez, how much have you been training, Sister Princess 1/12 Scale Model?!"

"That'd be a normal sister!"

Managing an appropriate rebuttal to my curse without letting her quipping distract her—I guess you could say she was built to different specs than me—she aimed at my head again.

A running, flying back kick—and you know, my head just happened to be right there!

And believe it or not, gruesome though it may be…it wasn't over with one strike.

I'd hate to say "wings on a tiger," but Karen almost seemed to defy gravity—still suspended in mid-air, she followed up with another pinpoint strike to my head with her other leg.

But it wasn't over with two strikes, either.

Still in mid-leap, Karen let the rotation take her, kicking me a total of three times—in the head.

I felt like Anpanman after getting a new face from Uncle Jam (Is that metaphor going to work?! It means: I thought my head had gotten blown off!)

The first kick had been so powerful that if I'd been standing up, it probably would have floored me instantaneously, but since my ass happened to already be on the ground, I took all three hits in quick succession—seriously, it was pretty devastating.

My brain was probably bean paste by this point, no exaggeration.

"What are you, a ceiling fan?! I'm gonna start talking like an alien at this rate, you Futakoi 1/6 Scale Model!"

"Me and Tsukihi aren't twins!"

"You were, in the original setting!"

"We were?!"

Yes, indeed. If you searched hard enough, you could still find a few remaining clues.

After a revolution and a half, Karen landed on one foot, but Karen, being Karen, most certainly did not stop to catch her breath. This time she spun in the other direction—and leapt back into the air in order to kick me on the other side of my head.

But apparently ergonomics were against her. As soon as she did, she was spun around by the force of her own kick, completely ruining her form—but wait!

I was wrong, it was another feint. She was just building up centrifugal momentum.

She leaned into her kick and executed a spectacular backflip before my eyes—and landed on me as I sat with my buttocks planted firmly on the ground.

She alighted on my shoulder—then, using me as a springboard, leapt straight into the air. Directly over my head.

"Wha… You!"

I glanced up reflexively—only to be greeted by the sight of Karen folding both her legs, ready to bring her full weight crashing down in a knee drop on the bones she'd used as her personal springboard.

"Y-You're kidding me, you'll rip my shoulder clean off—forget Anpanman, you Happy Lesson 1/5 Scale Model!"

"That one's not about sisters, it's about mothers!"

True. I guess I got carried away. What demographic were we going after, anyway?

Without a second to lose, ignoring the searing pain in my back, I somehow squirmed away—her point of contact was focused on a single spot, so I only had to shuffle a bit to avoid the blow.

It's your own jump strength that will be your ruin, girl!

Enjoy kneeing the asphalt instead of my shoulder—a couple of small stones are one thing, but demolishing an asphalt surface shouldn't prove so easy!

Your knees will be the thing turned to smithereens, this time!

Yet—from the corners of my eyes I witnessed an astounding sight.

I'd dodged her attack at the last moment, but in response, Karen twisted her upper body a mere foot and a half off the ground—creating a spiral with her 5'7" frame to stick a landing which, if not elegant, was plenty impressive.

Especially compared to just managing to crawl out of the way on your hands and knees.

Despite the fact that we were still in the middle of a battle, I couldn't help but gaze in awe at Karen's fluid maneuver—basically giving her a perfect opening.

She acted without hesitation, slipping behind me, swiftly twisting back my arms, and hooking them in place with her knees. Then she strangled me once again, with both of her arms.

A collar lock...no, sleeper hold? With her legs wrapped around my arms, it was an unusual variation, but this wasn't karate, either. It was clearly a judo move!

"Are you sure you're not studying judo...or maybe Jeet Kune Do?"

"Nope, it's karate... This technique is called the Choke Sleeper X!"

"Since when are they named like wrestling moves?!"

Uh oh. My sister had fallen prey to false advertising.

Well, considering her level, I guess it didn't matter what school or style she followed.

Either way, I was in big trouble.

I might be able to endure her punches and kicks, but even with vampiric healing, there was no way I could withstand a stranglehold—attacking the respiratory system directly is a surprisingly effective tactic. It had taken me so long to recover from Karen's first throw precisely because it had knocked the wind from my lungs.

When Karen said she was done punching—I thought she meant she was changing to a leg-heavy style. But if the idea was to use other variations with her arms, like throws and chokes, then I was screwed!

"Getting choked can be kind of pleasurable, I know from experience—I hope you enjoy it!" invited my sister.

"Who choked you?! I'll kill the bastard!"

"I'm talking about you!"

Right...

And I guess as part of training at the dojo.

"This is vengeance for all those years under your thumb!" declared Karen.

"Wait...didn't we have another reason for this?"

But no matter how much Karen flexed—and squeezed my neck—my breathing remained absolutely fine. I guess when push came to shove, she still wasn't feeling well.

Unlike striking techniques, where she could concentrate the impact into bursts, a chokehold required her to maintain continuous force with her arms. In her current condition, she just couldn't generate enough power.

The fact that she released her leg hook earlier, while still in mid-air, bolstered my theory. It wasn't long before Karen also realized trying to choke me was a mistake.

But this was my chance. As soon as she realized her mistake, I shook off her arms, stood up, and spun around.

Karen had also gotten back on her feet. I reached for her chest. I'd never beat her on technique. My one chance was to hook her by the jersey and drag her into an ugly free-for-all. Unfortunately...

"Where are you aiming, perv!"

Karen easily dodged my arms. And then, of all things, she planted her skull to my face.

A head-butt!

Girls weren't supposed to use head-butts!

The counter was well-timed, hitting me square in the bridge of my nose and temporarily dazing me—I closed my eyes reflexively and lost sight of Karen.

Karen, being Karen, did not let that opportunity go to waste.

She immediately stepped into my blind spot, turning her back to me for a moment before executing a 270 degree turn, using her full weight to strike me with a backhand to the temple—talk about a pin-point strike!

My brain shook in my skull. The single blow was enough to knock me down to the asphalt again. My body skidded, leaving my clothes tattered.

But I didn't have time to worry about that. If I didn't get up right away, she'd follow up—

"Ugh, my hands really hurt," Karen said. She stepped back to reassume her stance. "Honestly, I don't want to hit you anymore. This is just turning into senseless violence. You get it already, don't you? You really can't beat me."

"Hmph. Don't be stupid. Don't you realize I passed up at least five chances to take you down? You're the one who needs to wake up. It's you who can't beat me."

Obviously, the truth was that she was pummeling me. I just sounded like a sore loser.

Victory or defeat.

You win—or you lose.

"Justice must win, right?" Even as Karen spoke, her legs began to wobble again, probably from all the jumping around—but if I tried to make a move, she'd pull herself right back together, no doubt. "Doesn't that mean might is right? If I defeat you—why shouldn't I go?"

"Careful now. That kind of thinking is a far cry from justice."

"Huh?" A look of displeasure crossed Karen's face. Her eyes, which were slanted up to begin with, narrowed even further. She glared at me—harshly. "What's that supposed to mean? It's what you always say, like you know everything."

"Oh yeah? I said that?"

"About me and Tsukihi. That we're right, but not strong—justice always prevails, and losing isn't an option…"

That she and I are fakes, Karen added.

"Like you know everything, Koyomi, like you know everything! So I'm just making sure that I don't lose—"

"Oh, that," I said, stepping closer to her.

Well, no, I could barely move.

She was going to leave—I couldn't stop her. The next bus would be here soon.

"I meant it," I told her. "You're right. But you're not strong."

"I am. Stronger than you, at least."

"Are you? From where I'm standing, you seem pretty weak."

"Look who's talking. You're a mess."

"Physical strength is meaningless. What you really need—is strength of will."

That was what was amazing about Hanekawa. Her strength of will.

"You say you can't forgive Kaiki," I continued, "but is that even your own will? You two are always acting on someone else's behalf. For someone else's sake. I don't see your own will in it."

"You're wrong… We do what we do because we believe it's right. Other people just provide us with reasons."

"Don't make me laugh. Since when does justice seek its rationale outside itself? How can you take responsibility when you make others your reason? You two aren't anything like justice, or even defenders of justice. You're just brats—playing make-believe."

Fake. Fakes who'll never be anything else.

"You don't go after the bad guy, just the heel—am I wrong?"

"You are! Don't act like you know what you're talking about!" shouted Karen. At some point—she had lowered her fists. They were still clenched—but lowered. "Tsubasa would understand—she knows everything!"

"Not everything—she only knows what she knows."

Hanekawa's line. What she always said—almost as if to keep herself honest.

"If you aren't ready to acknowledge that it might only be self-satisfaction, and not self-sacrifice, don't bandy about grand words like justice," I admonished. "It's unpleasant."

"What's so wrong about doing stuff for other people? Is sacrificing yourself bad? If we're—so what if we're fakes? It's not like it causes you any trouble!"

"It causes me plenty of trouble, but…" There was no space left between us. I grabbed Karen, who still had her arms down. "I never said it was wrong."

"……"

"If you're willing to go through life wrestling with a sense of inferiority, then even if you're fakes, you're as good as the real thing."

My grip strength was almost gone. I'd grabbed Karen, but there was almost no strength in it. Although she didn't try to brush me off, I needed to be sure.

I pulled her into a hug.

Her body felt hot, like she was burning up. But even if it was weak—I could sense her will.

Everything would be all right.

They were brats, immature, childish.

But they had a whole future ahead of them in which to grow strong.

"Let me say one thing—I really can't stand you and Tsukihi. But I'm also proud of you. Always."

"K-Koyomi."

"You said it was disheartening. I'm pretty sure I heard you say that. But it's even more disheartening for me. I'm not letting anyone get away with disgracing my sister, whom I'm so proud of."

And so.

And so—

"Leave the rest to me," I said.

There was no need to say more.

Karen's body, which had been stiff moments before, suddenly went limp.

"Disheartening…" she mumbled. "More like pathetic. Needing my big brother to wipe my ass…"

"Says the girl who couldn't wipe her own sweat. Well, it's a great honor, as your big brother, to be wiping my little sister's ass."

Hugging her tight, holding her taller body close, I flashed a smile.

"It's my turn to show off," I announced. "Just don't go crushing on me. That would be incest."

Too late, Karen said. And—

"I'm leaving the rest up to you."

Just like the bickering siblings we were, we'd fought.
But what a right and fine, and gratifying, fight.

021

The whole thing played out so smoothly that it was almost anticlimactic. Whether or not that was fortunate, however, is another matter.

"Fine then, I cede the issue. No more deceiving middle-school students. I will cease spreading these so-called charms. And Araragi, if you are worried about that spirited young lady—your sister—you needn't be. Her condition is like a placebo effect. Instantaneous hypnosis, as they say—given her susceptibility to belief, I imagine her symptoms are quite severe, but she should recover within three days. Consider it a simple cold. As for you, Senjogahara, allow me to formally apologize for the situation with your mother. Legally speaking, I did no more than offer advice to you and your family. There is no law to indict me. But if I have hurt you, it would be untoward not to offer some consolation. Likewise, whatever money I took from your father I will do my utmost to return—as that money has nearly all been spent, however, doing so may require some time."

So said the ominous man dressed in a black suit, as if he was in mourning.

Deishu Kaiki.

Senjogahara had chosen the location of our rendezvous—the roof of perhaps the only department store complex in our town. Close quarters would have put us at a disadvantage, whereas any place too deserted would also be dangerous. Which is why she had chosen the department store roof—of course, she also had the benefit of learning from Karen's mistake.

It was the evening of July thirtieth.

After our fight I had carried Karen home piggyback. I figured she wasn't going to try and sneak out again, but just in case, I scrawled "Need good time—all men welcome" across her face in permanent marker to ensure she wouldn't leave the house (I also wrote "Hate bras—not wearing one" across Tsukihi's face. Joint liability).

Then I met up with Senjogahara and headed to the meeting spot.

There was a mini-amusement park atop, with a small stage adjacent to it. Since today was Sunday, a performance was scheduled (a Power Rangers-type show). That would allow us to pretend we were just there waiting for it to start.

A man dressed in the deepest black and two high school students. It wasn't the strangest combination, but it would draw some stares—which was probably desirable.

He may have driven her off, but Kaiki had already been confronted by Karen once. Even though he had answered his phone, counting on him to let himself be summoned again seemed like a gamble to me—for some reason, however, Senjogahara remained strangely confident.

In fact, it seemed less like confidence, and more like trust.

When we reached the department store roof, Deishu Kaiki was already waiting, alone. He was drinking a can of coffee.

When he spotted us, he tossed the empty can into the garbage.

"Hmph. You're the boy I met outside the home of Gaen's legacy. Come to avenge your sister? How rare these days to see a child with such chivalry," he addressed me in a somber tone.

Next he turned toward Senjogahara.

"You've lost your charm though, haven't you, Senjogahara. Such an ordinary girl you've become."

He didn't even smile.

"Excuse me?" Senjogahara spoke in reply. She stepped in front of Kaiki, her face still expressionless. "I'd say I never wanted to see you again—but I'd be lying. The truth is I never wanted to see you the first time. Still, I have to tell you—I've been looking forward to this moment."

"Well, I haven't been. Certainly not when you've become such an ordinary girl. When I met you before, you sparkled as the night—or maybe I should say you seemed enlightened. You were so worth deceiving," Kaiki answered glibly.

I found myself thinking of them again. Of Oshino and Guillotine Cutter.

They were all very different—and face-to-face like this, Kaiki had almost nothing in common with them. Except for one point.

Their confidence.

As if they were perpetrating crimes of conviction, registering and comprehending all, they chose to be silent or eloquent as they saw fit.

"Is this your fault, Araragi? Are you the one who solved this young woman's problem?"

"No—I just gave her a little push."

"Then you and I are the same," Kaiki remarked in a moody—an ominous—manner. "Of course, when I pushed her, it was in the direction of a cliff."

"Which is what you're doing now, isn't it? To middle-school students? Giving them a little push—and trying to knock them over."

Off the side of a cliff. Or a suspension bridge.

"Did your sister tell you? Yes, exactly. These country children have been saving up. I've earned a fair bit of coin in a very short amount of time."

Shift.

I noticed Senjogahara was slowly closing the distance between herself and Kaiki—I'd say she was gearing up for a fight, but then she had been for some time now.

Ever since we had arrived on the roof.

Or maybe, since she heard me utter Kaiki's name.

Or—ever since he deceived her.

"No, let's talk," Kaiki curbed Senjogahara's approach. "I'll listen to what you have to say. It's why I'm here. It's why you're both here as well. Am I wrong?"

"......"

"......"

Then, in fact—we listened to what Deishu Kaiki had to say.

Fine then, I cede the issue—he said.

He admitted to everything, promised to pick up stakes—and even offered to make reparations.

An anticlimax.

Everything had gone smoothly—it was a perfect outcome, more than we had hoped for, yet...

It was, indeed, more than we had hoped for. His response wasn't unexpected so much as unwanted.

"How very forthcoming of you," praised Senjogahara, sarcastically—to be honest it sounded hollow, like she didn't know what to say, and was making do. "But why should we believe you?"

"You wouldn't, Senjogahara." The man never seemed to bother with honorifics. He didn't with me, either. "Araragi, what about you? Are you able to believe me?"

"Asking me to believe anything a conman says is ridiculous. At the same time," I answered cautiously, "if we're not going to trust you even one bit, then this whole conversation is moot. It's like you said earlier, Kaiki. We came here to talk."

"Hmph. You're a very level-headed young man, aren't you? Not one iota of a child's innocent charm. Your sister was much cuter with her refusal to think. In that sense, I suppose you live up to your title as big brother."

Kaiki didn't seem to be trying either to provoke or to commend when he said this.

"To me, at least," Senjogahara cut into him curtly, "you don't look very repentant. I don't smell a whiff of remorse."

"Ah. I haven't offered any apology yet, have I? Nor begged for my life. A thousand pardons, I am most repentant, truly eaten up inside— well... I suppose it's not you two that I should be apologizing to, but your father and mother, Senjogahara—and all the children I deceived this time."

"You expect me to believe that shallow apology? Everything you say is a lie."

"Perhaps it is," Kaiki allowed, nodding. From his oppressive tone, you might think that he was angry—but something made me doubt that.

I felt quite certain that he was a man incapable of anger. And not just anger.

I had a feeling he didn't think about other people in any way.

"And if everything I say is a lie—so what?" he continued. "I am a fraud. It would be nothing less than sincere of me to only ever traffic in nonsense. And besides, Senjogahara..."

"What?"

"Isn't it overly hasty to label a mismatch between words and feelings a mere deception? If the words are not reflective of feelings, why assume that the words are false? Must the words be a lie—and the feelings true? Who is to say?"

"Could you refrain from intentionally aggravating me? In case you didn't know, I'm trying very hard to be patient." Senjogahara closed her eyes for a moment. Not a blink, but a long pause. "I'm having a tough time resisting this urge to kill you."

"So it would seem. And that's what I mean by 'ordinary.' The old you would have never shown such patience."

"At this point, what I want isn't to have our money returned—it wouldn't bring my family back."

"I see. That is a great relief. I am a prolific spender and terrible at saving. In order to pay back your money, I was going to have to cook up a new scam."

"Leave this town…immediately."

"Of course."

Once again, Kaiki assented with a readiness that was creepy and dubious.

"What's wrong, Araragi?" he said. "Why are you looking at me that way? You shouldn't. The results may not have been serious, but I did harm your little sister. If you're going to stare at me, shouldn't there be more enmity in your eyes?"

"My sister has herself to blame… She should have never gotten mixed up with someone like you. That goes without saying."

"You're wrong. Your sister's mistake was in coming to meet me alone—if she wanted to trip me up, she should have brought a friend or two, like you knew to do. Then I would have thrown up a white flag, just as I am doing now. On all other points, the young lady was more or less right."

"……"

"Or are you declaring her to be a fool and denying her as a fool?"

"I think she's right. But…"

"She isn't strong?" Kaiki beat me to the punch as if he'd already thought about it—as if he'd contemplated such trivial matters long ago and were done with them. "No, she certainly isn't. But there is no denying that young lady's kindness. What's more…"

For the first time—Deishu Kaiki seemed to smile. A smile as ominous as a crow.

"What's more, if it weren't for young ladies like her, I'd go hungry as a confidence man."

"And why," said Senjogahara, who unlike me, was fixing Kaiki with a highly appropriate stare, "is that conman now so quick to do as we say? Surely you could just wheedle your way out of this…like you did with me before. I bet no one has any proof that you're scamming these kids."

"Senjogahara, you misunderstand me." Kaiki was no longer smiling. Perhaps what I took for a smile had only been a trick of the light. "No, perhaps I shouldn't say misunderstand, but rather overestimate. It is quite natural to view someone you consider an enemy as being larger than life. I understand the impulse. But Senjogahara, life is not so dramatic. Rail against me though you may, I am but a middle-aged dullard. Even as a conman, I am small fry at best. A dismal man."

Hardly worthy of your resentment, he appended.

"I am not your enemy—just an annoying neighbor. Even if I did once seem like a monster to you."

"Don't kid yourself. You're just—"

A fake, spat Senjogahara. But it was true that the same fake had been tormenting her.

"Yes, precisely. I am that," Kaiki agreed. "A low creature whose mind is racing even now, desperate to get out of this fix. And the most effective means to that end is to be meek and submissive and to do as you say. Capturing your good graces is my only avenue of escape."

"……"

Then…why come in the first place? He was obviously under no obligation to answer a summons from Senjogahara.

"You see, Senjogahara, I am not obeying, so meekly and submissively, because of who you are—I would obey anyone, under comparable circumstances. If I may—until your call this morning, I had completely forgotten you. From my point of view, what happened to your family was just one con in a line of many that I carried out. I learned no lesson from you back then."

I had to wrack my brain to remember you, he muttered and looked at Senjogahara again.

"I am not special—and neither are you. There is nothing dramatic about me, and there is nothing dramatic about you. All the loose bills and small change I manage to gather are but a paltry amount in society's grand scheme. However momentous a decision it was for you to confront me, its outcome is as insignificant as today's weather."

You'll find no drama here, Kaiki reiterated as though to chastize her.

"And what of you, Araragi? Allow me to ask you. Is your life

dramatic? Is it a tragedy? A comedy? An opera? I sense something…
unsettling, in your shadow."

"……"

"Also—you seem to have somehow absorbed half of your sister's
condition. What madness. Such a risky thing to do, and without the
promise of monetary reward."

Could he tell? About Shinobu—and about my body? And if he
could—how?

"Just…which are you?" I asked him.

"Which… Which what?"

"For a fake, you did a pretty good number on my sister. Senjogahara's thing too—you could actually see what was wrong with her,
couldn't you? Kanbaru, too." It was starting to seem less like a matter of
which, and more like whichever. "Are you *familiar with* aberrations?"

"Hmph. I wasn't expecting such a silly question. My interest in you
is waning, Araragi. Do you, for instance, believe in ghosts?" Kaiki's lack
of enthusiasm was apparent. He seemed almost embarrassed to be having this conversation. "Even if you don't, I imagine you can understand
the psychology of someone who is afraid of ghosts. My case is similar. I
don't believe in the occult, but there is money to be made in it."

"……"

"I refute the existence of aberrations and anomalies—but there are
others in the world who affirm such things. Which makes said persons
easy to deceive. I may be a small-fry conman, but thanks to such su-
perstitious people I am able to eke out a living. So, in answer to your
question, no, I'm not familiar with aberrations. I simply know people
who are. Or to be precise, I know people who're under the impression
that they're familiar with them."

This time, he definitely smiled. Once again—like a crow—it hadn't
been a trick of my eye.

"Money is everything in this world," he said. "I would happily die
for money."

"When you take it that far, it sounds like faith…"

"However far I take it, it is a matter of faith. Faith is unswerving. Don't forget, people whom I deceive pay me money in compensation for my deceit. It is precisely because they believed that they paid a just price. To doubt what they once believed—what could be more inconstant?"

The Cinderswarm Bee, Kaiki suddenly said.

The name of the aberration he'd unleashed on Karen.

One of those aberrations he wasn't familiar with.

"Do you know of the Cinderswarm Bee?" he asked me.

"It's from the Muromachi period or something, right? An epidemic of unknown origin that people attributed to the work of an unidentified aberration—supposedly, a lot of people died at the time."

"You are correct. But you are also wrong." Kaiki nodded first, then shook his head. "The Cinderswarm Bee is actually a tale of the weird from the fifteenth chapter of *The Illustrated Compendium of Eastern Discord,* which was written during the Edo period. A fairly obscure text—but the fundamental point is that, Cinderswarm Bee aside, no such sickness as described in the compendium ever spread during the Muromachi period."

"Huh?"

"If such a thing had truly occurred, surely it would have been included in other texts—but the infection is mentioned only in *The Illustrated Compendium of Eastern Discord.* In other words, that 'epidemic of unknown origin' never existed in the first place."

"......"

"Since there was no epidemic, there were, of course, no deaths and no actual phenomenon to attribute to an aberration—the entry was a product of the author's passing fancy. A spurious invention penned to resemble historical fact."

No such aberration—ever existed in the first place.

Not as cause.

Not as effect.

Not as process.

It was all—fake.

"It's apocryphal," Kaiki explained. "Search as hard as you like, but the aberration known as the Cinderswarm Bee traces back not to the Muromachi period but to the Edo period. Foolishly enough, later generations came to believe in the author's *bullshit*. What do you think of that? An aberration born from a single person's lie—with neither grounds nor tradition to support it."

I stole a glance down at my shadow.

Oshino had to have known, too—in other words, Shinobu must have heard this story… But like she said, trying to remember all of Oshino's ramblings was a fool's errand.

Besides, even if she'd known in advance—it wouldn't have been particularly helpful.

Whether or not it existed, and wherever it came from—at the end of the day, the Cinderswarm Bee was still the Cinderswarm Bee.

"It's as true for these old tales as it is for today's urban legends. There are cases that spring from reality and cases that spring from fantasy. As a conman, I simply happen to make my living from the latter."

Placebo effect. Instantaneous hypnosis.

That was how he'd put it.

"But my sister…"

"Hmm?"

"My sister, who was stung by the Cinderswarm Bee… Will she really get better even if we did nothing?"

"Of course. The Cinderswarm Bee does not exist—these aberrations do not exist. By extension, neither must her condition. It only seems to because you people believe in it. To be blunt—don't drag me into your game of make-believe. It's annoying."

Who was he to talk?

Deishu Kaiki, that was who.

That settled it for me.

He was as fake as they came.

Just like Senjogahara said. Just like he, himself, said.

A proud fake—willing to go through life feeling inferior.

"What's more," he said, "you absorbed half of it—it may take even less than three days for her to recover. I don't know how you did it, but I'm impressed. It's proof enough, Araragi, that you and I are incompatible—we're not even like oil and water, but oil and fire."

"Who's the fire and who's the oil?"

"Who knows? But neither of us seems particularly fiery—how about we change it to rubidium and water. In that case, I would be the rubidium."

"So that'd make me…water."

In which case, Karen and Tsukihi had to be the fire.

Fire and fire. Put them together, and they made a conflagration.

The Fire Sisters.

"Araragi, are you familiar with shogi?"

"Shogi?" Not picking up on his sudden transition, I simply repeated the word. Shogi? "I'm as familiar with it as the next person… But what does that have to do with anything?"

"It doesn't. It's just idle conversation. But humor me. What about you, Senjogahara? Are you familiar with shogi?"

"Nope," she replied monosyllabically, but she was lying.

There was no way she wasn't familiar with our domestic version of chess. In fact—I bet she was quite good at it.

"It's a simple game, relatively shallow at its core," Kaiki continued unperturbed as if he'd seen through her. "The number of pieces is limited. The manner in which they can move is also limited. The board is clearly drawn. Every aspect is finite. In other words, the possibilities are extraordinarily limited from the start—it is very low-level, as games go, with no room for complication. And yet, the very best shogi players are, without exception, geniuses. A game that should be open to mastery by the most mediocre of intellects is mastered by none but the most intelligent. Do you know why that is?"

"No," I said. "You tell me."

"Because shogi is a contest of speed. In an official match, there is always a timer set on the table. That's why. If there's a time limit, the simpler the rules, the more exciting the game is. How expediently can the player consider his options? In short—intelligence is a matter of speed. However masterful a given strategy, with enough time, any player could mimic it… The crux lies in *not spending* that time."

"……"

"Like shogi, life is finite. How to spend less time thinking—or to put it another way, how fast you can think is key. As someone who's been alive much longer than either of you, allow me to give you one piece of advice."

"Save it. I don't need any from you," Senjogahara replied immediately.

"Now, now," Kaiki disregarded her comment. "Don't think too much. From my point of view, people who get too preoccupied with their own thoughts are as easy to deceive as people who don't think at all. Think in moderation—and act in moderation. That is the lesson for you to take home from this."

So said Deishu Kaiki.

"Your cell phone…" Ignoring his words as though in retaliation, Senjogahara held out her hand, palm up. "Give me your phone."

"Hmph."

Kaiki reached into his suit, drew out a black cell phone, and placed it in her palm as ordered. It was a flip phone. Senjogahara bent it backward with brute force—breaking it.

Then she dropped it onto the concrete and stepped on it as though to put it out of its misery.

"What a nasty thing to do." Kaiki's tone was calm. He didn't even seem upset. "There was a lot of information I need for my work on that phone."

"You mean—for your scams."

"Of course. But now I can't help those middle-school children, either. Because I no longer have my clients' contact information."

"Why should I care whether or not you help some middle-school kids I've never met? Araragi…" Senjogahara threw me a sidelong glance that I couldn't read. "I'm about to say one of the worst things I could say."

"Huh?"

"Wasn't it their own fault?" she declared.

She was addressing Kaiki—the confidence man who had duped her, too—but spoke the words without hesitation.

"I'm no defender of justice," she continued icily. "Only an enemy of the wicked."

"……"

"Besides, you couldn't help those victims, not you. Even if you tried, you'd wind up pulling a worse scam."

"I probably would. I am a conman—even my reparations are made in lies. You two may not want to understand this, but for me, making money is about more than profit and loss."

"Your problem is that—"

Senjogahara started to say something but changed her mind.

She suddenly stepped aside—out of Kaiki's way.

It seemed to be her way of saying the conversation was over.

This was it—the end.

All done.

Kaiki tilted his head. "I should thank you. I came here ready to get slain, but I must admit, I do not like pain," he said to Senjogahara, who refused to meet his eyes. "If there's a thing or two you need to tell me to my face, I'll listen. Surely you have feelings that have burdened you—these so many years. What is my problem, pray tell?" he solicited.

"……"

Nothing? muttered Kaiki. He sounded terribly disappointed. "You truly have grown into a very boring woman, Senjogahara."

"……"

"If not dramatic, back in the day you sure were the best. Truly worth deceiving, a rare treat for a con artist. Now you have become tedious. Heavy with excess fat."

"……"

"What happened to the seed that I sowed? Did it rot? If so, I wish you'd remained forgotten to me. That way, you'd have continued to shine on in the hazy recesses of my recollection."

"…Shut up," groaned Senjogahara. Her face was still expressionless—but it was a hard stare that she returned to Kaiki. "You can say whatever you like about the old me, but don't insult who I am now—Araragi says he loves me. This me. So I like this me. I'm not going to stand by while you slight what I am now."

"What, you two are in a relationship?"

Kaiki seemed genuinely surprised—he was a match for Senjogahara in how little his expressions changed, but a look of real astonishment had crossed his face. "I see, I see. In that case, I won't say another word. The third wheel is the first to crack."

He slipped past between Senjogahara and me and kept his back turned to us.

"Well then, if you say reparations are not required, I will not be making them. After all, I'd rather not engage in any activity that is not lucrative. I will slink away from this town. Come tomorrow, I will already be gone. Is that acceptable, Senjogahara?"

"Answer me one thing…" she said quietly to his back. "Why did you come back to this town? After you already left once?"

"I told you. I barely remember my last visit. It wasn't until I got your call that I recalled working this area before. That's how it is."

"How it is…"

"*A vampire,*" Kaiki said suddenly, startling me. "*I heard a ridiculous story about a vampire, the so-called king of aberrations, showing up in this town*—if I had to give you a reason, I guess that would be it. Such places are ripe for occult-related work, a hangout for aberrations—not that I actually believe in them, of course."

"……"

I glanced down at my shadow once more.

There was no reaction of any sort.

It was early evening—so she was probably still asleep. Either that, or she was listening, but staying quiet.

A vampire—king, and slayer, of aberrations.

An ironblooded, hotblooded, yet coldblooded—vampire.

"That reminds me, Senjogahara." Despite claiming he wouldn't say another word, Kaiki spoke one last time—without turning around. "I have a story I think you'd like to hear."

"I'm not interested."

"It's about that man who tried to violate you. Apparently he was hit by a car and died. In a place and manner that have absolutely nothing to do with you—and without any hint of drama," Kaiki reported indifferently as he started to walk away. "That's how it is with the past that's eating at you. It's not even worth settling. The man who hurt you won't be coming back as a worse threat, and the mother who left you will not repent and return. That is life. The past expires the moment it slips away. The lesson for you to take home from this—is not to expect the dramatic in life."

"That's probably just another lie, anyway," Senjogahara managed to retort in a level but subdued voice. "Why would a man who didn't even remember me until this morning know anything about the man who tried to have his way with me? And my mother—you don't know what you're talking about. Put a leash on your spite. Is trying to confuse me so amusing to you?"

"Not at all, as I don't stand to earn a single penny. But Senjogahara, don't see things so superficially—is it not possible that the lie was that I'd forgotten you?"

"A lie…"

That's such a lie, Senjogahara said.

Which statement was she referring to?

Kaiki—Deishu Kaiki—didn't even bother to ask. "Whether or not it's a lie, in the end there is no such thing as truth in this world. You needn't worry, the fact that *you once had a crush on me doesn't make you unfaithful*—don't hold a grudge against me in your exertions to be devoted to your current boyfriend. Let me repeat myself: the past is no more than the past. There is no value in overcoming—or overtaking it. A woman of your worth shouldn't be bound by petty concerns. Go live happily ever after with this young man."

Adieu, he bade.

Unlike Oshino, who never said goodbye, the swindler ended his speech with a farewell salutation, but without a shred of sincerity, almost as if it were slapped on in savage haste.

And so Deishu Kaiki went away.

I…Senjogahara, too…stood frozen for some time.

It had gone perfectly.

We couldn't have asked for a better outcome.

And yet—why were we left feeling so powerless?

Not defeated, so much as hollow.

Sadly, at this rate—Karen would never go crushing on me. It was a far cry from showing off.

Still, putting aside my own regrets…I felt like we'd been able to work through Senjogahara's. That deserved a passing grade.

"You had a crush on him?" I asked.

It wasn't the best way to break the silence, but that was hard to let slide without comment. Maybe it wasn't manly of me, but I had to put the question to her.

"Excuse me? Araragi, are you worried your girlfriend might not be a virgin?" a caustic reply came from her as expected.

There wasn't much I could say in response. That wasn't what I had meant, but I guess I had to admit to having given such an impression. But instead of taking me to task any further, Senjogahara answered me.

"Of course not. How could I? That was just his imagination. What a smug creep." There was a hint of annoyance in her stone-faced expression. "It's just—at that point in my life, I probably would have thought of anybody who tried to help me, whoever it was, as a prince. So I'd be lying if I said I didn't look favorably on that fraud at all."

He was only the first, she added.

True. This was Senjogahara, who had been more resigned but also more tenacious than anyone—who, resigning and giving it up, hadn't resigned or given it up.

"I brought this up before," she murmured, "and I don't mean to hash it out again…but if someone other than you had saved me—I might have fallen for that person instead."

She followed that up without giving me a chance to cut in.

"The thought makes me sick. I'm so glad—it was you who saved me."

"……"

I tried to say something, failed, and in the end just lamely repeated something I'd said before.

"According to Oshino, though, you just went and got saved."

Dammit, if only I could think of something cool to say at a time like this—I'd be a full-fledged man. Pathetic.

Senjogahara didn't object to my words, nodding and murmuring, "Maybe."

"After seeing Kaiki, I can understand why you disliked Oshino so much."

"I disliked Mister Oshino—I hate Kaiki. There's a big difference." She shrugged her shoulders. "Let's go home. The sun is already setting—I almost feel like this was all a waste of time. Still, it's good that you didn't meet that man under different circumstances. That's something, at least."

"True…"

Senjogahara made a good point. Kidnapping me might have been taking things a bit far, but I was lucky she had taken the initiative—the problem with me and Kaiki went beyond not mixing.

We couldn't be less compatible.

We weren't just enemies, but natural enemies.

"If we meet again, it will probably be to kill each other."

That probably wasn't the right thing to say in front of Senjogahara, but it was all I could. I didn't mean much by it. Those were my honest feelings when it came to the man known as Deishu Kaiki. In other words…

The lesson for me, Koyomi Araragi, to take home from this was that I should never meet Deishu Kaiki again for the rest of my life.

"Not that there was any big catastrophe, but I think this couldn't have turned out better."

"What kind of dish was that, again? Catastroganoff?" deadpanned Senjogahara—even though she must have felt that way even more than I did. "Araragi, once you start thinking that it might be a valid creed with its different form of justice—you lose. Watch out."

"I will…"

"Let's go home," Senjogahara repeated as if nothing had happened.

"Oh, right, by the way. Before we leave, what's this request of yours? You can't just foreshadow and then forget about it. To be honest, I'm on pins and needles here. What in the world do I have to do?"

"Nothing major. Maybe, like that swindler said, it wasn't worth putting an end to. But as far as I'm concerned, I just settled with my past."

"Settled, huh?"

It was something we all had to do.

Senjogahara, Hanekawa—me too.

And Shinobu.

"Tell me I did good," Senjogahara said.

"Is that…your request?"

"No way. Praise from the likes of you, Araragi, would hardly delight me. You seem to be forgetting to fulfill a basic duty, so I'm simply reminding you."

"……"

This woman—was she actually made of iron?

"Iron?" she asked. "Of course not—I'm a soft, cute girl. And after listening to that man go on and on, I feel very fragile. Look at me, I'm in shambles."

"Liar."

Who's the con artist here, I quipped.

"I mean it," she said. "So…"

Her face as expressionless as ever, or maybe a bit angrily expression-less, and in a supremely flat tone—Senjogahara voiced her request.

"So tonight, be kind to me."

022

The epilogue, or maybe, the punch line of this story.

The next day, in a reversal of our usual roles, I was the one to rouse my two sisters, Karen and Tsukihi. They were both on the top bunk, naked, holding each other in their slumber. The idea that the warmth of skin-to-skin contact could help cure a cold was, itself, a kind of urban legend, but as the one waking them, I must say it was a shocking sight.

You guys are way too close.

But—an aberration for an aberration, an urban legend for an urban legend, and, to borrow from Shinobu, a charm for a charm—indeed, just as Kaiki had said, we didn't have to wait three days. Karen was already back to her old self that morning.

If anything, she was too energetic.

I guess for Karen, the picture of a healthy kid, being under the weather must have been pretty stressful.

"Hai-ya!" she shouted senselessly in kung fu mode.

Seriously, though, what kind of dojo was this? I needed to check it out sometime.

By the way, Tsukihi was more than a little cross at Karen for sneaking out despite being ill (not for the sneaking out, but for not telling). How they managed to make up and wind up sleeping lezzie sisters-style remained a mystery.

Well, it must have been a right and fine fight, too.

After breakfast, my parents left for work, so I called Karen and Tsukihi to my room to give them a quick rundown of yesterday's events.

Kaiki was no longer in town.

As a result, there would be no more victims.

Those two points.

As for the aberration itself, I thought long and hard about it but decided that for now, at least, I should leave it out. Karen's condition could be explained well enough in terms of the placebo effect and instantaneous hypnosis, and for the moment, telling them about Shinobu just seemed reckless. It may have been indirect, but Karen had given Shinobu a major beating. I didn't think now was the right time to introduce them.

But I had a weird hunch that I'd be doing so before too long.

Keeping a secret from my sisters—was probably beyond me.

Monday, July thirty-first—it was an odd-numbered day, so my tutor was Hanekawa. I was curious as to how she'd make up for Saturday's cancellation—but it also scared me.

As I prepared to head to the library and reminded myself that I needed to get my bike back from Hanekawa today, Karen and Tsukihi slipped past me.

"Koyomi, I'm heading out for a little bit."

"Koyomi, I'm heading out for a lot of bits."

Karen was dressed in her school jersey, and Tsukihi was dressed in her school uniform.

"Where to, lezzie sisters?"

"Just because the conman is gone doesn't mean all the charms are suddenly gone, yeah? Or that all the relationships he ruined are gonna suddenly recover? There won't be any more victims, but it's not like all the kids who fell victim have been saved, am I right?"

It was Karen who said this as she slipped on her shoes.

Tsukihi was already standing outside the door.

"I suppose," I admitted. "He did say that with his phone smashed, he couldn't help—not that he was ever going to."

"Exactly. Which is why it's up to us to take care of the aftermath," Tsukihi stated with a crisp smile. Her words didn't betray the slightest doubt.

"Don't get carried away playing at defenders of justice," I warned like always.

"We're not playing at it, we are the defenders of justice."

"We're not defenders of justice, we are justice itself."

See ya—they left with parting words that didn't remotely hint at having learned anything the hard way, my little sisters—

My pride and joy—

Quite possibly closer to the real deal than anything, thanks to their fakeness.

Like fireworks lit by a spark, the Fire Sisters made their sortie.

Afterword

This is something I've been thinking about a lot lately, but people are not one-sided but rather multi-dimensional creatures, which is of course what makes them so very complex and wide-ranging, and a person seen through my eyes and through another person's eyes is practically a different individual, which gives me headaches. You could take it further and say that the you that you understand to be yourself and the you that others understood as you are not the same person, either. And there's no single image of how others see you, but instead a you made up of image upon image, and each of those persons must be different from the next. Which is synonymous with saying they are like strangers, so it's hard not to sympathize with young people who ask "Who am I?!" and set out on journeys of self-discovery. It would be easy to say they're mistaken, but obviously no two eyes see the same, and it's impossible to flat-out reject the phenomenon. The fact that one man's fakery is another's real deal and one man's real deal another's fakery is prevalent in our cosmos, and maybe bothering to discuss such a universal is the real mistake. First and foremost, humans are creatures that act differently depending on who they're dealing with, so being judged differently depending on who you're dealing with seems like the most natural thing in the world, meaning, perhaps, that the person most capable of assessing you is you yourself. But wouldn't that amount to saying that to know yourself is to know your place?

And so I bring you the first half of *BAKEMONOGATARI*'s sequel:

NISEMONOGATARI—finally introducing the long-awaited Araragi sisters, who have been making a splash in certain corners since the original *BAKEMONOGATARI* and its prequel, *KIZUMONOGATARI*. To share some of the inside story, this novel was never intended for publication, and after writing it, I didn't tell anyone about it for some time. I'd planned to leave this work buried in obscurity, never even printing it out—in other words, to keep it all to myself, which is to say I wrote it two hundred percent as a hobby. Working on a novel in complete freedom, absent any pesky restrictions or fetters, is highly enjoyable. Some might ask what kind of attitude that is for a professional writer to have, but the amateur spirit (in the best sense of the word) is something that I, personally, never wish to lose. And thus "Chapter Six: Karen Bee," *NISEMONOGATARI: Part 01.*

The artist, VOFAN, really did it this time. His illustration of Karen Araragi is truly phenomenal, and as the author I cannot begin to express my gratitude. For indulging my wish to write fiction brimming with so much silly banter, dear readers, you likewise have my gratitude.

May we meet again in the latter half of *NISEMONOGATARI*, over another follow-up story, Tsukihi Araragi's—that is, if I decide to make it public.

NISIOISIN

ANIPLEX
傷物語
II 熱血篇
-KIZUMONOGATARI-
PART 2: NEKKETSU
Blu-ray Set
NOW
AVAILABLE
PART 1: TEKKETSU
ALSO AVAILABLE
ART SUBJECT
TO CHANGE
FOR MORE INFO, VISIT US AT:
WWW.KIZUMONOGATARI-USA.COM
© NISIOISIN/KODANSHA, ANIPLEX, SHAFT